Praise for
MURDER ON THE GRAVY TRAIN

"Food is Richman's passion, writing her profession. Both qualities stamp her second novel, *Murder on the Gravy Train*, with a flavor all its own. . . . There is much to be enjoyed. . . . When Richman cuts loose doing what she does best—evoking food as a metaphor for human passion, as a tool for ambition and as a setting for social jockeying—the pages really begin to sing."

Washington Post Book World

"It's always fun to be taken inside a particular world, and the world of food is so deliciously devious that this is a delightful trip."

Dallas Morning News

"Tasty."

Baltimore Sun

"Suspenseful."

Book magazine

"As good as *The Butter Did It*."

Stuart News (FL)

THE BUTTER DID IT

"What fun! . . . Features a memorable case of foodies, and a unique look at the goings-on behind the swinging doors to some of those famous restaurant kitchens."

Diane Mott Davidson, author of *Prime Cut*

"[A] tasty first novel. . . . A lively tale told with wit and high spirits. . . . [Chas is] a heroine we want to spend time with and a gourmet we'd be happy to join for dinner."

Washington Post

"Please control yourself and try not to gobble this down all at once."

Miss Manners (Judith Martin)

"Richman's prose is as smooth and easy to swallow as premium ice cream. . . . She brings a welcome angle and authenticity to the expanding menu of culinary mysteries."

Publishers Weekly

"Great fun."

Pittsburgh Post-Gazette

"Murder, mayhem and meals. . . . A thoroughly fun read, with an unexpected ending."

Portland Oregonian

"A delicious summer read. Mystery-reading food lovers can hope that Richman will be whipping up a second helping of Chas and her friends."

Ft. Worth Morning Star-Telegram

"A rare find—a book you find truly hard to put down. Richman's culinary expertise and familiarity with the world of restaurant reviewing is evident throughout this delicious novel (which you won't want to read on an empty stomach or if you're on a diet). *The Butter Did It* grabs your attention from its opening pages. . . . A masterful whodunit."

Journal Inquirer (Springfield, MA)

"A promising debut. . . . [She] has followed the cardinal rule—write what you know—to give us a delightful confection. . . . Add lots of insider Washington for flavor and color, season with eccentric culinary characters, sprinkle with Miss Richman's rich imagination, stir well, simmer and serve with a flair."

Washington Times

"Fast-paced . . . bubbles like a good glass of Veuve Clicquot."

Jacques Pepin

"Sue Grafton meets Wolfgang Puck? Sam Spade meets Julia Child? Warner LeRoy dines alone? *The Butter Did It* is great fun and food for thought."

Mark Russell

Also by Phyllis Richman

The Butter Did It

MURDER ON THE GRAVY TRAIN

PHYLLIS RICHMAN

AVON BOOKS
An Imprint of HarperCollins*Publishers*

This is a work of fiction. Names, characters, places, and incidents are products of the author's imagination or are used fictitiously and are not to be construed as real. Any resemblance to actual events, locales, organizations, or persons, living or dead, is entirely coincidental.

AVON BOOKS
An Imprint of HarperCollins*Publishers*
10 East 53rd Street
New York, New York 10022-5299

ISBN: 0-06-109783-7
www.avonbooks.com

First Avon Books paperback printing: July 2000
First HarperCollins hardcover printing: August 1999

Printed in the United States of America

WCD ❖10 9 8 7 6 5 4 3 2 1

To Joe, Matt, and Libby

Curious minds, generous hearts, willing forks

Acknowledgments

Dreaming up murders is easy enough. But trying to relate them in credible detail and weave them into a cohesive plot sends me running for help. The first person I turn to is Bob Burton, who shares my computer as well as the rest of my life. Next I reach out for my children—Joe, Matt, and Libby—and siblings, Howard and Myrna Chasanow and Ruth Heitin, imposing on their sympathetic spouses as well. When I wear them out, I toss around plot ideas with friends. Karen Levy always comes up with just the right bizarre twist, while Leila Kight and John Ballou help me to find out practically anything. Mark Furstenberg is endlessly willing to talk food and Washington lore, and Susan Friedland offers the New York perspective. Then there are the medical experts—Kevin Cullen, David Rabin, David Rall—who help keep my plot honest, and such specialists as J. Russell Stilwell on kitchen design, Denise Klein on senior citizen issues, Mark London for legal insights, and Quintin Peterson of the D.C. police on homicide department procedures. My informant on credit card scams wishes to remain anonymous, but I won't forget his help. Many colleagues at the *Washington Post* have been an inspiration and support, but I want to specifically thank my restaurant column editor Susannah Gardiner, theater critic Lloyd Rose, and the entire computer systems department. Most important, I'm especially lucky to count generous and talented writers among my friends; Anne Tyler, Jody Jaffe, and Russ Parsons have offered their literary insights and invaluable advice.

A manuscript is not a book, I've learned. It needs such alchemists as an agent and an editor or two or three. I'm grateful to Bob Barnett, my agent, who gets more done better and quicker than any other Washington powerhouse. He's amazing. At HarperCollins, Vice President and Associate Publisher Gladys Justin Carr and Associate Editor Erin Cartwright made the transformation from manuscript to print so smooth that I, uncharacteristically, was unable to come up with any complaints.

1

"Just coffee, please. A decaf espresso." I wasn't going to spend unnecessary calories on this encounter. Nor was I going to risk losing sleep.

"I'll have the tiramisù," said my companion—I use the term reluctantly. I should have guessed that this sallow, twitching guy with a frayed collar and happy-face tie would order tiramisù in a deli.

Ottavio Rossi, despite the poetry of his name, was about as Italian as SpaghettiOs. I speculated on whether a man could be sued for false advertising in a personals ad. This "freshly divorced, optimistic, and glad-to-be-alive architect, recently moved to Washington, seeking company on walking tours of new city and new life" was actually a depressed-looking waiter whose feet hurt. And he wasn't much of a talker. I wondered—not for the first time—how I, nearly fifty years old, could have been so crazy as to answer an ISO and arrange a meeting with a strange man just because he sounded funny and wise in his forty-three paid words.

Anger and curiosity make a dangerous stew.

For three weeks I'd been simmering, since I told my boyfriend, Dave—by now, my ex-boyfriend—that we needed to take a breather from our relationship until he was ready to pay it more respect.

What's made the breakup more complicated is that we both work at the same place, the *Washington Examiner*. I'm the restaurant critic, and Dave is—or was—the star investigative reporter. In the past year, his star began dimming in favor of a newer, younger—and female—reporter, who uncannily scooped him at every turn. Understandably, he'd grown irritable. What's worse, he was increasingly uncommunicative.

My usual view is that relationship problems should be solved within the relationship, but that wasn't happening.

"I've got to work this out myself," Dave would answer when I tried to get him to talk. Mr. Independent Go-It-Alone. Bob Woodward without Deep Throat.

He didn't even try to argue when I suggested a trial separation. He just stopped calling, started treating me like a stranger in the office, and immersed himself in his work. Then he wangled an out-of-town assignment to cover a long-running trial in San Francisco.

So I decided to pretend this breakup was an opportunity—a time to satisfy my curiosity about those ISO ads my office mates and I often read to each other. At the moment, though, adventurousness seemed like an astonishingly bad idea.

Here I was, Chas Wheatley, a restaurant critic ever

ready to mince a chef's ego to a duxelles, in this case too cowardly to make an excuse and dump Ottavio Rossi. I couldn't hurt the poor guy's feelings, even though he had virtually lied in describing himself and had almost nothing to say.

I'd been careful to arrange our meeting in a place that was public, but one where I was unlikely to cross paths with anyone I knew. I suggested we meet for coffee, which seemed like a safely limited encounter. And I'd never told him a name he might recognize, just introduced myself as Charlotte Sue, which is my real name but one that nobody ever uses.

The really frustrating part was that although I'd scrupulously avoided the ads of any men who might be connected with the restaurant business, and assigned Ottavio extra points because he was new in town and we were unlikely to have acquaintances in common, now he told me he'd just made a career change. No sooner had he placed the personals ad in the newspaper, he said, than he'd lost his job. He was afraid of falling behind in his child-support payments, so he'd turned to the emergency income source of countless out-of-work actors and downsized corporation lawyers. He'd immediately—after telling a few lies about his experience, I suspected—snagged a position as a waiter "in a big-time restaurant," he bragged, one where his Italian name had been "a major plus."

It got worse. Ottavio hadn't had an ordinary mainstream architecture job when he came to Washington. He was a kitchen designer. For restaurants.

I sat over my undrinkable bitter espresso and tried

to make the best of a bad situation. Maybe I could learn some worthwhile restaurant gossip. I quaked at the idea of Ottavio regaling his fellow waiters with having met a restaurant critic through a personals ad, but since he hadn't asked a single thing about me yet, I hoped I might get away without his knowing who I really am.

Silently willing him to hurry up with his tiramisù, which he hadn't touched yet, I asked him where he was working.

"It's a pretty weird place, Charlotte. . . . May I call you Charlotte?"

What else could he call me, since that was the only name I'd given him? I nodded and smiled, assuming he would elaborate, but he didn't.

"How is it weird?" I prodded.

"Just weird. If only people knew what restaurants get out of them, they'd sure watch their backs."

Ottavio's eyes were riveted on his coffee and he silently stirred it. I began to count the intertwined boomerangs on the Formica table. Just as I was about to try again to pry a detail or two from him, he blurted, "I couldn't believe they'd fire me because of one single mistake. They had it in for me. I'm sure of it."

"Who? At the restaurant?"

"No, my design firm. Kitchen Works. Just one drawing, that did it. I got the scale wrong on one drawing, and they fired me. You'd think that since I was the only CAD . . ."

"What's that?"

"Computer-aided design operator," he answered, and went on as if there'd been no interruption. "Since I was the only CAD who knew how to get the most out of the new custom-designed range suites . . ."

"Range suites?"

"Yeah, that was my specialty. I knew more than anybody about those pricey French stoves that all the top chefs are installing now. The ones that look like miniature luxury liners and come with everything—broiler, hot plate, fryer, induction top, electric and gas burners—in one unit. I've designed kitchens where the range suite alone cost a quarter of a million dollars."

I knew a little about such stoves, but wanted to hear more. "A quarter of a million dollars?"

"Oh, sure. You ever hear of the Inn at Little Washington? The chef there installed a green-and-black one to match the restaurant's colors, and it was a prototype but in its final form is bound to cost that much. The Culinary Institute of America at Greystone in Napa Valley has a bunch of them in a kind of deep burgundy. Jean-Louis Palladin installed a bright blue one at the Watergate, though his wasn't the most extravagant. Charlie Trotter has one in Chicago, Gray Kunz at Lespinasse in New York. In the old days, the big guys had to have a duck press. Now it's a six-digit stove."

This conversation was actually getting to be interesting. In fact, as Ottavio began to talk about his former job, his face took on more color and he stopped twitching. He was even starting to look good to me. I'd have to be careful, though, not to betray my restaurant expertise and blow my cover.

"You must have gotten to work with some pretty good chefs," I prodded.

"Pretty good? Not with these stoves. I'd say none

less than great. So far, I've done the drawings for two French restaurants, a fantastic Italian trattoria, and a Vietnamese restaurant that's making a run for the big time."

Ottavio had shed his dreary expression. His darting washed-out eyes had settled on my face and looked a little more blue. He'd totally ignored his fluffy brown-and-white dessert and was using his hands to gesture rather than twitch or pick at his napkin. Whereas at first I'd have called him gaunt, now I saw him as slim. He did, after all, know how to smile, however tentatively. Most surprising, his gaze seemed less concentrated inside himself; he was giving me the once-over.

He even asked me a question: "So, what do you do, Charlotte?"

Oops. How was I going to handle this one? Now that I knew he was in the restaurant business, I wanted to be more sure of his interest and discretion before I gave him my full name or told him I was a critic. I could just imagine the knee-slapping guffawing in his restaurant when he spread the word that Chas Wheatley was searching for love in the classified section.

"I'm sort of . . ."

My pause gave him the opportunity to sneak a peek at his watch. Ottavio leapt to his feet, upturning his cup and sloshing coffee on his shirt cuff. "Omigod," he said, grabbing a napkin. "It's late. I've got to put more money in the parking meter." He lunged out of the room. I noted the clock on the wall: 3:20.

His sudden departure gave me time to think of

how I was going to answer his question. I'd try to return the focus to him while I sized him up better. He had me confused. Was he the schlemiel he first seemed to be, or had I underestimated him? He actually was kind of attractive, once he loosened up.

What was I thinking? I couldn't date a waiter. That was a total conflict of interest. Besides, what kind of jerk parks at a twenty-minute meter when he meets a woman for coffee? When he comes back, I told myself, I'll just have to politely deflect personal questions and extricate myself as soon as I can. I could only hope he'd never spot me in a restaurant and make the connection. Before I left, I'd have to find out the name of the place where he was a waiter.

He must have parked some distance away. He was taking too long. Way too long. And I wasn't the only one who thought so. The waiter approached Ottavio's chair and swept a towel across the spilled coffee. "You want me to clear this stuff, lady?" I looked up at the clock: 3:40. I looked at the waiter's face: a half smile.

My cheeks burned. I wasn't going to give in to that smirk. "My friend forgot he had an appointment, so just take his cup." He nodded curtly, but the look remained. I took another swipe at him. "I'll have another espresso. This one's grown cold."

After the waiter turned away with a shrug, I reacted exactly the way rejected women have throughout history: I reached across the table and slid the tiramisù to my side. It looked more like marshmallow than mascarpone cream. Barely any chocolate or espresso, tiramisù aimed at the lowest common denominator. Hating myself as I did it, I forked up the metallic white fluff as if it could soak up my frustration.

Why did I have to save face before that turnip of a waiter? I turned over the check that had been sitting on the table, added the price of my second espresso, and calculated a stingy 10-percent tip—before tax. I straightened to my full five-foot-four inches and swept out the door. I'd never felt so old before. My toe caught on a napkin that lay crumpled on the sidewalk. I started to pick it up, then just kicked it into the gutter.

I felt at my worst, but Washington was having a glorious day. Spring had come early, and the cherry blossoms were in full bloom well before their annual festival, which meant that we who lived here got to enjoy them privately before the busloads of tourists arrived. I decided to bypass my office and walk to the Jefferson Memorial. Walking is my drug, my solace, my addiction. I crave a walk the way other addicts grow desperate for a drink or a smoke. And on a day like today I surely needed to take advantage of every morsel of good fortune that blew my way.

To have a man dump me was humiliating enough. Being rejected by a man I found only barely tolerable made me feel I'd had my feathers plucked one by one and my carcass left bare.

Years ago I'd come to terms with being overweight. Now I felt fat.

I'd never minded growing older, figuring that wiser came along to compensate. Today I felt as if I'd begun to decay.

My long, gray-streaked blonde hair looked to me like drought-seared corn silk, the breeze whipping it into my eyes. My normally loose gait felt stiff, as if I, the inveterate hiker, were unused to walking. Somewhere behind my eyes I ached, the way I'd felt as a child after I'd been crying for a long time.

As soon as I swept my hair from my face, the wind picked up again and tossed pink petals, like big, soft flakes of rosy-hued snow, into my eyes. They drifted down my nose, into my mouth. Warm, silken snow, never to melt. I was in a forest of cherry trees, the air filled with blossoms shimmering pink and white, beyond them the calm sparkle of the Tidal Basin. I slowed to a standstill, breathing deeply to fill my head with the fragrance.

A Japanese couple approached me with an embarrassed giggle, offering their Polaroid camera and asking me with gestures to take their picture. They stood barely touching, stiff and smiling while I aimed the lens. As soon as I snapped the picture, they rushed to me and pulled the square of film from the camera, shifting their gaze affectionately between the paper and each other as the image blossomed. I edged away, ready to leave, but then the wife swooped to my side to show me the photo, bowing in excessive gratitude for such a meager favor. I signaled my thanks for her thanks and again started to go, but the husband caught up with me, waving a second photo. This was of his wife and me. She looked like a doll in the long slim silk shirtdress that she somehow wore as if it were a kimono. Next to her, I saw myself as a teddy bear, round and lumpy. My pained smile was saying, "I want to get out of here."

So I did. I bowed, they bowed, and I backed away, waving the photo like a handkerchief until I bumped into a tree and automatically apologized to it. I turned to make a more rapid retreat. As I waited impatiently for a walk light on Pennsylvania Avenue, I took one last look at the photo, then dropped it in a trash can, where it settled on a blob of ketchup, and was thus glued to a thicket of limp french fries. RESTAURANT CRITIC DROWNS IN KETCHUP, I imagined the headline.

My life was a bloody mess.

I was in no mood to face the newsroom, so I gave up and went home. Maybe in my beloved Seventh Street loft I could pull myself together before I had to review tonight's restaurant.

I rooted through drawers until I found just the CD I needed, folk-bluegrass-gospel in Gillian Welch's plaintive voice. An hour in my old red plush platform rocker, my bare feet tucked under me, and a corduroy pillow behind my head, lulled me to a slow rhythm of dozing and waking. As I watched puffy white clouds, like the flowery caps of cherry trees, drift past the Washington Monument, I tried to lecture myself out of my misery.

Couldn't life be beautiful without my being beautiful?

2

Sherele would never have to ask herself that question, I thought as I watched my best friend make her way across Machiavelli's dining room to my table. Most theater critics would hardly be noticed if they walked across a stage, much less a dimly lit dining room. But most theater critics are nondescript, middle-aged men. And white.

Sherele is a showstopper. She keeps her wiry black hair closely cropped and wears her skirts long and clinging, all the more to accent her shape, as lean and riveting as her prose. If I didn't know what a generous heart beat under that ribbed silk sweater, I'd have to hate her.

"Was he a keeper?" she asked, with a leering smile as she slid into a chair across from me.

"Didn't stick around long enough so I could find out."

The low, silk-shaded lamp on the table had left my

face in shadow, so apparently Sherele hadn't noticed my glower. But once she caught my tone, she leaned across the table for a better look. Her smile vanished. "Oh, Chas, what happened? You dumped the poor guy?"

"Poor guy?" Just what I needed. Sherele's words derailed my self-pity in favor of more cathartic anger. "The twerp didn't even stay to finish his coffee. He's the one who dumped me." I suddenly felt surprisingly better.

Sherele reached over to pat my hand, but before she could say anything, the waiter grabbed his chance. "What shall I bring you beautiful ladies to drink? How about a nice sparkling glass of *Prosecco*? Yes. And you must taste a few slices of our specially imported prosciutto. With this wonderful ham I have some little sticks of fried bread–like an unsweet doughnut but very light, very crisp–which you will wrap in the ham. *Bellissimo!* You must try this before you even think of looking at the menu. Right?" He looked from Sherele to me, and nodded decisively as if we had given him a clear answer. "Right."

No time for hesitation at Machiavelli. The waiter dashed off, taking our awed silence as agreement.

Sherele and I shrugged at each other. "Right," we both said to his back, already four tables away. At least he'd managed to get us started on our favorite social activity: laughing.

Sherele wasn't fooled by my laughter, though. She immediately returned to the painful subject. "What do you mean he dumped you?"

I told her all. Every twitch. The frayed collar, the happy-face tie. I even confessed that Ottavio had begun to look almost good to me. I went on about his pretending to put money in his parking meter and never coming back. I told her about the sneering waiter. I didn't tell her about my eating the tiramisù.

"Even losers aren't interested in me," I finished, once again deflated by the retelling.

"No such thing." Sherele waved her hand impatiently as if my complaint were a puff of smoke. "You've always had men interested in you. The longest I've ever seen you without a guy was two years, but that was only because you were keeping your romance with Dave a secret. And remember, you were the one who broke up with Dave. So it's sheer masochism to read major rejection in this. Maybe the poor creep found a ticket on his car and it did him in. Maybe he was such a jerk that he couldn't find his way back to the restaurant. There's no way for you to know what actually happened, so there's no point thinking the worst. Besides, he's not the real problem here."

"If he's not, what is?"

"The real problem, my friend," said Sherele, holding up the little lamp as if to interrogate me, "is that you ate the tiramisù. Am I right?"

As if on signal, the waiter skidded to a stop at our table with two champagne flutes in one hand and in the other a plate the size of a medium pizza, filmed with thin slices of prosciutto under a tangle of golden branches. He placed the plate and glasses in front of us with such a flourish that I felt as if my hand had been kissed. Keeping up a steady murmur of compliments, he signaled each of us to pick up a branch of fried dough, then he speared slices of prosciutto with a fork and draped them around our fried bread with a little twirl, finishing with a slight bow.

"I'll be back in a moment with your menus," he said as he vanished again.

One bite and Ottavio didn't matter anymore. The contrast of ham and fried dough was startlingly delicious. Cold against warmth. Chewy, salty, and earthy against puffy, bland, and yeasty. Sherele and I wrapped and nibbled, taking sips of sweet, bubbly wine to heighten the saltiness and prickle our tongues, not even talking until we'd nearly finished the ham.

"We probably should have saved some for Homer," I suggested belatedly. "Or isn't he going to get here before dessert?"

"Not even then, I'm afraid. I'll tell you, going out with a homicide detective is the next best thing to not having a boyfriend at all, at least if you live in the murder capital of the U.S. of A. Homer's gotta work late again tonight. He sends his apologies."

"Then we'll just have to drink another glass of wine in his honor," I said, looking around for the waiter. I caught his eye and signaled that we wanted two more glasses of *Prosecco*.

"I'd happily settle for nothing more than this prosciutto and wine tonight," Sherele said as she picked at the last shreds of ham.

The waiter delivered two more glasses of bubbly and our menus without slowing his gallop to the next table. Sherele and I swallowed the last drops from our first glasses, then held up the new ones in a toast to Homer.

"I don't think our waiter would be happy if we made

dinner out of just a couple of glasses of wine and some fried bread and ham," I said. "Besides, I'm working, remember? I've got to try as much of the menu as we can possibly order without looking like fools."

"Good God!" Sherele wasn't answering me; she was talking to the menu.

I opened mine and looked, too.

PROSCIUTTO DI PARMA WITH FRIED BREAD—$18 PER PERSON

"What a scam!" I blurted. "Thirty-six dollars and he didn't even tell us." I did a quick calculation. "I don't know how much the *Prosecco* is, but I'll bet we're running more than sixty bucks and we haven't even ordered yet. No wonder they named this place Machiavelli."

"They should have named it *Glengarry Glen Ross*," Sherele said, after a long sip of her wine. "I, for one, have just lost my appetite."

"Sherele, have you ever walked out of a play after the first act?"

"If you were my boss asking me, I'd say no."

"But since I'm merely your best friend, I'll assume your answer is yes."

Sherele shrugged.

"I don't have the stomach to review this restaurant tonight. Let's go someplace else. I know a new little Persian restaurant with a ten-dollar buffet and the best baklava south of Brooklyn." Sherele is a dessert freak. I knew that would get her.

I waved to the waiter and asked for the check. I guess the glare in my eye warned him away from voicing any protest. I signed my credit card slip—a whopping $92.40 with no tip—and we left.

An hour later Sherele was finishing my baklava. We'd discussed the Machiavelli scam to death and we were back to talking about that never-tiresome subject: men. Her first baklava hadn't sweetened her complaints about Homer, who'd become the main subject of our conversation after we'd talked my afternoon disaster into the ground. "Three hundred and ninety-seven homicide cases last year. The city's murder rate is killing my romance," she said, as she stabbed the last chunk of nuts and phyllo with her fork.

"Here we are," she wound up, "two women with jobs that are the envy of anybody who's ever seen a play or eaten a doughnut, with lives that most people would consider the stuff of fantasy. Two women who sit in judgment of world-class artists. Who make people tremble and cower when we walk in the door. And what turns us to quivering Jell-O? A man not falling for us. Or standing us up. Or even not calling us. The world sees us as lionesses, and we see ourselves as mice."

"You're right," I said, resolved. "No more quivering. I'm going to be the person everyone thinks I already am."

"Right on," Sherele said, as she dabbed the last sticky crumbs with her finger, then licked them off.

"Waiter," I called, "we'll have another baklava."

3

Homer Jones unwrapped his sandwich of true prosciutto di Parma, gorgonzola, and mascarpone with watercress and fig jam. He said thanks for the good luck that had taken him over to Pennsylvania Avenue for a meeting this morning, so that he could stop at the Bread Line for his current favorite sandwich. He'd been salivating for prosciutto all morning after Sherele had told him about the overpriced appetizer he'd missed at Machiavelli last night.

The walnut bread smelled like fresh-ground whole wheat. Homer smiled to himself as he tucked a big cloth napkin into his collar and spread it across his teal blue shirt. Wouldn't want to stain his imitation Hermès tie. Homer kept a stack of cloth napkins in his bottom drawer in anticipation of many savory lunches to come.

Most homicide detectives at lunchtime settle for a hot dog on the street, at best seeking out a Sabrett's. Not Homer. If he didn't have a thermos of soup and some bread he'd made at home, he looked for the best he could buy. He devoted as much attention to the style and taste of what he put in his body as to the way he clothed it. He'd long ago determined to eat well no matter what the circumstances, even if he had to do it while he wrote up his death reports.

Like today.

DECEDENT'S NAME (Last, First, Middle):
unknown
SEX: male
RACE: white
AGE: 40 to 50
HOME ADDRESS: unknown
POSSIBLE MANNER OF DEATH: homicide
ADDRESS AND LOCATION OF DEATH: 1855 Wisconsin Ave. NW
FOUND DEAD TIME: 19:45

Most of it Homer had to leave blank. No next of kin. No occupation. Unknown yet whether the decedent was an alcoholic or a drug addict. In fact, the only other detail Homer could add was that the guy had clearly been strangled. And apparently robbed. No wallet. Band of pale skin on his wrist left by a watch. Poor slob had been dressed like every low-level bureaucrat in Washington: rumpled no-color suit, slightly frayed white shirt in need of a good bleaching, godawful tasteless necktie, in this case covered all over with those stupid yellow smiley faces.

This one was going to get a lot of attention. It had been found in a garbage bin behind the Social Safeway, Georgetown's famous all-night supermarket that served as an alternative to a singles bar for those who preferred to meet over a stack of Spago pizzas rather than a bottle of

Sam Adams. There would be no way around it: A body among the romaine leaves and beef trimmings was going to make news.

Everything was sunny about the next morning but me. My eyes felt puffy and my stomach heaved with an echo of baklava.

No matter what the weather, my path to the *Washington Examiner* is impeded by a parade of picketers complaining about something the newspaper did or hasn't done. But today even they seemed to have spring fever. They carried their placards at a rakish angle as they marched with a jaunty step. And instead of photos of bloody carcasses or emaciated inmates, their placards showed cartoon characters.

Being the newcomer among Washington newspapers, the *Examiner* had for its first decade been at a disadvantage in acquiring comic strips. Now, after long and painful gains in circulation and clout, it was taking advantage of every opportunity to catch up. Thus, the newspaper had just dropped its least-read strip in favor of an immensely popular one that unexpectedly came on the market. As a result, we were learning that every comic strip is loved by somebody.

Unlike middle-aged women.

I must have looked like a storm cloud as I passed the cheery protesters. Several shifted their eyes downward as they made way for me.

In a job like mine, where my work is to eat and drink night after night, I've grown used to coming to work with the bloat and headache of overindulgence. Today, though, my hangover was primarily emotional. I felt like an old napkin, thrown out rather than washed and pressed back in service. Washington's sparkling spring day was wasted on me.

The best I could hope was that nobody would bother me until the rhythm of work lulled me into a better mood. But no sooner had I clicked on my computer than I was summoned by the boss, Bull Stannard.

He couldn't have picked a less welcome moment to talk about my upcoming dining guide. After yesterday afternoon's sneering waiter and sludgy tiramisù, then last night's bill padding, I didn't feel in the mood to contemplate my annual search for Washington's finest restaurants.

It turned out that my sour mood was just right for what Bull had in mind.

Most newspaper editors have offices, merely offices. Not Bull Stannard. You'd have thought we were meeting in the Metropolitan Club. Madeleines were being served.

Bull, whose name is no exaggeration, sat anchoring his oversize chair with several hundred pounds of solid meat in a custom suit. Generally, men his size look as if they are about to burst their seams and their armchairs. Bull has both his suits and his furniture custom-made, so he looks perfectly normal until you notice his context: the stapler, the book, the teacup on his desk that appear doll-size, the pastry that seems but a crumb in his massive hand. Bull loves to play up the contrast. No Redskins mug of joe for him; his caffeine break is properly brewed tea, in a Meissen cup, accompanied by buttery French dainties.

Helen Marden, the lifestyles editor, was already settled on the damask sofa, sipping some of the effete brew. Normally, Helen's an outpost of serenity in the newsroom; but this morning even she looked fierce.

"The hell with fun and games for young readers," Bull was saying as I stepped through the door. "Good news sucks."

It was an old argument. Every newspaper in the country is suffering because of the same dread disease—attention deficit. When kids are diagnosed with this, their doctors give them Ritalin. But the symptoms aren't so easy for newspapers to treat. Newspapers' readership is draining away. Even more alarming, it's the young adults whose interest is slipping; thus, no future audience is developing. The adults of the future are growing up without the habit, and are learning instead to satisfy whatever craving they have for news via television or the Internet.

All in a panic, newspapers are scrambling to compete on the Internet and to establish their own presence on television and radio, but that doesn't secure a place for newsprint in future society. So the battle cry, from the *Seattle Post-Intelligencer* to the *Miami Herald*, is: Attract Young Readers. That's why newspapers are packing their shrinking news holes with more graphics. It's the reason the old, gray *New York Times* has gone Technicolor and the politics-heavy *Washington Post* fills Sunday Style's inside pages with contests for bad song lyrics and silly T-shirt slogans. Newspapers are looking for fun news, cute news, E-Z reading. And fearful of letting a single subscriber slip through their hands, they dread offending.

Bull sees it differently. He doesn't think a newspaper can compete with television by being more fun. He has no illusions about the fact that reading is simply harder work than watching. Furthermore, a newspaper can almost never hope to scoop twenty-four-hour television or radio, much less the instantly accessible Internet. He thinks the only chance a newspaper has is to go beyond reporting news and to be the news.

That's why Bull is at his happiest when those picketers outside our door are at their loudest. He loves to make the world angry, to churn things up. His most exquisite joy is forcing other media–newspapers, television–to report on the *Examiner*. Getting sued makes his day.

"Best madeleines in town, Chas. Try one." Bull held the plate toward me and nodded for me to take a seat. "You look like you need something stronger, though. Recovering from a Pepto night?"

I shook my head no to both questions and lowered myself gently onto the sofa next to Helen. She's a calming presence, which makes her a standout among newspaper editors. But today she definitely wasn't her usual serenely attentive self. In fact, she looked as if she were suffering from my hangover.

"Let's get it over with, Bull," she said, taking the plate of madeleines from his hand and setting it firmly out of his reach.

This looked like really bad news. Was Bull canceling the dining guide? Was he canceling me?

"Gotcha, Helen. Chas, I've got a new idea for the dining guide this year," Bull started.

That might be bad news, but it wasn't a pink slip.

"Everybody is doing a top ten since you started it," he continued, "so it's time to do something different."

"Or something more," Helen chimed in.

Top fifteen? I didn't say it, but that would be in line with Bull's usual innovations.

Instead, I launched my defense. "I personally think the readers will riot if we change one crumb of the top ten," I said, having learned that the only thing Bull likes better than a doormat employee is one who gives him a good fight.

"A riot over restaurant reviews . . . I like the idea. Do you think *Newsweek* would pick up on it?" Bull was actually smiling. I'd taken the wrong tack.

"Bull's not suggesting you forget the top ten altogether," Helen started to explain.

"Naw, that's your signature. But I think we need to vary it a little. This year, let's tell readers what to avoid," Bull interrupted.

"A bottom ten? That's impossible. There are too many," I protested.

"Slow down. That's not exactly what I had in mind. Not the ten worst. Too predictable. And too narrow, I agree. No, I want you to tell our readers about all the worst. All those dirty, sneaky, cheating things restaurants do to soak innocent diners. You're always showing me letters you get from customers who've been scammed. And didn't you find some credit card bill hiked last year? Hunt them down. Dig them out. When you finish, I want every reader from Gaithersburg to Herndon to start carrying a magnifying glass to restaurants to read the fine print."

"Look, Chas . . ." Helen was about to mollify me. Her brow wrinkled in concern.

But I didn't need mollifying. Machiavelli was in my sights. I loved the idea. And it wasn't because I wanted to compete with Dave as an investigative reporter.

My headache suddenly disappeared, and for the first time that day I smiled. "That's a great idea," I told Bull, as I unclenched my shoulders and sat back. I quickly recounted last night's experience at Machiavelli, which he agreed was a perfect example. "Can I write about cockroaches, too? I've got a whole file on them."

"Write about maggots if you like." I couldn't remember ever seeing Bull with such a wrinkly grin. But then, I couldn't remember ever agreeing with him before, either.

"I've got only one problem with this," I continued, thinking fast. To give in to Bull so easily is always a mistake. "Readers may love to be given something new to hate, but they also might feel deprived if we don't also tell them where to find some good food. Not to mention advertisers . . ." Now I was really playing to Bull's vulnerable spot.

"That brings me to the big brass ring I've got for you, Wheatley." Bull always tries to sound more gruff, calling you by your last name when he's got something nice to say, so this meeting was looking better by the moment. Even Helen's tense eyebrows had relaxed. "We're gonna syndicate your Table Matters column. Take it national. Not only are you gonna review a Washington restaurant every week, you're gonna tell our readers about restaurants everywhere in the country. Readers everywhere."

I was so shocked, I reached for a madeleine. Eating is my inevitable reaction to strong emotions. For a moment I couldn't think of a thing to say. This didn't sound believable.

When I finally found a response, it was exactly the wrong tack. "Who outside of Washington is going to buy a restaurant column from us?"

Bull didn't even look offended. He'd probably asked himself the same question at one time, and he beamed so proudly that he obviously relished the chance to explain his brilliant solution.

"Not many people know this yet, Chas, but we've formed our own syndicate. All of us number two newspapers around the country have been working out a new way of competing with the big dailies by pooling our resources. Instead of every one of us covering national issues, network TV, professional sports, health care, food trends, and all that, we're picking the best columnist in each field and all running with him. Or her. You're food; we all agreed. And we're going to launch you with this exposé of dirty practices. Every restaurant in the country will be talking about you."

"And what did you have in mind to keep them talking the second week?"

"The best restaurants in the United States. That's column numbers two and three up to fifty. You can write about anything you want, and part of that is going to be the most interesting places to eat around the country—giving us your take on them. You'll also have the chance to show off Washington restaurants to the rest of the world."

That I liked. For years I'd been trying to impress Bull with the crucial role restaurants play in Washington life. They're more than feeding stations or community centers or sites for seduction. In Washington, restaurants are the places where secrets are exchanged, deals are made, careers are launched, coups are planned. What would Watergate have been without those innocent-looking meeting grounds where money and information could be shared along with the chocolate soufflé?

I started to thank Bull, but he cut me off.

"Get out of here and start digging up dirt." He wiped his mouth meticulously with his napkin.

I felt like a lottery winner. One who hadn't even bought a ticket. No, it was better than the lottery. An Oscar—an award, not merely a lucky accident. When I'd walked in, I already had just about the best job in the world, and now I was about to walk out with one ten times better.

Under normal circumstances, one might shriek with joy. Whoop with glee. Dance. Leap madly about. But this was a big-city newsroom.

"Sounds good to me," I said. I wasn't about to make a fool of myself just because it was the happiest moment of my life.

Bull reached out his hand to shake mine—a rare display of affection.

I thrust out my hand to meet his. "One problem, though," I said, as he wrenched my bones.

Bull cocked his head and raised his eyebrow. He looked like a massive dog who had just heard a faint meow heading his way.

"We've got to keep this restaurant-scam story absolutely secret," I brazened, figuring this was about as powerful a moment as I was ever going to get with Bull. "Nobody, not one single reporter or editor outside this room, is to know what I am doing until it is finished."

"Hardly anybody does have to know," Bull said, as usual not really listening.

"No, 'hardly anybody' is too many. I mean none. This has to be taken as seriously as any investigative story this paper does, because to the restaurateurs it is every bit as dangerous."

"I like that." I'd hit just the right note with Bull. The meeting was over.

As I walked out with Helen, I saw Andy Mutton, the food editor, hanging outside Helen's door. He had spotted us through Bull's glass wall and was undoubtedly ready to pump Helen about our meeting. If it was about food, Andy was hungry.

"Helen, I especially don't want Andy to know anything about this story," I said, turning my head away from his direction. Maybe I was paranoid, but I didn't even want to risk his reading my lips.

"But, Chas, he might be helpful."

"I don't need him. And I don't trust him," I pleaded with her.

"It's your call," Helen assured me.

Good. I didn't really want to have to tell her about the time I'd found him leaking one of my negative reviews to a restaurant before I'd even finished writing it.

The first thing I did when I reached my desk was an unconscious reaction to exciting news. I picked up the phone and dialed Dave's number. Before it rang, I caught myself and, with a smidgen of self-pity, put down the receiver.

Next best: I called Sherele, who spends her mornings cooking at home because she thinks better in a room with a simmering pot of black-eyed peas. Before I could get a word in, she poured out her frustration over Homer being wrapped up in yet another insoluble murder. This time it was particularly ironic. Found behind the Social Safeway was a dead man who—like most Washington bureaucrats—had no distinguishing features and apparently no friends or relatives who missed him. To Homer's great surprise and relief, the news media were underplaying this murder in a fit of political correctness. They feared that highlighting a murder of a white man in Georgetown would leave the media open to criticism for not having given equal play to three recent murders of blacks in Anacostia. Even so, Homer was working around the clock to identify the body and the murderer. It's hard keeping up a relationship with a homicide detective in the murder capital.

My little bit of sympathy was generously repaid. For twenty minutes I had the rare treat of sharing great news with a colleague who reacts to it with pure joy and no jealousy whatsoever.

Then I called my daughter, Lily. I even called my ex-husband, Ari, who couldn't wait to tell the story all over again to his second spouse, Paul. When I let him in on the example of Machiavelli's dirty deed, he was so delighted I'd shared that bit of gossip that he volunteered to be my secret scout for more such examples.

By then it was approaching lunch hour, and I still hadn't started my real work. It was time to settle down and connect myself to my daily routine.

That takes me so long each morning, I wonder what reporters did with their first hour of the day in the "olden" precomputer days. First, I boot up. Then I enter e-mail, the electronic newsroom, the archives, and the Internet by typing my password a few times, probably a few more times than most since I am a sloppy typist. While the computer percolates, I walk over to the mail corner to retrieve the first of the day's paper-and-ink accumulation. Half of it I can always toss away unopened, but that still leaves a stack of books, press releases, and letters to deal with before the early afternoon delivery.

As I leafed through and organized the contents of my mailbox, I set aside two pink phone messages from the central switchboard and stacked the more personal-looking letters on top of the press releases. Three envelopes were from private schools, certain to be requests for auction donations ("lunch with the critic"). I opened the lone interoffice envelope immediately, just in case it was a notice of a merit raise that Bull had forgotten to tell me was going to accompany my syndication. Of course, I knew that wasn't the faintest possibility. Instead, the envelope contained my expense account, shipped back to me because I'd forgotten to sign it. The problem was, I'd submitted it two weeks before, and my unpaid American Express bill was waiting impatiently on my desk. Even the infamously slow U.S Postal Service could learn a few delaying tactics from the *Examiner*'s mail system.

I was ready to approach the electronic postal service. First, the newsroom's message system: This month's expense accounts are due (hah!). Everyone's invited to bid good-bye to the obit editor and eat some cake in honor of her departure (I couldn't wait to see how that cake was decorated).

Next, e-mail. Eight of the messages were from readers, the typical mix of complaints, compliments, requests for dining suggestions, and suggestions for where I should dine. Plus junk mail, of course, which meant a virus alert, a chain letter, a political message, and some religious tract that reminds me every few days that the world is going to come to an end if I don't eat lower on the food chain. A good friend who's a food writer in California alerted me that a wonderful LA pastry chef was relocating in Washington and went on to tell me that last night he'd eaten some outrageously overpriced ravioli that worked out to ten dollars a bite. I replied with my thanks for the pastry-chef tip and countered his ravioli with my thirty-six-dollar plate of prosciutto. I knew he'd call for the juicy details as soon as he read this.

It was time to tackle voice mail. By now, though, I was already tired of suggestions, and my mental pencils were sharpened and ready to write. I considered putting off my voice mail until later, when I'd need a break from writing my column.

No, I couldn't do it. Just as I can't ignore a phone ringing and let the answering machine deal with it. Communicator genes.

The phone itself was uncharacteristically quiet, I thought, forgetting for the moment that it was too close to lunchtime for restaurateurs to call. In another hour they'd be finding excuses to remind me about their restaurant—a new menu, an upcoming wine dinner, a visit by some star performing at the

Kennedy Center or Arena Stage. They'd ring me after the height of the lunch rush.

The publicists would start in full force later, since they linger at lunch. I'd be their afternoon's project. Hotels, pricey restaurants, and chains keep publicists on retainer, and I am one of their prime targets. Several had beat the rush and already had chats with my voice mail: "How are things going?" "Whadda ya think of this weather?" "I've got some really big news, and I'm passing it on to you before anybody else." By Friday they'd be desperate enough that they would call with no better reason than to ask whether I'd received their press releases.

I found nothing personal among my messages this morning. Nothing I was vaguely tempted to answer.

The waste of all this meaningless communication made me itch to get some real work done. I fished for last night's menus in my purse, where I'd folded them and wedged them under my makeup kit. As soon as I pulled the kit aside, Machiavelli's laminated menu popped out and unfolded itself like a bouquet of flowers from a magician's hat.

I'd finished writing my Friday restaurant review yesterday, so I had just enough time before lunch to pull together my notes for my Sunday column—a warm-up for my soon-to-be-syndication.

Table Matters
By Chas Wheatley
Examiner Staff Writer

Generally it's viewed as a sign of progress that our food has no seasons. We can eat fresh produce throughout the winter, and find every kind of meat, fish, and vegetable on our plates in February as easily as in August. We can enjoy raspberries on New Year's Eve and corn on the cob for Thanksgiving.

We know there's a price to pay. Nobody expects to encounter winter tomatoes with a midsummer aroma. We're even willing to buy what looks like a pale pink tennis ball and tastes like the packing material as long as it behaves like a tomato. Over the decades we've been educated to concede that winter tomatoes must be bred for sturdiness and shipping quality if we are to have them at all. And we've lately accepted without protest that cherry tomatoes—which once arrived sweet and flavorful every day of the year—no longer have any taste.

This week at Morton's I was reminded how far backward we have come. The waiter proudly touted a beefsteak tomato—with the option of purple onion or (not and) blue cheese for $5.50. Admittedly it was sliced to order, but it was featured (and priced) as if this were midsummer and the tomato came fresh from the fields of New Jersey.

To make matters worse, I've had equally winter-pale beefsteak tomatoes at Morton's in summer, when the restaurant must have to go to some lengths to find such hard, tasteless ones at the time of year when vine-ripened fruits are for sale even on downtown street corners. Maybe Morton's is aiming to provide consistency year-round and from coast to coast. Or does its management believe that a generation raised on cottony tomatoes now prefers them that way? Could it be that I've missed the point and will be chided for not recognizing the brand-new cross between a tomato and a cucumber?

4

The next morning, I woke up euphoric about the new direction in which my career was heading. I decided to celebrate by making a reservation at one of the best restaurants in America—taking up Bull on the second part of his promises for my column. And since it would take a month or two to get a table at one of these superstars, I could have all that time to look forward to it.

I watched the clock carefully. The switchboard at Jean-Georges, Manhattan's hottest ticket, opens at nine A.M. At that moment, people flood the phones with calls begging a reservation for exactly a month ahead. Since I don't live in New York, I would be at a disadvantage. I'd have to dial 1 and the area code, four more numbers than New Yorkers needed, and that would slow me down in the race to get my call through. Fortunately, I have a redial button on my phone, so I could at least compete with any out-oftowner who had a speed dialer. Even luckier, I don't live in California, where I'd have to get up by six A.M. to make the call.

After forty-five minutes, I was so hooked on the rhythm of punching redial and hanging up that I nearly cut off the voice when it came.

"Jean-Georges. May I help you?"

I was too late. The reservations for that day—a month from now—were already filled. I wrote on my calendar to try again another day.

I strode into the newsroom ready to complain to anybody who'd listen about what a bothersome job restaurant reviewing is. Of course I knew there'd be nobody who'd listen to such privileged whining. Even if the newsroom hadn't been empty.

Given that state, I allowed myself to stop at Dave's abandoned desk, piled with mail and memos but stripped of all mementos of me. I sat in his chair and imagined him in it, too, tugging me onto his lap. Somehow I'd expected to miss him less as the weeks went by, but instead I was growing steadily hungrier for him.

The ding of an arriving elevator startled me to my feet. I didn't want to get caught with my resolve down. I scurried to my desk and was swiveling in my own chair by the time colleagues began trickling into the newsroom.

People don't expect you to look for sympathy when you're the one to break up a romance, but in this case I'd thought I was splitting up to save it rather than to scuttle it. I hadn't really expected Dave and me to stay apart this long but thought the breakup would shock him into appreciating what we'd had. I'd expected a fresh start long before now. Would I have been so cavalier if I'd thought that once Dave was out the door he'd keep walking?

Never.

And now recollections of his caressing voice and his belly-shaking laughter drowned out my memory of his silences. Long, lean body, hazelnut-colored hair falling over seductive gray eyes—why had I cared so much about his forgetting to show up one night?

"Where are you, girl?" Sherele dropped my mail on my desk and gave me a quizzical look. Rarely did she check the mailboxes before I got to them.

"Huh?" I said noncommittally, blinking at the noise of briefcases, bags, and stacks of mail being thumped on desks around the newsroom and computers issuing their bell-like greetings to their handlers. Last time I'd surfaced, I was nearly alone, and now the room was humming like a meadow full of bees in clover, with little stand-up meetings in the aisles and phone conversations at almost all the occupied chairs. Everybody was communicating. That's what we do.

I was just about to give Sherele a more complete answer, when Andy Mutton curdled my view. I should have heard the slap-slap of his footsteps—the sole had come loose from his left shoe—as he walked up behind me. But I didn't spot him until his food-stained tie was six inches from my nose. Strawberry jam on his toast, it told me, with crumbs on his belt buckle to back it up.

"Tomatoes are my department," Andy growled at me, shaking a computer printout in my face. Andy, as the *Examiner's* food editor, sees as his competition, not the *Post* or *Washingtonian* magazine, but me. I'm the one he hides information from, spies on, and sabotages every chance he gets. He sees every word I write as one less for him, every breath I take as using up his air. And he's always trying to enlist Helen and Bull in shrinking my territory.

"*Your* department? Are you trying to tell me I can't write about the tomatoes a restaurant serves? What about the lettuce? The fish? The meat? Maybe I should leave my columns full of blank spaces, like obscenities. Tomatoes deleted." I scooted my chair forward, forcing Andy to edge backward, then I backed up to make some space between us.

"You're not talking about eating tomatoes or cooking tomatoes," he grumbled back at me. "You're talking here about buying tomatoes. And shopping is the food section's turf. I'm going to get Helen to kill this column of yours. Mark my words, Wheatley, if you continue to step on so many toes, your column won't be all that people want to kill." He was still rattling the computer printout as he stalked off to Helen's office.

Sherele and I shook with laughter. I reached into my bottom drawer for two napkins to wipe our eyes.

"I can't wait to read your next column," Sherele squeaked in between bursts of laughter. "'The lettuce and bleep salad tasted fresh. The pizza needed more bleep sauce. Be sure to try the bleep-LT.'"

"Then there's that old song, 'You say tomato, I say bleep.'"

I felt much better. It wasn't until later in the day that I began to wonder about how Andy happened to get hold of that column, which was stored only on my computer.

Being a restaurant critic sets you in the opposite direction from your colleagues—in fact, from most people. When I'm working hardest, everyone else is playing. My job is what the rest of the world considers entertainment. Of course that's also true for movie critics, sports writers, all kinds of reporters. But for me life is even further out of step. People refer to food these days as sinful. Some consider my work a form of pornography.

Look what happens at lunchtime here at the *Examiner*. Instead of putting on their suit jackets to go out for lunch, more and more of my colleagues put on their sneakers or grab duffel bags they carry off to the gym. Lunchtime is not for eating, but for working off their past and future eating. My fellow reporters duck into the rest rooms to change into shorts and T-shirts for a jog to the Mall. They swim, they read a news magazine or a government report on the treadmill, they work off their editorial frustrations with free weights.

Some, of course, eat lunch at lunchtime. But it's not the lunch a reporter would have eaten in the days when I first started reading newspapers. No double-scotch or three-martini meal at a seedy bar, or even a burger at a twenty-four-hour diner. Lunch is a salad, hold the dressing. Midday interviews with sources, bitching sessions with office mates about heavy-handed editing—these days they're conducted against a background of turkey on toast, mustard not mayo. A real splurge means a dish of sorbet.

Thus my colleagues are eager to go to lunch with me once. But even though it's a free meal, few volunteer for a replay. Almost nobody is comfortable ordering the three courses I need my companions to try so that I can sample a full range of the menu. I feel their disapproving scrutiny when I order veal marengo, or french fries, or even mashed potatoes. My guests greet every new dish with an apology: "I haven't tasted fettuccine alfredo in years" or "I certainly won't eat any dinner tonight." I feel as if I've dragged an innocent into an X-rated movie.

Vince Davis had been to lunch with me before, so I had to promise to let him order just a salad this time in order to rope him into joining me again. It was worth the compromise because he's not only one of the best reporters in the business section, he's secure enough to share his information and ideas with other reporters. And I could trust his discretion. I wanted to pump him about consumer scams.

"What you really want is a mole," Vince said, as he tasted his Evian and nodded to the waitress approvingly, as if she had just poured him a wine to sample.

"I wish I could find one." I winced as I said it, thinking of Ottavio Rossi. My pain over being dumped was magnified by the recollection of how eager he'd been to tell me about the "weird" things that were happening behind the scenes in his restaurant. Maybe I should swallow my pride and track him down. "In the meantime, I hoped you could give me some examples of how scammers work. A place to start."

"I'll begin with a classic in my department: Here's a surefire way for a sleazy stockbroker to pick up clients," he said, as he cut a leaf of arugula into four pieces and lined them up with quarters of cherry tomatoes he'd already dissected. "He starts with as large a mailing list as he can accumulate and divides the group into halves." He illustrated with the greenery on his plate.

"Why halves?" I asked the question to give him a chance to take a bite. His orderly food was beginning to make me feel uncomfortable as I forked up long, sloppy strands of tomatoey fettuccine puttanesca.

Vince swallowed and launched into his explanation. "That's how he proves himself to be an infallible stock picker. He chooses a stock, say Merck. He writes to half the prospective clients, introducing himself as a broker with a revolutionary new method and a finger on the pulse of the market. He tells them to buy Merck today because it is going to go up. He writes a similar letter to the other half, but tells them that his stock tip of the day is to sell any Merck they might have since it is definitely going to go down. Then he waits until Merck goes up or down and writes a follow-up letter to the half for whom he predicted correctly. In this letter he picks another stock, say, Amgen, and tells half of them it is going to go up and the other half that it is going to decline. Then he waits for Amgen to move up or down and writes to those for whom he has now predicted two right moves. That's a quarter of his original group. After two more stock picks—half right and half wrong—he's got one out of sixteen people in his original group believing that he's predicted what would happen to four stocks in a row with nary a miss. They've found themselves the stockbroker of their dreams, and they can't write him checks fast enough."

"Gruesome," I said. "Just the kind of thing I want."

5

Procrastination sometimes pays off. My file drawers are filled with complaints about restaurants, letters that readers have been sending me for a decade. I tend to just stuff them in folders, promising myself that I'm going to weed them out when I have time. Now, instead of feeling guilty about never getting around to a cleanup, I was relieved that I'd never thrown away any of the letters. Maybe I wouldn't need an Ottavio Rossi after all, at least not yet. My files were a mountain of raw material for my exposé of restaurant scams.

"Raw" is the significant word here. The letters weren't organized, just randomly dumped into a series of folders. It took me weeks to review and sort them, devising categories as I went along. Overbooking reservations. Wine list misinformation. Excessive charges. Portion sizes. Ingredients. I ran out of space on my desk and began arranging papers into piles on the floor, labeling and stacking them at the end of each day and hoping that the cleaning crew would treat them gingerly.

That was just the beginning. I cross-referenced the complaints by restaurant, and grouped together those with common ownership, looking for clusters and patterns. I kept a tally of complainers, and flagged a few chronic ones for a future article on restaurants being plagued by troublemakers. I even tried reorganizing the material chronologically to look for patterns in the dates when particular problems recurred.

The task filled all my free time and became an obsession, like doing crossword puzzles or playing solitaire. These stacks of letters papered over thoughts I didn't want to notice anyway. To be exact: missing Dave.

All I could talk about was wine.

"Have you ever wondered why wine prices in restaurants are so much higher than in liquor stores?" I asked Sherele, who had moved her chair to the far side of her desk in deference to my stacks of papers edging over my desk into her territory. I couldn't see her computer screen because she'd had to turn it to face her new position, but I didn't think she was working on anything important.

"Not really." She didn't even look up.

She must be writing something important after all. I got up and circled my paper landscape to stand behind her and get a look at her computer. No wonder she had sloughed off my question.

"I didn't know you could get that stuff on the Internet here at work," I said. "Aren't you afraid of somebody catching you at this?"

Sherele instantly hit ALT+TAB, and the succulent male flesh that had occupied her screen turned to notes on the summer theater season. "Fastest keyboard in the newsroom," she boasted. "Now, what were you saying about wine?"

I sat on the edge of her desk, half wishing we were discussing her topic rather than mine.

"It can be big money for a restaurant. The restaurant buys it wholesale—about half the retail price—and marks it up as much as three times, to well above retail. Already we're talking about greed."

Sherele leaned back and gave me her full attention. "You know, Chas, we've been going out to dinner together for a lot of years. And surely you don't think I haven't been listening all that time. I know what it costs a restaurant to serve wine—the up-front money for bottles it might not sell for a decade, the storage space, the occasional bad bottle. I know how much breakage there is, how much a really nice wine glass costs. It seems to me that last time we discussed this, you were defending those triple markups."

"You're right, but only for low-end wines. The problem is that while tripling a wine to twenty dollars could be warranted, tripling the price of an eighty-dollar wine is outrageous. That would be like charging sixty dollars for a steak. And the charges for wine by the glass are really disgusting. One-fourth of the bottle price is normal, even though a bottle will yield five or six glasses. Yet some restaurants charge as if there were only three glasses per bottle, and then they pour short, so they serve as little as two or three ounces."

"Interesting subject," Sherele agreed, "but hardly a

major scandal. After all, the job of capitalists is to make money." Sherele was one of the very few people I'd told about the story I was writing.

"That's just the warm-up. The commonplace irritant. What's really appalling is how often restaurants overcharge on top of the overcharges."

The newsroom buzz had grown louder, as it tends to late in the afternoon, when deadline pressure builds. I realized I'd been raising my voice to keep pace. So I lowered it again as I continued.

"Wine provides the easiest opportunity for overcharging a diner. The reason is that diners are insecure about wine. It's a complicated subject. It involves geography, chemistry, meteorology, and geology. Just for a start. Most diners don't understand labels, they haven't the foggiest idea about which wines should cost more, they can't compare vintages, and they are afraid of being embarrassed publicly. So they just pretend they know what they are doing."

"Sounds like me," Sherele said.

"I hope not. Here's how it works. You look over the wine list and figure it's a nice restaurant, so you'll splurge a little and order something in the middle range of the list. You've heard that Rhônes tend to be good values, so you pick a Côte du Rhône for forty-five dollars. 'Very good choice,' the waiter says. You're ready for some fine drinking.

"The waiter returns with a bottle of wine, and he interrupts your conversation to show it to you. You're distracted; what's more, the light is dim. Still, you can see, plain as day, that it's a Côte du Rhône. He pours you a taste, you swirl it as if you know what you're doing, you sniff the cork—which is a meaningless gesture—and you sip the wine. Delicious. Everybody's happy.

"Until the check comes. The charge for the wine is a hundred and thirty dollars. You ask the waiter about it, and he says with assurance, 'That's for the Côte du Rhône blankety-blank.' He might even bring the wine list to show you that, sure enough, it was one thirty. You're too embarrassed to tell him that you meant the forty-five dollar wine listed just above it. The mistake must have been your fault. You were too ignorant to realize that he'd brought you the wrong bottle, and you accepted it without complaint. You pay up and shut up, just to save face."

"This really happens and people quietly go along with it?" Sherele looked skeptical.

"Ask Homer sometime. If he's willing to admit it. I'll bet he's had it happen to him, and he knows a lot more about wine than most people do. Of course, this trick is usually pulled with men, especially when they are on a date or showing off in some way."

"What happens if the waiter is called on it?" Sherele asked.

"He'd have to have been called on it when the bottle was brought, not when the check is presented," I explained. "That's assuming he really did serve the more expensive bottle. Sometimes he'll just bring the cheaper bottle and charge for the expensive one, claiming it was a simple error and apologizing profusely if he's caught."

"This is great stuff, Chas. Tell me more." Sherele's phone rang, but she just looked over at the caller ID and ignored it.

"There are many variations on the theme," I continued, settling myself more comfortably on her desk. "You might order a Fetzer sauvignon blanc and be served the chardonnay—or just be charged for the chardonnay, which is considerably more expensive. Also, switching vintages is commonplace. The diner has to remember which year was on the wine list and check that the one on the bottle matches. Or there might be a seemingly tiny difference on the label such as the nonreserve instead of the reserve, or the wine from the winery's lesser vineyard rather than its premium one. Some restaurants take advantage of the fact that people forget the prices on the wine list. A restaurant could add on five or ten dollars and it probably wouldn't be noticed, or charge for a full bottle when only a half was ordered."

"I've got one for you," Sherele said, practically rubbing her hands in glee.

"The floor is yours."

"You know that Italian restaurant over near Union Station, the one with the greasy water glasses and the huge platters of sausages and peppers?"

I nodded. It's one of Washington's classics.

"One night a bunch of us were there, eating and drinking up a storm. Well, the place doesn't really have a wine list, as you'll recall. It just brings you a bottle of the one red or white wine it always serves. I guess you'd call it the house wine, though it comes in a bottle rather than a carafe.

"That night, we were in the smoking section. One of the guys looked around for an ashtray and saw that all of them had migrated to the other end of the table. So he just put out his cigarette in an empty wine bottle."

"Yeecch." I shuddered. I hate the smell of wet cigarettes.

"We kept ordering more wine. It was one of those long, messy evenings. The waiter would bring more bottles of wine and we'd pour it ourselves into those little tumblers they use for wine glasses. At one point I poured for everyone around me, then poured myself the last of the bottle. Out came that cigarette butt."

"Yeecch," I repeated.

"That's what comes of, as Thomas Hardy put it, 'putting new wine in old bottles,'" Sherele said with a smirk.

"Hardy? Which play? You're not usually reduced to quoting a novel," I chided her, since Sherele hardly ever ends a conversation without an exit line from a play.

"He cribbed it from the Bible anyway. Substituted 'bottles' for 'wineskins,'" she said, as her phone rang again. "It's Homer," she mouthed when she picked up the receiver.

Mine rang, too, and I reached behind me to pick it up.

"Chas Wheatley," I said, as I looked at the caller ID. It was a "private number," which meant it came from some switchboard.

"Good day, Miss W. I have some information that might interest you." The voice was male, accented. West Indian? Jamaican? I had no time to figure it out. The next words were replaced by a dial tone. He must have changed his mind about talking to me, because he'd hung up.

My friends tell me I make people nervous.

6

Homer Jones didn't look good. His glossy dark skin had an ashy cast and was puffy under his eyes. Most telling, he didn't bother to protect the razor edges of his pants when he sat down again after greeting me with a kiss.

I didn't even have to look at Homer to know he was in bad shape. I could see his fatigue in Sherele's eyes.

"No wonder we haven't been able to get together lately," I said to Homer, as I slid into the banquette next to Sherele. "You look exhausted."

"Hey, thanks, Chas. Is that the way to talk to a guy who's wearing his best knock-off Armani just to have dinner with you?"

"I didn't say you don't look handsome. Just tired. What's going on?"

"Nothing that will take away my appetite. And nothing that a bottle of *viognier* can't fix. What do you think of this one?" At least Homer wasn't so worn down that he hadn't thoroughly examined Coastline's twelve-page wine list before I arrived a mere five minutes late. He held out the leather-bound volume to me.

Gianni Marchelli got there first with another copy of the wine list. The owner of Coastline is as quick and smooth as melted caramel. "No need to share. With a list like this, you should both take your time. And you, Miss Travis, would you like one, too?"

Sherele shook her head. "I'd rather have a Bloody Mary to examine while these two prolong the foreplay."

Gianni gave her an appreciative smirk as he slid away to order her Bloody Mary.

Coastline, an extravagant New England restaurant, had been an immediate hit when it opened two years ago. Since I wait at least a month before visiting a new restaurant, I had a hard time getting a reservation. Then I dreaded going back. The chef seemed taste-blind, for all he understood about combining ingredients. Shiso leaves and Frangelico have no business consorting on a rack of lamb. Four million dollars in fish tanks, brushed aluminum walls, and cigar vaults can't hide silly food. I panned the place.

It didn't surprise me when Coastline's chef eventually left, but I was taken aback to learn that his downfall wasn't his cooking but his attitude. The salad girl (the fact that they're still called that tells a lot) had complained that the chef wouldn't keep his hands to himself. And once he still had a knife and fork in them. She had scars to prove it.

Gianni had to act fast, not only to oust the chef,

but to reestablish order in the kitchen. I wondered whether he was acting too fast by simply promoting the sous chef, Benny Martinez. That's what I was here to find out.

The preliminary signs were good. The menu had been shortened and simplified. I couldn't find shiso leaves anywhere. And from the first bite I saluted Gianni's wisdom. The wild mushroom and scallop pan-fry was such a remarkable appetizer—crisp-edged chanterelles throbbing with flavor, scallops caramelized at the edges but still slightly translucent inside—that after we passed plates, Homer suggested we order another portion. Since the first had restored him as if his interior lights had been turned back on, I agreed.

By the last bite of Indian Pudding Tart, which sounds heavy but tasted like shoofly pie gone to Harvard, Homer, Sherele, and I were groaning as well as laughing. We'd eaten well beyond our fill, while Sherele had led us in devising new lines for old plays. A politically correct *Othello* was the pinnacle of our giddiness. Homer looked as though he'd been on a vacation. And I was mentally rescheduling my week so I could return and write about the new Coastline as soon as possible.

Homer rolled his shoulders as if enjoying the aftermath of a massage. "I didn't think I could feel this good this week," he said.

"Will it set you back to talk about what's going wrong?" I ventured.

"No, it would probably help." Homer swirled the bit of wine he always saved for the end of the meal and took a sip. "Too many unsolved homicides. It's bad enough when witnesses won't come forward to help us nail murderers. But lately we're having trouble even figuring out who the murder victims are. Take, for example . . ."

Gianni Marchelli interrupted with a bottle of Armagnac. "Any table that orders a second round of appetizers in my restaurant always gets free Armagnac," he said, as he put the bottle down and snapped his fingers to signal the waiter for glasses.

I started to protest, but Homer's eyes looked too happy for me to continue. Sherele, who knows what I'm thinking almost before I do, shrugged at me in sympathy. It's not always easy to fend off freebies, especially when a restaurateur insists that he offers the same to all his customers.

"I've been meaning to try out your legendary cigar room," Homer was saying to Gianni as his Armagnac was being poured. "You get a pretty good crowd, I hear."

"The cigar room does even better than the dining room," Gianni said, his cheeks dimpling from a contented smile. It's those dimples that soften his Italian-banker dignity and make him look approachable as well as fourth-generation handsome. I found myself hoping for another wink. "I've even opened it for breakfast. I'd be glad to show it to you; but if nobody minds indulging me, I would first like to introduce my new chef to you. Chas, he tells me his mother has been lighting candles in your honor ever since he took over the kitchen."

Gianni nodded in the direction of the open kitchen, where I now noticed someone hovering at the edge of the window. A short, wiry man headed our way so hesitantly that he seemed to be waiting for someone to yank him back.

"Meet Benny Martinez."

Gianni's arm around Benny's shoulder might have been all that was holding the chef upright. His hands flexed and clenched; his smile faded in and out. He kept nodding his head as if someone were asking him a barrage of questions. Benny Martinez looked about twelve years old and mighty nervous.

"Miss Wheatley, I have been reading what you write for many years, and I think you are a big help to all chefs who want to know how to please the customers. That is what I want to tell you. It is an honor to cook for you," Benny recited as if he had been rehearsing.

"He knows better than to ask how you liked your meal," Gianni interrupted. "But I don't. How was everything?"

"It's been a lovely evening," I answered, embarrassed as always and skirting the question.

"I do not need to know yet, Miss Wheatley. I want to get better each time I cook for you. Then I would like to hear what you think of my cooking only after you have tasted everything I can do," Benny said.

"You see, he's not only a great chef, he's more of a diplomat than I." Gianni recovered control of the conversation. Benny caught his hint and took his leave.

When he was gone, Gianni continued, "Benny's so shy that he's moved his station to the back of the kitchen, where he can't be seen by the dining public. It's a problem when guys like the Speaker of the House or the CEO of Comsat want to meet the chef."

He brushed a stray crumb from the tablecloth and smoothed it unconsciously while he talked, his hand so close to mine that I could feel its warmth. "When people hang out in the cigar lounge they like to show their friends how well connected they are with the restaurant world. It reassures everybody of their importance when the chef greets them personally. But give Benny time. A couple of good reviews and he'll be conducting his orchestra from the front with headphones like Bob Kinkead wears."

"I like a good cigar myself on occasion," Homer hinted broadly.

Gianni beamed and bowed slightly in Homer's direction. "Let me set up a table for you. This Armagnac tastes all the better in the company of cigar smoke." He backed away from our table, as if he didn't want to seem overanxious to leave.

As soon as he was gone, Homer looked from Sherele to me. "Would you mind? Is it getting too late for you?" But Gianni was back to fetch us before either of us responded.

"You were going to tell me about your horrible week," I reminded Homer once we were settled, he and Sherele puffing cigars while I just swirled and sniffed my Armagnac. It did taste better with cigar smoke, as long as it was forty-dollar-a-stogie Havana cigar smoke.

"Yeah." Homer sighed, but it was a sound of contentment rather than complaint. The meal had done its work. "But first I have something I want to say to you, Chas. I didn't want to talk about it with waiters hovering over us." He looked around; none of the staff was within eavesdropping distance.

"I hope you don't mind that I told Homer about your assignment," Sherele interrupted, looking sheepish.

I did mind, but I knew I was feeling overprotective, so I kept silent.

Homer's gaze had fallen lovingly on his cigar. He twirled it and smiled seductively at it. Then he looked at me and his mouth went serious.

"I'm sorry I didn't get to say this sooner, Chas, because Sherele has told me how much work you've already put in this investigation of yours. But I think you should reconsider writing this story."

I was stunned. "Reconsider? Not on your life. Why would I want to drop this? It's a great project. You wouldn't believe the dirt I've been finding out about restaurants."

I told him about the stealing with credit cards and the wine scams, talked about the sources I'd interviewed. We talked about Sherele's and my experience at Machiavelli. He listened carefully and asked thoughtful questions.

"If this goes as well as I'm hoping," I concluded, "readers will never think of restaurants the same way again."

"Exactly. That's the point."

"What's the point?" It wasn't fair. Homer had his cigar to soothe him. I suddenly wished I smoked.

"The point is that you love restaurants. You want them to thrive. You appreciate their art and you understand their hardships. What you're doing is going to hurt them, not just the bad restaurants, but the good ones, too."

I couldn't believe this starry-eyed speech from

Homer, who not only tore into homicide investigations with the same gusto he devoted to a stack of barbecued ribs but didn't even back off from chewing out other detectives when they struck him as too passive. And I told him so. No minced words.

Sherele, to her credit, didn't either take sides or try to mediate. She just sat quietly, smoke curling slowly from the edges of an amused mouth, her eyes bouncing from one of us to the other as if we were a tennis game.

"I'm not defending the restaurants that cheat the public, but they are a small minority, the exceptions rather than the rule," Homer summed up his argument. "More important, I'm worried about your being seen as part of the food police, with all of those crusaders against rare beef and milk-fed veal and hollandaise sauce. And I'm worried about you. This is big business you're attacking, and in my department you see how far some of the worst elements will go to defend their profits."

My voice grew metallic. I could hear it myself. I was turning chilly and defensive. I was worried that he was right.

Sherele understood. The more shrill I sounded, the more I was taking Homer's point. So she stepped in.

"Give the girl a little space," she said to Homer.

That lowered my defenses. "Setting aside your views as a homicide detective, you have an important point, Homer. The fact is, restaurants are my life. I don't want to suggest that most—or even many—of them cheat the public. I intend to put my complaints in perspective. And I need to help readers to distinguish between legitimate cost-cutting or pushing the profit margin and cheating."

Homer was nodding. "Smart business versus sharp business."

"Exactly. The good, honest restaurants should appreciate my explaining to the public that cheating goes on, but most restaurants wouldn't dream of doing it."

"You got it," Homer agreed.

"And now, my sweet," Sherele took Homer's arm and tucked it under hers as she changed the subject, "let's see if we can dissect your work. Tell Chas about this mystery victim who has you in such a sweat."

"Not much to go on there," Homer started to say. Then he stopped and reached inside his jacket to pat his waist. I knew that gesture; he'd been beeped.

Leaving the poor unknown murder victim undiscussed and his Armagnac unfinished, Homer—with his cigar—was off to the next emergency.

7

"Mama, let's go to dinner."

Lily's call took me aback. I'm always the one suggesting dinner to Lily. I'd long ago accepted that in a mother-daughter relationship, it is the mother who inevitably seeks more contact. And given my job, I'm continually and frantically looking for dinner companions.

Countless people volunteer that they would love to go to dinner with me. After all, I'm picking up the check. And it's fun to see a meal you've shared written up in the newspaper. But all too often they want to dine out only in theory, not necessarily in practice. A trip to Rockville or Fairfax on a Tuesday night to an unknown Peruvian restaurant? They ask for a rain check. What's worse, too many potential companions don't eat red meat, or shellfish, or can't take spicy food, or are allergic to nuts, or are on the Ornish diet this month. For a restaurant critic, trying to find a dinner companion can be like living in a neighborhood filled with teenagers and looking for a babysitter on a Saturday night.

"Tonight?" I couldn't believe my good luck. A ready companion just when I needed one, and my favorite companion at that.

Lily wasn't quite so available as she'd sounded. "Sorry, I can't make it tonight. Pick another night. I have someone I want you to meet."

"You and Brian haven't broken up, have you?" My mercurial daughter's boyfriend is a waiter, and that poses some ethical problems for me as a restaurant critic, but he's worth the trouble.

"No, not a guy. Well, yes, a guy, but not a date. Brian and I are just fine."

"That's a relief."

"This is a guy I went to school with. I ran into him at Tower Records. He used to be a musician, too, but guess what he's doing now?"

"Opening a restaurant?" Usually when my friends and relatives have "someone I want you to meet," it means someone needs advice.

"Much better than that. He's an investigator for a credit card company. And I think I can get him to talk."

I never get over the pleasure of watching my twenty-three-year-old daughter enter a room. Tonight she was wrapped in filmy layers of cotton billowing like gentle white waves in a blue sea. Lily puts together outfits that seem like merely bits and pieces of cloth writhing around her in beautiful and changing patterns. She sometimes looks pre-Raphaelite, sometimes newly arrived from ancient Greece, and occasionally as if she'd been evicted from a homeless shelter. Her mood shows not only in her blue eyes, her posture, the set of her mouth, and the bounce or limpness of her curly black hair, but in the very texture of her clothes. Tonight she was wearing something peaceful.

"Mama, meet Josef," she said, as she gave me a kiss and slipped into her seat. She reached over for my glass of Matanzas Creek sauvignon blanc, swirled it and sniffed, then raised her eyebrows in approval before she took a sip. Lily knows wines like most of her generation know espressos, lattes, and cappuccinos.

Tonight I'd chosen a Chinese restaurant—with family-style service—in case Josef might be squeamish about our sharing food from each other's plates. I need not have worried. Lily passed my glass to him, and he also swirled and sipped. I realized Lily and Josef had that ease together that comes from more than shared classrooms and concerts. Theirs was the intimacy born of coed dorms.

How quickly our world has changed. I once amazed Lily by referring to a men's dorm on my college's campus. She'd had no idea that in "the olden days" of my youth men and women weren't allowed to live under the same roof—not even permitted to visit the upstairs of each other's buildings. In turn, I was taken aback to find that some of her school's dorms had coed bathrooms.

Whatever else those revisions had wrought, they seemed to have led to friendships with a brother-sister closeness quite different from those in my day.

And since Lily is an only child, I've been grateful for the change.

I already liked this string bean of a young man. And that was before I witnessed his huge, uncritical appetite. My perfect dinner companion.

It took some urging and substantially more wine before we could loosen his tongue. Relaxed as Josef might be about sharing spoons and eating sea slugs, he was stiff and hesitant about leaking information. I helped him along by talking about some of the scams I already knew—starting with the prosciutto pricing at Machiavelli and going on to the bill hiking I'd found in my files—so he would think he was only filling in insignificant details, not revealing brand-new material.

"From what I understand, all it takes to apply for a credit card in somebody else's name is the right social security number, and anyone can copy that from a D.C. driver's license," I prodded Josef.

"In some cases you might need the mother's maiden name and the date of birth," he added, scraping the last bits of the Hunan lamb.

"You can get that plenty of places, can't you?" I passed him the near empty platter of salt-baked shrimp.

"Oh yeah. Doctors' offices, gyms. Some fraud rings even plant employees there to gather the data." He nudged the last few shrimp onto his plate.

"I think the neatest trick is the simplest, just running a credit card slip twice. Then if you're caught, you can claim it was an accident. What could work better?" I was hoping he'd feel challenged to top me.

He did. "Old-hat. That's hardly worth the risk with

today's technology. You know, Chas, fraud has its trends just like everything else." Josef was sucking the last of the shrimp heads as he said this, but once the distracting food was polished off, he seemed to come to his senses. He abruptly closed his mouth tightly. He'd said enough.

I tried a new tack. "How'd you like the scallops?"

"Pretty good. A little stringy, though, or am I wrong?"

"Good catch," I reassured him. "They were definitely stringy. And if you looked closely at them, they were all exactly the same size and shape, perfectly round and equally thick."

"What's that mean?"

"Even I know that by now," Lily chimed in. "They weren't scallops. They were machine-made fake scallops cut from some large fish, probably pollock. Kind of like those fake crab legs."

"Well, I'll be." Josef broke into a sticky grin. "Cheaper, huh? This happen often?"

"Not so much that you could call it a trend." I reeled in the line. "That high-tech fraud you mentioned—the one you were calling a trend—isn't it just a wee bit of an exaggeration to call crimes trendy?"

"No, really. The popular tricks become so widespread that you can even buy the equipment in places like Radio Shack."

"You can't honestly mean that crooks shop for the tools of their trade at discount stores." I reached across the table to fetch the last platter that had any food on it. I spooned the final drops of black bean sauce over Josef's rice and, in desperation, searched the bowl of discarded clam shells to find for him any that might still have a clam attached.

"Have you ever heard of a magnetic strip encoder?" Josef looked hungrily at the two intact clams I transferred to his plate.

"Hmm. I remember reading something about it." I lied to encourage him to refresh my memory.

Josef was licking the clam shells clean of their garlic and black bean barnacles. "It's a simple gadget that installs the numbers on that black magnetic strip on the back of your credit card. You can take your own credit card—or any fake one, even one from a dead person—and change the numbers on the back so the charge goes to another person's account. Waiters, of course, have access to many credit card numbers in a single evening and can observe their owners' habits so as to make a good guess whether they're the types who check their monthly statements. The best cards to use, of course, are corporate accounts, where there may not be any checking at all."

"Sounds so easy," I prodded.

"Not always. Some cards have built-in protection. And when the forger uses the card, he risks running into a sales clerk who compares the number on the receipt with the one on the card. Usually it's easy to divert such a clerk's attention. But the landscape is always changing. Now that word of this fraud has gotten around, credit card companies are beginning to require clerks to key in the last four digits from the card, but for the time being, this is a pretty easy scam to run."

"How much can a scam like this net?" I risked a question now that Josef was on a roll. I was wondering whether it would be too obvious to order another platter of clams.

"A couple of million dollars a week if you work fast."

"Yow!" Lily chimed in at this, unable to keep out of it any longer. "Where can I get one of those machines?"

"That's nothing," Josef said, absentmindedly licking his garlic-sticky fingers. "If you're ready to skip the country, you can really make it big. And that's where restaurant owners shine."

"You mean closing down in the middle of the night and skipping town?" I knew of a few restaurateurs who had done that.

"Exactly. Usually it starts small. Restaurants find themselves cash poor, so the owner begins to pay employees by crediting their credit card accounts, which gives him a little time. The employees don't mind because they figure they can save the taxes that the owner would have had to deduct. Then the owners escalate to debiting their own accounts to get instant cash. It's like a free loan, at least until the end of the billing period. After that, they can pay the minimum each month to keep the loan afloat and eventually default or start debiting fake accounts. The smarter ones learn how to time their actions: When a charge is put through, it goes into the restaurateur's bank account within forty-eight hours. So when the owner is ready to bail out, he takes all the credit cards he can get ahold of and posts charges on them, then skips the country at just the right moment. I've seen hundreds of thousands of dollars charged in one day."

I was getting terrific information, but it was missing the crucial piece: specific cases. I hoped the wine and stir-fries had done their job and loosened up Josef enough for the next step.

"How about some examples," I ventured, trying to sound offhand.

"Not a chance, Chas. This is dangerous stuff. When this much money is at stake, lives are considered cheap. Even murder is part of the program, from what I hear. These credit card scams have grown into industries, with gangs fighting over territory. In fact, I'd caution you to be mighty careful in handling this information."

That brought Lily back into the conversation. "You're not going to write all this, are you, Mama? You just need little bits to make it sound scary, right?"

"Don't give it a thought. We journalists know how to defuse this kind of explosive material," I assured them, trying to keep a straight face as I invoked that pompous "we journalists." At the same time, I was hoping I could find a more experienced journalistic bomb squad to give me guidance. I was wading in deep water. "Besides, I'm looking for balance here. I'm going to reveal some scams that are used against restaurants, too, and throw a little sympathy their way."

"That's easy," Josef said, reaching with his chopsticks to Lily's plate, where he'd just noticed a stash of Hunan lamb. "The same scams work sort of in reverse. Someone will call the credit card company at the end of the day, pretending he is the merchant, and ask that the charges be credited to his account."

"Mama, tell him about the cleaning bills," Lily said, trading her plate with Josef's to save him reaching for the bits of rice he was chasing.

"Ahh, that's a classic. It's happened twice in Washington in the past year, maybe more times that I don't know about. Usually it's an out-of-town customer and often a receipt from a dry cleaner is included. The customer claims that a waiter spilled food on him or her during dinner and asks that the restaurant reimburse the cleaning bill."

"Sounds like small potatoes," Josef said.

"It is, except that this letter goes to dozens of restaurants in one city alone. And it is probably sent to several cities. So a couple of hours' work and a stack of postage stamps can net many hundreds of dollars. The important part is that the restaurants usually pay because it is such a small amount that it's not worth risking the customer making a fuss."

"So how do you find out about it?"

"The scam is unmasked when the customer sends the same letter to two restaurants that have the same owner. Then the restaurateur calls me, hoping that I'll write something about it to warn other restaurants. Usually it's too late, but at least they'll be wary the next time.

"The same process is used with a more lucrative variation: the 'I got sick on your food' scam. In that case the so-called diners are looking for reimbursement for a full meal they never ate and threatening to sue for substantially more money, along with bad publicity for the restaurant. Again, they are caught when they are greedy and make a claim against one too many restaurants."

The plates looked as if they had been licked clean. I signaled the waitress for the check and pulled out a credit card.

Josef nodded at the credit card. "If they didn't know you at this restaurant already, they will now when you pay the check, right?"

"Guess again," I said, handing him the card. It didn't say CHAS WHEATLEY or even CHARLOTTE SUE WHEATLEY. It had the name R. MATTHEWS.

"Who's that?"

"That's me, for the moment. I change it frequently, every time I get a new credit card."

"You must have a ton of them by now. How do you get them in pseudonyms?"

"All I do is ask for a supplemental card, as if it were for my daughter, who has a different surname."

"I'll have to look into the legality of that."

Josef scooped up a handful of mints on the way out.

Lily and I said good-bye to Josef and walked down Connecticut Avenue toward her Dupont Circle apartment. The balmy air had brought to the streets a sense of celebration. From the steps of a market closed for the night came the drumbeat of teenage boys living out musical fantasies on upended plastic buckets. A block away, the piercing trill of an Ecuadorian flute played in accidental counterpoint. The sidewalks were more crowded than the streets, so the Rollerbladers sailed down the spacious avenue nearly unimpeded.

I felt good about the evening, and not just because I'd had a reviewable meal and gathered some useful credit card information. I'd enjoyed getting to know one of Lily's friends. Nice kid, Josef. What would it be like to have such a son?

Other women tell me that relationships with daughters are very different from sons. Sons don't talk about relating, they just do it, their mothers say. I could see that might be less tricky than the kind of relationship Lily and I have. And sons are very direct about their boundaries. They say no if they don't want to go, they are silent if they don't feel like talking, and if you piss them off, you'll know it, but they'll forget it faster than you do. A relationship with a daughter tends to be closer, more complicated, more emotional. In my experience, it's a minefield—for both mother and daughter. I find that it is alarmingly like trying to have a relationship with myself.

For example, not for the first time, Lily spoke as if she'd been reading my thoughts.

"You know, Mama, I've always wished I had a sibling. I think brothers are great. And they eat so much. Life together probably would have been easier on you and me if you'd had a couple of sons as well. You'd never run out of possibilities for dining companions."

I turned my head away because tears sprang to my eyes. Was I that overwhelming to Lily? And was she that lonely in dealing with me? Then I looked back at her. She was laughing. Once again I'd taken her too seriously. I quickly covered my dismay and met her head on. "Sorry, sweetie. I'm not about to have another baby now, even for you."

Lily and I strolled with our arms around each other's shoulders, lurching as first she pulled me toward a window to view the shiny chrome coffeepots, next I tugged her to a stop in front of the darkened window of Mystery Books; then we both were drawn to the all-night glow of Kramerbooks.

"I love living in the same city with you, Mama." Lily ventured into a difficult subject in the very nicest way. She'd only recently moved back to Washington from Philadelphia, and we were still feeling our way toward new mother-daughter patterns.

I was buoyed with pleasure, not only to hear that Lily was glad to have me around, but even more because she could tell me this without fearing I'd make too much of it.

In the next instant, experience reminded me that her confession sounded less like a statement than a prelude. Lily was softening me up.

"But it's hard to know exactly how to be an adult daughter," she continued. "I feel I have to protect my time and my privacy, even though I'm glad to see you. On the one hand, you're one of my best friends; on the other, I keep being afraid of your expecting too much from me."

"I'm just as afraid as you are of my expecting too much," I told her for the first time, though I'd thought about it a lot. "After all, the last time you lived here you were a student, a dependent. And we lived in the same house. I saw you every day, so we didn't have to plan ahead or make appointments. I knew what your life was like without having to ask you directly about it. I knew who called you and what you ate for breakfast. I knew if you were sick. And it was pretty obvious to me whether you were happy or miserable on any particular day. I automatically had a role in your life without having to get your permission."

"I liked that," Lily reassured me, though she'd dropped her arm from my shoulder. "It was comforting to me that you could keep tabs on me, even when I acted secretive and hated to answer your questions. And although I know I didn't act interested in your life, I felt secure knowing that even when you had problems you really were handling things and that even though you were single you didn't seem lonely or scared of being alone."

My life in those days would have been a whole lot less anxious if I'd known then that Lily had such a keen interest in my well-being. She'd hidden it most effectively. But I didn't want to throw cold water on her candor now, so, for once, I swallowed an accusation. Instead, I made a proposal.

"Now that we know we are both afraid of my expecting too much, it's time for an experiment. Let's agree to suspend judgment for the time being while we figure out how to share the same turf. We'll just see what works."

"A kind of no-fault relationship. I like that." Lily cocked her head and wrinkled her forehead the way she does. "A laboratory. No nursing hurt feelings."

"That part may take monumental effort. Hurt feelings are kind of my specialty."

"Well, then, this experiment is just what you need. It might improve all your relationships."

"Who says my other relationships need improving?" Five seconds into the experiment, and I'd already failed at the no-hurt-feelings rule.

"You do, as a matter of fact. Who was it who

recently broke up with the love of her life?" Lily, in her inimitable way, had swooped right down on my next area of vulnerability.

Then one parting shot: "Mama, promise me you'll find some guy like Dave to help you with this investigation. I'm getting scared for you."

Guy like Dave, indeed! That from my liberated daughter!

8

I was so preoccupied as I walked into the *Examiner* that I didn't even notice who was picketing the paper today. Josef's warnings had gotten to me after all. By four A.M. I had been huddled in my red platform rocker with a yellow legal pad, making a list of everyone who knew about my investigation: Bull, Helen, Sherele, Homer, Lily, Josef, Vince Davis. Andy Mutton suspected something, but didn't quite know what. Seven was enough. More than enough. I decided to be even more careful to keep the circle small—maybe one more investigative reporter to advise me, and then I'd keep my mouth closed to everybody else.

Even though I'd eventually fallen back asleep, this morning I was feeling dim and sluggish. Thank goodness I didn't have to go out to lunch. Bull had scheduled one of his "enlightened leader" staff seminars at noon, and we were all expected to attend. The subject of this meeting was to be the "glass ceiling," a forthright and open discussion of why no woman is ever likely to occupy Bull's office. As forthright and open as any woman who wants to keep her job would dare to be.

Bull schedules such meetings at noon so that the time counts as lunch break rather than work time. That doesn't mean the company provides lunch. No, we all bring our own from home or the cafeteria.

I made the mistake of taking the noon starting time literally. Journalists are never on time, except perhaps when they're on assignment. Most of my colleagues figure that if somebody is going to wait for somebody else, they don't want to be on the waiting end. And they cultivate the impression that their lives are lived at breakneck speed, which they expect to justify their always running late.

Thus, at 12:15, the room was only half full and staffers were still arriving. Those of us who showed up first took the rear seats, and latecomers were forced to sit closer and closer to the speakers' table. Even so, the first four rows were empty. Bull, playing host, kept inviting people to move in and fill up the front. It wasn't working. As soon as people sat down in the farthest seats, they opened their brown bags to establish their place firmly.

At the speakers' table, the other editors and guest speaker had also brought their own lunches. All except Bull. While we, the audience, sat whispering and waiting for the meeting to begin, Bull's secretary tiptoed in, carrying a cafeteria tray. Looking as if she wished she were invisible, she delivered the lunch to Bull. Glass ceiling, you betcha. A wave of giggles rolled toward the front of the room. Bull looked puzzled, then pasted a jovial grin on his face, as if he knew why everyone was laughing.

After the speaker's dour presentation of the historic situation of women in corporate America and innovative projects for improving it, Bull followed with a recital of self-serving statistics at the *Examiner* and boasts of soul-searching to root out even the subtlest barriers to women's advancement. Smug from his pep talk and full from the lunch his bright and underutilized secretary had delivered to him, he invited questions and "frank discussion, with gloves off." (Was that boxing gloves or white gloves?)

The women shifted in their seats, waiting for somebody else to start, at most ready to risk being the second challenger. I didn't even have that much courage; I'd wait to see if any real discussion got going. Finally, Michiko, a frail and shy-looking new reporter on the metro staff, raised her hand and stood up at the same time.

"I'm new here, so maybe I should wait for somebody more senior to ask the first question."

"Not to worry," Bull responded. "Sometimes the newest reporters have a fresh perspective. Go right ahead, Keiko."

We all flinched. He had confused Michiko with another Japanese-American reporter. Michiko herself blushed and looked miserable, but bravely went forward.

"I have observed that women here are offered very good assignments. In most cases equal to men."

Bull smiled. He started to thank Michiko, but she interrupted. She wasn't finished.

"When it comes to assignments that have any danger, though, I wonder whether there is some reluctance. I have never seen women offered the opportunity to pursue crime stories in Anacostia or organized crime beats. They are more likely to be assigned to softer stories. I know that I have asked . . ."

Bull didn't bother waiting for her to finish. "That's just a misperception on your part, little lady."

Whatever he said next was drowned out by shouts from around the room. That "little lady" had detonated a fierce reaction. A dozen women and nearly as many men were on their feet, some shaking their fists, others with hands at their hips or arms crossing their chests as if restraining themselves. Helen, the lone female editor at the front table, stood up to help placate the crowd.

"Let's not lose this opportunity," she pleaded. "You all clearly have a lot to say and to ask. We'll only get somewhere today if you all sit down and ask your questions one at a time."

Bull looked at Helen in grateful silence as she calmed us down. One by one, people took their seats and raised their hands to speak, waving them at Bull impatiently. He held up his arms, palms outward, as if to fend off the barrage.

"I'll get to your questions in a minute. But first I want to address this woman's legitimate concerns." He'd already learned something, at least for the moment. "It is undoubtedly true, or it was in the past, that we were too protective of our female reporters. Some of us were raised in an age of chivalry, and those habits die hard. That doesn't mean that we continue to react the same way. Trust me; things are changing."

A faint groan followed the "trust me," but Bull continued uninterrupted.

"I'll give you a good example. Not so long ago, newspapers had separate women's sections. You all know that. Even now, most newspapers' food sections are staffed by women, maybe with a token man. The big change, though, has been in restaurant coverage. That being a high-profile, glamorous job that involves big-time money, it's always been staffed by men. We at the *Examiner* were pioneers in this city when we hired a woman, Chas Wheatley, to review restaurants for us."

I was beginning to feel like window dressing, the token minority paraded in public to make the company look good. My fellow reporters were pointedly not looking at me, in order to avoid further embarrassing me. But it got worse.

"That's not all. We've made her job one of the most important ones at the paper. In fact, we're going even further. We're making Chas our first syndicated columnist."

All eyes turned to me.

"And as for dangerous assignments, how about this: Chas's first syndicated column is going to be about how restaurants lie, steal, and cheat. It's going to blow wide open the dirty secrets of one of the country's biggest industries."

I've never heard of a reporter carrying a gun. Clearly it would be far too dangerous to editors.

I was livid. Outraged. Furious. And, yes, scared. That was just for starters. My most immediate problem was that I wasn't likely to meet the deadline for my column this afternoon, not with half the newsroom coming by to congratulate me.

Since that was the fun part, I didn't want to respond by waving away their good wishes in favor of writing. Besides, all inspiration had flown after that cataclysmic lunchtime seminar. I couldn't even remember whether the potatoes I was writing about had been mashed or french fried.

What's more, I was so angry with Bull that I didn't care. He didn't deserve to have my restaurant column on time after he sacrificed me like that, just to make himself look like an equal opportunity hero.

Andy Mutton couldn't keep away. He'd stopped by my desk three times so far, on flimsy pretexts such as wondering whether I had a copy of Marcella Hazan's first book, then bringing me a press release on Emeril Legasse's summer menu, as if I wouldn't get the same press release or would even have any use for a summer menu from New Orleans. The latest drop-by was to ask for his press release back, so I fished his and mine from the trash and handed him both.

The real reason for his visits was to taunt me with how restaurateurs are going to hate me and stop returning my phone calls, and to express his sincere concern for my safety and his hope that I was going to be careful, extra careful. The latest visit was also a snooping expedition. He'd seen several reporters hanging around my desk and wanted to know what they were talking about.

My colleagues' response was the unanticipated bonus of Bull outing my secret project. My wonderful, generous fellow reporters were bringing me juicy bits of restaurant lore for my collection.

One reminded me about the ticket-scalping story, which I'd forgotten even though it was only last year. A federal judge had taken a friend for a pre-theater dinner around the corner from the National Theatre. After the two women were seated, the waitress asked to check their coats. When they'd finished dinner, they retrieved their coats from the closet and hurried to the theater, only to find that their tickets were missing from the judge's coat pocket. They explained to the theater manager that they'd lost their tickets but remembered the seat numbers. The sympathetic manager showed them to their seats, even though the show had started by then. But the seats were already occupied. Somehow the people sitting in the seats had the judge's name on their ticket envelope.

The restaurateur, when confronted later, claimed he had no responsibility for the judge's property because he didn't maintain a supervised coatroom. Patrons hang coats there at their own risk. That might be true when the patron actually hangs the coat, but not when the waitress has taken charge of it, countered the judge. Furthermore, the waitress hadn't warned her that the coatroom was unsupervised. Eventually the restaurant agreed to compensate her with new tickets to the theater, though it made no promises about looking into the problem.

What I found most interesting was how quickly the stolen tickets had found a taker. What's more, the incident reminded me that the same people who carefully remove their house keys from the ring when they give their car keys to the parking attendant neglect to protect the contents of their pockets—or briefcases—when they check them at restaurants. In most cases, missing valuables aren't likely to be spotted as readily as theater tickets. And one might never know what secrets have been stolen from a checked coat or package.

The stories kept coming. Another reporter volunteered to check his files for that long-ago tale about the lobster and the cocaine. As the legend goes, a Washington steak house, one of those that also specializes in four-pound lobsters, was reputed to be a drug market. As I heard it, the cocaine was delivered in lobster claws, wrapped in little foil packets tucked inside those four-pounders. No wonder they were so expensive. Since that story made the rounds, I've always wondered about the people carrying foil swans out of restaurants, even from the high-style restaurants where the entire portion wouldn't fill an earring box. Are they always leftovers?

By the end of the day, after I'd warned my editor that my weekly column wasn't going to be in until late tomorrow morning (she didn't blink an eye, knowing well the damage Bull had inflicted on me at the seminar), my mood had turned. In fact, I was feeling buoyant. The secret was out, but I'd gathered some terrific material and had great fun doing it.

My computer screen was filled with messages.

"Remind me tomorrow to tell you about the restaurant that bumped my husband's office party because a bigger party requested its private dining room. Gotta run now. Congrats."

"I caught a waiter inflating his tip on my credit card bill last month. I'll bring you a photocopy tomorrow."

The last message was one of those that had been forwarded from the wrong address, so there was no way to reply to (or even find) the sender. The circuitous path was obviously intentional. It read:

> Before you destroy restaurants, you should consider how much easier it would be for them to destroy you. You're going to need to watch what you eat, watch where you walk, check your car for tampering, and keep your door locked.

I took a taxi home.

9

Transcribed from Communication Between Chas Wheatley and Unnamed Companion

CW: They're getting more brazen.

UC: You'd know better than anyone.

CW: Sometimes I wonder how dumb they think we are. I can't get over this one. It's a new level.

UC: They don't stop to think, do they?

CW: Machiavelli. Perfect name for the place.

UC: It's supposed to be such a great restaurant.

CW: That's what makes it easy. Everyone wants to try it.

UC: But you'd think people would notice.

CW: Maybe they do, but they are afraid to say anything.

UC: You mean because it might be embarrassing?

CW: They're not even sure they're right. They're afraid maybe they're already supposed to know it's so expensive. That it's their fault.

UC: You mean they might feel ignorant or unsophisticated?

CW: Not to mention cheap.

UC: Have you tried to figure the profit on this sort of thing?

CW: Well, if the standard food cost is twenty-eight to thirty-three percent, and that allows, say, ten-percent profit, and in this case the food cost is . . .

"Are you a good cook?"

That's the most frequent question I get from strangers when I'm introduced as a restaurant critic. People no longer ask, "How do you stay so thin?" But when you have a job as terrific as mine, there's always some price to pay.

"I think I once was a pretty good cook," I answer. "It's hard to remember." I rarely have the opportunity, much less the need, to cook anymore since I spend every possible mealtime reviewing restaurants. When I am at home and hungry, like tonight, I don't even feel like going out to buy groceries. So I just scrounge around in my kitchen eating the leftovers, if I've brought any, from restaurants, or looking for surprises in the freezer.

Today I'd canceled my dinner plans. I needed time to think, to unravel the strands of anger, fear, excitement, and adventure that were knotted inside me. I needed a plan.

A night at home is always a good start to putting my life in order. For me it smacks of the thrill of playing hooky, the unexpected freedom of an exam canceled. I won't have to make small talk and can eat just what I feel like having . . . within the limitations of my larder.

Olives, cornichons, and mung bean noodles didn't look like dinner, but hidden behind them at the back of the cupboard, fusilli and a jar of grilled artichokes in olive oil did. When I discovered an unmoldy lemon in my crisper, I knew luck was beaming on me. A little grated peel was just what my artichoke-and-pasta combination needed. I didn't want to waste a good wine on artichokes, which make every accompaniment taste sweet, so I opted for a Rolling Rock, left over from my days with Dave.

It was a meal to enjoy with candlelight and Vivaldi, which I did. Sure enough, by the time I finished I felt calm and directed. I'd thought through my restaurant column enough to know I could finish it by noon tomorrow, I'd mentally adjusted my schedule to account for this night off, and I'd decided to make up for it by going through my own credit card bills looking for errors.

"I've been overreacting," I lectured myself after comparing a year's credit card statements with receipts and not finding a single mistake. I was feeling both relief and disappointment. My passion for the restaurant business competed with my determination to find a great story.

At last I found a fifty-dollar overcharge. A thirty-five-dollar tip had been transformed into an eighty-five-dollar tip. An example that substantial would go a long way. Then I came to the charge from my dinner with Lily. It seemed higher than I remembered. I compared it with my receipt, and it matched, but it still seemed more than it should have been. I dug through my file and, as I'd hoped, found that I'd saved a copy of the itemized dinner tab. Sure enough, we'd been charged double for the wine. That was an expensive mistake—or scam.

I checked my watch. The restaurant would still be open. I called and asked for the manager, then told him I'd been charged twice for the wine. He didn't even seem very surprised.

"Oh, that happens sometimes with our new computer system," he said. "Just fax us a copy, and we'll credit your account."

Old story. The computer did it.

I asked for his name, thanked him without telling him mine, and hung up. It crossed my mind to worry that he might have caller ID and track me down. But that moment of paranoia passed quickly. I did a little victory dance and congratulated myself on an evening well spent.

I would have been happy enough, even without the call.

I'd done the dishes and rewarded myself with another beer, even written the lead for my review so I had a head start on tomorrow morning's work. I was dozing off in peaceful anticipation of a solid night's sleep for a change.

When I picked up the phone, at first I thought I was dreaming Dave's voice.

"Did I wake you? I didn't think you'd even be home yet."

"Who is this?" As if I didn't know.

"Oh, I must have wakened you. I'm sorry. It's Dave."

He sounded so crestfallen that I didn't have the heart to give him a hard time. I lowered my defenses—an inch.

"No, I really wasn't asleep, just dozing a little.

Besides, it's nice to hear your voice. How are you?"

"I guess I'm all right. Working hard."

He paused.

I paused.

I didn't want to say anything more until I knew why he was calling.

"You probably want to know why I called."

I relented. "You don't need a special reason. How are you doing, really?" His voice. It was as if I'd opened an oven door, and heat radiated toward me. My face warmed, my fingers tingled. The heat pulsed down my body, detonated a throbbing between my legs.

"I'm fine. More or less. A little lonely."

That was good news. "Aren't you dating?" I couldn't resist. Not after he'd given me an opening like that. I hoped Dave couldn't hear my heavy breaths. I tugged my pillow from under my head so I could wrap my arms around it

"Dating?" He sounded subdued, or thoughtful. "Not anybody special."

That was like a dousing of ice water. I'd hoped for a simpler answer.

"Getting back to the point, why did you call?"

"I don't want to intrude. But this time I couldn't help it. I heard about your restaurant project. I heard about Bull hanging you out to dry."

"Just like him, isn't it?"

"I just wanted to make sure you'll get some help where you need it. Now that the whole newsroom knows about your investigation, the restaurants are going to know, too, of course. Journalists are the world's busiest gossips. You can't trust Bull to protect you."

"Who says I need protection? Isn't that just a little bit patronizing? I'm a girl, so I need somebody to take care of me?"

"That's not what I meant, Chas. Or not because you're a girl. I mean woman. I mean . . ."

Why was I doing this? The minute I heard his voice, I'd wanted to tell Dave to come back. Instead, I was pushing him away. I was punishing him. And punishing myself.

"Oh, hell," Dave concluded. "I knew it was a mistake to call. Besides, I can see that you are fully capable of taking care of yourself. Sorry I woke you."

He hung up. He hung up! He'd climbed out on a fragile limb to reach me, and I'd given it a good shake. How could I have done that?

I called him back. I'd secretly found his number and kept it in my address book, not under *Z* for "Zeeger" but in *F* for "fools." But I'd kept it too long; that number had been disconnected.

I slept no better than any other woman who'd managed to stab herself in the back. Dave was constantly vivid before my eyes, and not just when I was dreaming. His steady interest in encouraging me to do my best, his knack for turning even tedious tasks into rollicking fun, his curiosity about everything from my nail polish to the State Department's encrypting procedures–I missed every bit of it. We had been so cautious about allowing our love to develop at a measured pace, not telling even Lily or Sherele what was happening for nearly two years. After that, our relationship had seemed so solid. I couldn't believe it had dissolved.

By morning I couldn't stand my own company, so I skipped the usual and went to the office early, even beating the picketers to the *Examiner*'s entrance. I bought breakfast in the cafeteria—a bowl of grits with extra butter and pepper, grapefruit juice, and coffee—and took it to my desk, along with the morning's paper.

To my surprise, a few other early birds were at their desks. Vince Davis waved at me, and as soon as I'd arranged my breakfast on my desk, he wandered by.

"I wondered what you'd find palatable from our four-star kitchen," he said, eyeing my tray. People are always curious about what a restaurant critic eats.

"I figure that any restaurant that serves grits is doing so for a reason," I said. "What are you doing here so early?"

"I'm following up on a little crisis in the business community. The head of the Jamaican Coffee Consortium committed suicide last night. We had time to get just a small item in the late edition, and I'm following up for tomorrow. On the face of it, that might not sound like big international news, but the guy was the most charismatic young politician in the country. A kind of West Indian JFK. And nobody has the faintest idea why he did it. I've been drafted to work on it because I spent some time with him when he was here this spring. You would have loved the guy. He was your kind of restaurant-goer. He even read some of your reviews before he came and asked me for your number so he could tell you about some place he thought you'd like."

"Poor guy. I'll never understand suicide."

"Yeah. I'd better get back to work. See ya."

* * *

Sometimes my instinct for self-preservation amazes me. Despite my sleep-deprived brain having slowed to a crawl, and my gnawing frustration over the aborted conversation with Dave, or maybe because of them, I threw myself into writing my column before I did anything else. The diversion felt so good that I churned it out in record time. As often happens when I write as an escape, it read better than some of the columns that I craft meticulously over two days. With a tiny exultation, I pushed the button to send it to Helen.

Now it was time to restart my day. First, belatedly, today's newspapers. I turned to our front page to read the few sentences about the suicide Vince had mentioned, then turned to see what pap Andy Mutton had cooked up for Food Day.

The scumbag had scooped me.

How in the world did he get to Machiavelli so fast? On second thought, that wasn't really a mystery, since it was a much-ballyhooed new restaurant. And I didn't mind that he was writing about it before I did, since I wait a couple of months until a new restaurant settles down before I review it. Besides, he writes up restaurants only as features and recipe stories.

In this case, though, he was stomping around on my turf. He'd written a scathing little item about how expensive Machiavelli's prosciutto and fried bread was and about how the waiters sometimes offered it before they showed the menus so that diners were gouged without warning. I could have written the item myself.

I should have written it myself. In fact, I had planned to write it myself.

It was as if Sherele had told Andy every detail of our experience.

Sherele swore she hadn't breathed a word. She came in blustering about it herself after she read the paper at home. She was as outraged as I was and equally mystified.

"Andy always makes reservations in his own name," she reminded me. "He'd never miss a chance to get VIP treatment. Surely they wouldn't pull on him that trick of not telling how pricey the prosciutto was going to be. More likely, they gave it to him for free."

I couldn't have agreed more.

"I have an idea." Sherele reached for the phone and dialed information. "Washington. A restaurant called Machiavelli. That's M-A-C-H-I-A-V-E-L-L-I."

"What are you . . . ?" She waved away my question and dialed the number.

"Hello, Machiavelli? This is the accounting department at the *Examiner*. I wonder if we could get a copy of the bill for Andy Mutton. . . . Yes, I did read it. . . . No, I'm not the person who can handle that kind of complaint–I'm sure you'd never do such a thing without telling people. You might call the editor on that; I'm just the accounting department. But could I get a copy of his bill? Are you sure? Maybe it was under another name. Oh, I see."

She burst with pent-up laughter as she hung up the phone. "He was never there," she spurted out, choking on the words.

"How can they be sure? It could have been in another name."

"No, the guy knows him by sight. And so does

every maître d' on every shift. Besides, he did make a reservation in his own name. For tomorrow."

"I bet he doesn't show for that one." I turned to my computer to search for my notes on Machiavelli. "The question remains, how did he know about the restaurant pushing the overpriced prosciutto on customers before they get the menu? You didn't tell him, I didn't tell him, and I haven't even entered those notes in the computer, in case he has tapped that. Maybe some friend told him."

"That's not enough of an answer. The restaurant is denying it, so he would have to check it out firsthand before he wrote it the way he did."

Sherele was right. It would be too big a risk for Andy to make that unattributed charge without either the restaurant admitting it—which it wouldn't—or verifying it himself. Unless he knew I had it pinned down enough to write about it.

Lily brought a useful perspective to my fury. She called as soon as she finished reading the paper, wondering how I'd let Andy scoop me. She, too, knew his habit of making sure a restaurant knew he was coming so he'd be certain to get the best table and the most obsequious service. "He's certainly shot himself in the foot this time, Mama. I can't imagine why he did it. There goes his VIP status."

"I guess sometimes even Andy would rather look like a hero to his readers than have a good meal."

"You mean, sometimes he'd rather scoop you than have a good meal. In this case, though, he's done you a big favor."

Not in any way I could see. "How do you figure that?"

"You know how you taught me to always cook a sample—a tiny bit of sausage or a small matzo ball—to test for seasoning and texture before I did the whole batch? Well, Andy's your test. You can see how the restaurants react to his having blown the whistle on one of them."

"A kind of stalking-horse. I like the idea. And if he shows up floating in a pot of minestrone, I'll be warned to lay in some heavy protection for myself."

"If I were Andy, I'd keep away from kitchens for the time being, especially Italian ones." Lily started laughing as she said this. "You know what dangerous places they can be. All those knives."

That was a subject I could get into. "They're benign compared to the French kitchen, what with crème brûlée being so popular. Just think of the blow-torches used to caramelize the sugar." I'd begun to laugh, too. Sherele's eyebrows were raised as she stopped typing and looked questioningly at me.

"The pastry room. That's the real arsenal," Lily continued.

I knew exactly what she meant, but I reminded her, "Sauce painting isn't just for dessert plates anymore, my dear. Squeeze bottles are used for stripes and curlicues and zigzags of sauce in every course. Even for the soup."

"Right. Just fill one with acid and accidentally squirt in the wrong direction. Good-bye to Andy's typing hands or his spying eyes."

Far from grossing me out, Lily's vision made me laugh all the louder. An aisle away, the click of key-boards stopped. "Squirting is just the beginning. Chefs now use brushes and sponges and dish mops to paint their sauces on the plate. Just imagine the whole crew armed and attacking. Each with a different color. Permanent colors."

"A fate worse than death. More visible than the scarlet letter: The mark of the culinary stool pigeon."

Lily had turned my anger around. For about five minutes. Then my rage at Andy flared again, though I was beginning to admit that it was fueled by my bad temper over Dave.

Andy was merely a skirmish. Dave was the one who was really ruining my day.

The guy was cheating on me!

Of course, that charge was hard to sustain, since we weren't even seeing each other. But he was cheating on his memory of me. Somehow, I'd held the image of Dave being with me or nobody. It wasn't a rational idea, but before today I hadn't been motivated to examine it, knowing deep in my heart that we'd eventually be back together.

I'd also buried my previous suspicions that even when Dave and I were together he might have been cheating on me. Without him here, I could turn him into any person my mind wanted to create, without the inconvenience of a reality check.

10

Fortunately, it was lunchtime, time for a walk. And another stroke of luck: I'd planned to scout a restaurant on Pennsylvania Avenue way east of the Capitol, and instead of subjecting one of my colleagues to a long trek for what might be a dreadful lunch, I'd decided to try it by myself. That allowed me to go by foot, my favorite mode of transportation but one that few of my friends willingly share.

I hadn't counted on a thunderstorm.

The only thing that cheered me up about having to take a taxi was that it would be costing Bull money. The guy owed me big-time.

I avoid taxis simply because I crave walking. Other Washingtonians avoid them because our cabs tend to offer no more safety and comfort than skydiving. Many of Washington's taxis are a home away from home for immigrants. They bring along their kids when school is out, they eat their lunch, they talk to their wives and/or girlfriends on the cell phone, and they listen to everything from Howard Stern to Fresh Air at top volume. The radio often turns out to be primarily a vehicle for learning English, since some of these cabbies have only a rudimentary knowledge of the language. They nod and smile and haven't the faintest idea where you are going. Not only can't they understand what you're saying, they wouldn't know how to get there if they did.

These are mere inconveniences. It gets worse.

The major objection to Washington's new-immigrant taxi drivers is that many seem to have just learned to operate a car. They use their horns instead of their turn signals or brakes. They careen, they curse (I presume, since I can't understand their language), and they drive as if their shoes were weighted with lead. After a ride in a blizzard with a driver who had never seen snow before and sped down slippery streets in his delight, I've always carried rubber boots in winter and dealt with snowstorms on foot.

Today, though, I was lucky. My driver was a young Lebanese with an elegant English accent and a gentle way with the gas pedal and the steering wheel.

"You work at the *Examiner*?" he asked, while I leaned forward to read his name on the visor: Robert Said. He looked about thirty, though it was hard to tell with his beard, which followed along his jaw in a well-trimmed line from a slim goatee.

Usually a cabbie follows that introductory question with a complaint about the way the *Examiner* writes about taxi drivers or a query about how he can get a job at the newspaper. Mr. Said, though, wanted to know about me. When he heard that I was a restaurant critic, I suddenly had a friend.

"I have always been extremely fond of restaurants. Beirut, where I spent my childhood, has many excellent ones. Its French restaurants are among the best in the world, even compared to those in Paris."

After a few minutes of trading the diner's version of six degrees of separation (You've also eaten at Ducasse? In Paris or in Monte Carlo?), I asked him about something I'd noticed when I'd leaned over to read his name. "How come you have a jacket and tie in the front seat? Are you going for a fancy lunch?"

"No, I had an interview before I started my shift. A job interview. I'm about to become a consultant—the only profession more common in Washington than lawyer. I think I will celebrate, after I finish my shift."

"Congratulations. How will you celebrate?"

"A good meal, of course. Do you want to know my real celebration or my virtual celebration?"

"The virtual, definitely. That sounds like the most fun."

"It is a long story, but with this storm's traffic, it looks as if I'll have plenty of time to tell it."

We were stopped. It had taken four green lights for us to get through the last intersection, and this block was equally snarled. I felt sorry for Robert Said, whose fare would be the same with or without a traffic jam, since Washington has a zone rather than meter system. I vowed to give him a huge tip. On Bull.

Mr. Said seemed cheerful despite the mess outside his window. "Just before I picked you up, I had taken a couple from Union Station. He was a senator; she was his girlfriend. He was in a very angry mood. He could hardly sit still he was so agitated. She kept trying to calm him down, telling him that it didn't matter so much."

"What didn't matter?" I wondered whether this meandering introduction was actually going to link to Robert's virtual celebration. In the telling, he grew younger and more naive in my eyes, so I'd made a mental leap from "Mr. Said" to "Robert."

"I was getting very curious as to what was the senator's great disappointment."

Me, too.

"You can imagine my surprise when I finally realized."

Not yet.

"I eventually ascertained that the senator was missing a very fine dinner."

"Go on." Now I could begin to see the point. Or feel hope that there was one.

"The senator had dinner reservations at what he thought to be the very best restaurant in New York. His secretary had gone to great lengths to procure these reservations. He had planned to fly to New York with his lady friend, but National Airport was closed. And so he had rushed to the train station to take the Metroliner. But there was no Metroliner, either."

"This storm isn't bad enough to stop the trains," I protested.

"No, it was not the storm itself, which in any case will be over soon, but the storm has blown the roof of a house across the tracks in New Jersey. So the trains will not be running for many hours. And with the trains not running, this senator did not think it would be possible, even when the airport opens, to get on a flight in time. The airport will be too crowded."

"Poor guy. I know how he must have been feeling. Did you ever find out the name of the restaurant?"

"It is called Jean-Georges. It is a restaurant I have read much about. I often go there in my daydreams. Today I think I will start with the scallops and cauliflower in caper-raisin emulsion, go on to the squab with corn cake and foie gras, and finish with the dark chocolate soufflé. The lobster with pumpkin seeds and fenugreek was first-rate, as I imagined it on my birthday."

"I've been trying to get into Jean-Georges myself," I said, growing hungry from his descriptions of the dishes. "The secretary is the one I feel sorry for. As I've heard, it's quite a chore to get a table there, even with pull."

"I would think that a restaurant critic such as you could easily get a reservation."

"Not at all. I can't make a reservation under my own name, since I always try to dine anonymously. I have to go through the same procedure as anybody else."

"What a shame for this reservation to go to waste."

"It won't go to waste. I'm sure the restaurant has already filled the table from its VIP waiting list."

"No, I'm certain the senator has not bothered to cancel his reservation."

"How can you know that?" By now, we were finally past the Capitol, and my lunch was in sight.

"I can assure you that he is too preoccupied to bother with such a telephone call. His girlfriend wanted to cheer him up, so she suggested they stop at a little hotel for the afternoon rather than go back to the office. I dropped them at the Tabard Inn. Definitely not for lunch."

Robert's revelation was interrupted momentarily as he swerved to avoid a driver who'd pulled out of a parking space without looking. That diversion apparently jolted a new idea to the surface.

"You know, this could be your big chance. Why don't you take the reservation?" he suggested.

"I don't even know the name it was made in," I answered, wishing I did.

"I do. I heard his girlfriend call him by an odd first name. Simon. So I looked it up in my *Congressional Directory*." He held it up for me to see. Enterprising young man. "Sure enough, there's only one senator with that name: Simon Elias."

Too often we don't give fate the time of day. We are so fixed on our schedule, our routine, that we let opportunities slip by without taking them seriously. Here I was, with my column done and nobody to answer to for my time. And here was this restaurant reservation, one I'd be chasing for months to duplicate if I didn't act quickly. Why not? An impulsive trip to New York would no doubt be an improvement on my solitary Capitol Hill lunch and a day of obsessing about Andy Mutton and Dave Zeeger.

The taxi had come to a stop in front of the restaurant I'd been intending to scout. The interior looked dark, and there was a hand-lettered sign in the window. My eyes weren't young enough to read it from the taxi, but Robert's were. "'Closed. Flood. Sorry.'

That's all I can make out. Would you like me to go out and read the rest?" he asked, as he turned off the motor.

"No, thank you. I got the message. If you don't mind, I need a minute to think."

I pulled out my notepad. Reporters think best on paper.

"Is there some way I can help?" Robert had been watching me making a list.

"Let me bounce some ideas off you." I went down my list. "If the trains are stopped and the airport is so overcrowded that the senator was frightened off, how could I get to New York in time for dinner?"

"That's simple. By taxi."

Robert didn't even wait for me to respond, but immediately picked up his phone and called a supervisor. After a short conversation, in Lebanese, I supposed, he hung up and turned to me.

"It will cost $320. Round trip. That is $84 less than the shuttle. And more comfortable. Besides, there is no shuttle after nine-thirty, so you would have the expense of a hotel room."

"You could drive up and back in one day?"

"I drive far more than ten hours on a normal day. It would be no problem for me."

"We don't know what time the reservation is. It could be late. We might not get back until the middle of the night."

"I am a very good driver, even very late at night. I would be most pleased to drive you to New York and back. Then you could tell me all about your meal."

"You don't think I'd have you drive me all that way

and then leave you outside while I dined alone, do you? I would insist that you come with me. After all, my newspaper pays for me to take companions so that I can taste more dishes. And you already have a jacket and tie in the car."

"Now that would be a celebration."

11

Robert waited in the taxi in front of my building while I changed into a very New York black dress and heels. I called my office to tell Helen my plans and agreed to phone the copy desk later to go over any changes in this week's column.

Next came the tricky part. I called Jean-Georges to reconfirm—a procedure I correctly guessed would be necessary to hold the reservation. I also warned the receptionist that Senator Elias's administrative aide had been asked to cancel the reservation when the storm started but that the senator had changed his mind. So if someone called later to cancel the reservation, they should ignore that. To my delight, I found that the reservation was for the first seating. We'd arrive in Manhattan at just the right time, and could expect to be back in Washington by two or three A.M.

Robert jumped out of the taxi to open the door for me; this time I sat in the front. We smiled at each other and he took off with a squeal of tires as if we had a train to catch. When we passed the Capitol, I blew a kiss to Senator Elias and Robert saluted.

We suddenly didn't know what to say to each other, as if we'd been two strangers dancing cheek to cheek when the lights were turned on. Perhaps both of us were wondering what foolishness we'd undertaken.

After a few exchanges about when the rain was going to stop, we gave up and fell silent. I stretched my legs and leaned my head back as the hum of the road lulled me into half-dozing.

My sleepy thoughts were so preoccupied with mentally shifting gears that I didn't think of Dave at all until we hit Perryville, and then only because he'd once picked up a new car at Colonial Motors there. After that, I forgot Dave entirely. I found myself wanting to get to know Robert. He was whistling the most soothing and elaborate melodies as I dozed.

It had been a long time since I'd been with a man who made an art of whistling. What's more, it had been a long time since I'd been so close to any man, and there were hours of proximity ahead of me. Even in my sleep I was aware of his smell, a faint perfume of spice mingling with musky sweat. My head was barely six inches away, and I longed to rest it on his shoulder.

At the Delaware Memorial Bridge, I woke up ready to talk. Or, more my style, to ask questions.

By Camden I'd learned that Robert was an electrical engineer, although before he'd changed countries and languages he'd hoped to be a writer. Robert and his four older sisters and their husbands had left professional expectations behind in Lebanon, along with two large houses and the habit of dining out well. His mother had died years before the family left Lebanon, but there were plenty of servants and sisters to watch over his upbringing while his father traveled.

"What did your father do?"

"He never talked about it." Robert gave me a sidelong glance, checking my reaction.

"You must have wondered," I probed.

"I did more than wonder. I investigated."

This was sounding interesting. "What clues did you have to work with?"

"Constant travel. Plenty of money. Mysterious phone calls and meetings. He loved to fiddle with electronic equipment."

"That's how you got into electronics?"

"I suppose. But not the same kind. Not communications equipment or explosives."

"You don't mind telling me all this?"

"No, it was long ago, and I've come to terms with it. I've even grown rather proud of him."

"Did you ever pin it down?"

"Eventually, yes. Kind of a James Bond thing."

"For which side?"

"The most I can tell you is that although we had to leave everything of value behind, we were welcomed here."

"You never talked to your father about it?"

"Sure. Now we talk about it all the time."

"You do? Is he here?"

"He's in a nursing home. He has bad circulatory problems that have affected his brain, and now he's getting more and more forgetful."

"Oh, Robert, I'm sorry."

"I'm not . . . in a way. Anyway, he'll love hearing about our meal."

As we passed Trenton, Robert turned the subject to me. He started with questions about how I became a food critic, but my responses must have sounded rote. He took the hint and shifted conversational gears. Not gently. "Why aren't you married?" he asked.

"What kind of question is that? People don't know why they aren't married." I didn't bother to hide my annoyance.

Robert laughed. "Haven't you even considered what an interesting question it is to ask yourself? It's not an accusation, it's an invitation to explore your luck and your society and the messages your body is expressing to the world. It is obvious to me that you have been married. And that you could be married. It's certain that you have some choice in the matter."

"How do you know that?"

"Because you remind me of my older sister."

"The one who raised you, the mother figure? Maybe that's your answer. I'm old enough to be your mother. I'm old enough to be everybody's mother."

"No, you remind me of her because you are so beautiful. I have a very great passion for my older sister."

That shut me up all the way to Metuchen.

There's one subject women never talk about with men. As we rolled through northern New Jersey in what felt to me like the Detroit version of a magic carpet, the topic loomed large and irresistible. When would I ever feel so free to explore forbidden fruit? How much did I have to lose?

"Is your sister overweight?" I held my breath after the words came out.

"She's just like you."

"You mean, on the plump side?"

"Exactly. Just the way a woman should be." Robert's eyes were on the road. Mine were, too, but risking sidelong glances at him.

"That's not how most men see it," I ventured, stiffening a bit as if ready for a hasty retreat to my side of the car.

Robert ignored the road for an instant and looked me full in the face, caressing me without touching me. "You must be talking about American men. They like their women to look as if they have been ravaged by tapeworms. They prefer women with the bodies of little boys or victims of famine. I think every body is beautiful in its own way, but that nothing is more lovely in a woman than roundness and softness."

I felt round and soft and beautiful as Robert spoke. His words were polishing me, making me feel as if I glistened. Now that the conversation was moving in such a pleasant direction, I pushed him to say more.

"Do you mean that Lebanese men have no fear of fat?"

Robert took another long look at me. "You don't consider yourself fat, do you?"

"Well, I'm not exactly skinny."

"Thank goodness. Do you know, there is a marvelous word that is going out of use. It is one of the most pleasing and expressive words in the English language, but I fear it is becoming extinct."

"What's that?"

"'Voluptuous.'"

I liked it. I rolled it around on my tongue and in my head. I repeated it to Robert. "Voluptuous."

"Yes. It is a word that sounds like you. And looks like you."

I sank back into the upholstery and savored feeling more like a woman than I had in a long time.

"Are you married?" I'd been planning the question for thirty miles. He had no ring on his finger, and he hadn't called anybody to say he'd be home late, but you never know.

"I thought I would be by now."

"What happened?"

"She found somebody else. A doctor. An American doctor."

"How awful."

"For me or for her?" Robert flicked his eyes in my direction with a crinkly smile. I liked that he'd bounced back from rejection so thoroughly that he could suggest those alternatives.

Robert's recovery hadn't been so easy. I learned by Newark that he'd been more or less expecting to marry Layla for as long as he'd been expecting to be a writer: from childhood. They'd both emigrated around the same time, and their adjustments to America had dashed both Robert's dreams. It wasn't until a long time after Layla had left that Robert was ready to admit that theirs had been a love of proximity more than natural harmony.

Before we passed the Holland Tunnel, Robert knew Dave as well as I knew Layla. And I was marveling that a near-fifty American restaurant critic and a thirty-something Lebanese taxi driver had souls that meshed far more comfortably than I'd ever have guessed.

After we'd gotten all the relationship bitching and moaning off our chests, we found ourselves pouring out more playful words, ideas, and, eventually, fantasies. We filled each other to overflowing with reminiscences and observations. Robert loved not just scintillating women and fine food, but books in three languages, plays and opera librettos, American folk music and Japanese films. By the time Robert got us to the George Washington Bridge—which he preferred as far more scenic than the Lincoln Tunnel—I wondered whether a three-hour dinner and the ride home would give us enough time to talk. I also wondered whether, after a bottle or so of wine, I might dare to suggest we stop at a motel along the way.

New York's streets sparkled with damp puddles under an exuberant sun just beginning to set. The parking attendant was surprised to have Robert ask him to take the taxi rather than just usher me from it. Robert shrugged on his jacket and hung his tie around his neck and we, as previously agreed, immediately headed for the rest rooms to groom ourselves for an evening of power dining.

As I came out of the ladies' room and slid my eyes over the crowd, I was attracted to a lean slouch against a far window. Sexy. A second glance confirmed it was Robert. I knew everything about his life one could hope to learn in one afternoon, but I hardly knew what he looked like standing, walking, or talking to anybody else. He looked like a man very comfortable, not only in his clothes, but in his body. And as he walked toward me I saw that he not only moved as if he considered life great fun, but his posture seemed to issue a welcome. Come and join me, it said. I did.

"Going my way?" Robert flashed me a most delicious and intimate smile.

"You already asked me that five or six hours ago." I tried for an equally fetching one. "And here I am."

Restaurants carefully orchestrate their lighting, their music, their color schemes to establish a dining mood, but most forget the most critical of all senses: smell. Not Jean-Georges. For all its imposing height and chilly glass walls, this dining room greeted you like a host who's been cooking all day in anticipation of your visit. It welcomed you with aromas of sizzling meat and duets, trios, orchestras of spices. Chef Jean-Georges Vongerichten has returned the ritual of tableside finishing—sauteéing, deglazing, and flaming—to the dining room. As a result, every mogul in a three-piece suit, each matron or boy-toy in sedate black dress quivers with the excitement of a party. This is a clubhouse for the Masters of the Universe where everyone grows drunk on aromas.

Robert and I sat side by side on a banquette, the easier to share bites from each other's plates. As Robert slowly chewed a crackly corner of potato lace from the silky Arctic char, I noticed his left hand stroking the glove-leather upholstery. My legs quivered in sympathy. I nearly had to stem the bursting juices from the crisp brown duck breast as I cut into it and it released the perfumes of an Arab spice market. I felt my juices bursting, too. I wanted to stroke Robert's beard.

We finished our dinner with serious espresso and playful pink and green marshmallows–homemade, of course–which the waiter snipped from long strips into puffy little cubes. Robert scraped a last streak from the bottom of his chocolate soufflé and then, holding his empty spoon aloft and raising his eyebrow in a question, he nodded at my litchi sorbet, the last melting nubbin of it. I picked up my own spoon and scooped it up, then fed it to Robert. He reciprocated with a kiss on my cheek.

"Such a celebration. I'd gladly have given up my new job if I had to trade it for this evening. Chas, I've never had better food. Or company."

Robert's eyes didn't waver from mine. Suddenly I felt the young one.

The dinner cost more than the taxi ride. Both were worth every penny, even had I been paying.

"Maybe we should stay here tonight after all," I ventured when we were back in the taxi.

"No, I am fine for driving," Robert assured me. "All the alcohol has worn off, and I am not tired at all."

"That's not really what I meant."

"I know. And it's not really what I meant, either."

"Oh." I felt embarrassed. Hurt, to be more precise.

Robert didn't miss that. "I haven't said that very

nicely, have I? I could have done a better job of it in Lebanese." And he tried.

"What does that mean?"

"It is a very old saying, but I don't think I can translate it exactly. It includes something about letting experiences unfold and linger at several stopping places rather than hurrying them along and trying to cram them in all at one time."

I stopped feeling hurt. "Tell me more."

"Chas, I have had a very wonderful time. I meant what I said. This has been one of the most exquisite dinners I have ever tasted. But more important, I have had a time of—how can I say it?—enchantment with you."

"That's very sweet, and I—"

"I don't say that so easily," Robert interrupted. "And I do not want it to be all gone when I wake up tomorrow. Maybe if you and I went to a hotel, you would wake up and say, 'Well, that was fun but you are very young, so now good-bye.' We would have gone through the whole relationship in one day, from start to finish."

"That doesn't mean—"

Again Robert interrupted. "I know that right now I seem very young to be a boyfriend to you, at least for more than one adventurous day. But this is not necessarily so. And the only way to be sure is to leave something more for us to want until after we have had a chance a see whether such silly things as age are really important."

What a reversal. He was afraid that all I wanted was his body. He didn't want to be an easy lay, but to hold out for some possibility of commitment. Was this a gentle rejection, a cover for his not wanting to imply that I was too old to tempt him? I looked over and was caught in his hot eyes, noticed the tiny lines of tension at their edges. That was undeniably a look of yearning.

I was intrigued. If horny.

Once we'd maneuvered our way back to the New Jersey Turnpike, I needed something to take my mind off those muscles rippling under Robert's loosened shirt and the clenching of his thighs as he moved his foot from gas to brake.

I told him about my investigation of restaurant scams. At first he didn't understand the word, so I gave him some examples.

"Oh, you mean cheating."

"Exactly."

"But why single out restaurants?"

Good question. The obvious answer was that restaurants are what I write about, but I'd quickly learned not to bother with obvious answers when it came to Robert's questions. Besides, I ought to be sure myself that I had better reasons.

"Dining, by its very nature, implies trust," I said, thinking aloud. "It seems to be a rule of human society—all human societies—that a host promises a guest's safety at his table. It would be unthinkable in any part of the world at any time in history for a host to intentionally poison a guest or to knowingly allow any harm to come to him. There's an implied safe passage."

"I see what you mean." Robert took up my thoughts. "A restaurant, even though it is a business, takes on the responsibilities of a host."

"Right. So in this case, deceit is doubly reprehensible."

"It also seems particularly despicable to cheat people when they are celebrating," Robert added. "And to do so in public, to take advantage of their social insecurities."

"That's what makes it so easy for restaurants. They are dealing with people exactly when they have let their guards down. If ever people are not going to notice a discrepancy or be unwilling to call attention to a problem, it is when they are dining out with other people, especially when it is a date or a celebration or even a business meeting."

"People would rather lose money than lose face," Robert agreed.

"What makes it easier," I continued, "is that pricing in a restaurant is vague. Who asks the price of the bottled water? Who remembers how much the coffee was on the menu? And often the desserts are not listed anyway, so the restaurant can change any prices at will."

"I could never bring myself to ask about the prices."

"And there are other ways of maximizing profit besides hiking the bill. A savvy restaurateur knows how to direct his customers to getting the least for their money."

"You mean like featuring pasta, which costs much less than meat or fish?"

"Certainly. And consider the salad bar."

"An American invention I do not like very much. Those piles of conflicting foods all stuck together with thick dressing." Robert shuddered. I could feel it in my left thigh, which had somehow edged over to his.

"The arrangement of the salad bar is an art, not an aesthetic one but a financial one. The cheapest and most bulky ingredients come first—the lettuces. Then come vegetables cut to take up space and make it difficult to pile on much more—those big, awkward bell pepper rings, whole slices of onion or beet. Next are shredded vegetables, the carrots prone to landslides if you try to pile something on top of them. Only at the end are there the expensive and compact olives, cheese, bacon, nuts, and seeds."

"I hadn't noticed the arrangement of salad bars, but I see the same thing happening at buffet brunches." Robert dropped his right hand to my leg as if accidentally, then removed it immediately with a sheepish glance.

I put it back.

"Of course," I went on, as if our limbs had nothing to do with our conversation. "On a buffet, first come the salads. Fill up on lettuce, if you please. Or kidney beans. They're cheap. Next the breads. The pancakes and French toast—flour and water cost practically nothing. If you're looking for the shellfish or the meats, or for the luxuries like smoked salmon, you'll have to make your way past the scrambled eggs, the fried potatoes, the pasta of the day. Even the fluffy cream cakes—which are often cheap layerings of cake mixes and low-cost white fluff—are sometimes arranged to tempt you on the way to the carving station so you'll save room for dessert rather than filling up on beef. The arrangement of the buffet tables can spell the difference between Sunday brunch's profit and loss."

I had an afterthought: "Still, nothing spells profit more easily than water."

"But water is free."

"That's less and less true. Restaurants thrive on getting people to pay for what they might get for free. Notice how hard it is to order tap water nowadays. The waiter seems to be disappointed in you when you spurn his offer of Evian, Perrier, Pellegrino, Saratoga. You're made to feel like a hillbilly if you order plain city water."

"A hillbilly?"

"A peasant."

"Oh, yes. I know what you mean. When I have dared to ask for plain water I feel as if I am uneducated, as if I don't belong. Or that I am willing to endanger my health."

"Did you notice how the waiter at Jean-Georges pretended he didn't understand when I said I preferred tap water?"

"I, too, was surprised. I thought that a restaurant critic would have such a refined taste that even her water must be the best."

"At a six-hundred-percent markup, that's just what every restaurateur wants you to think."

We were talking business, but I had scooted closer to Robert and was finally, after twelve hours of imagining it, resting my head on his shoulder. Every once in a while he stroked my cheek or kissed the top of my head. It felt as if we were dear old friends. To me, anyway.

The night was warm and peaceful as we passed the NASA-Greenbelt exit of the Baltimore-Washington Parkway. Our conversation had trailed off along the dark, forested highway after Baltimore, and I felt as if the two of us were soaring alone through space. Now the road signs began reminding us that we were about to land back on earth. Landover. Bladensburg. Cheverly.

Robert got back to business, sounding as if he'd been rehearsing his question. "Will you write about this?"

"About the restaurant, definitely. Not about us, of course."

"How will you remember it all?"

"What do you mean? How could I forget this night?"

"No, I mean the restaurant. How will you remember all the food, the way it was cooked. You didn't take any notes."

"First of all, I have the menu." I reached over for my purse and pulled it out.

"I wondered what you carried in such a large purse. But I didn't see you take it."

"When I went into the ladies' room, the maître d's stand was empty for a moment, so I grabbed one."

"When you get tired of writing restaurant reviews, you could have a second career in burglary. But the menu isn't enough to tell you every nuance of what we ate."

"That's true, but I never have to take notes. Haven't for years. I'm so used to it by now that my mind just registers everything automatically—the food, the flowers, the paintings on the walls, and the design in the carpet. Sometimes I make small lists in my head and turn their first letters into sentences if there is some complicated series of spices or if the waiters have some special routines they follow. Or I create little imaginary scenes, like that Arctic char sliding right down your tongue because it was so silky, then slipping down to shatter the potato cake, which was like a crispy disk of lace."

Robert was flushing. I could feel the heat on my cheek, then saw it when I looked up.

"Don't worry," I said, putting my cool hand against his warm face. "I won't forget a thing."

12

When I woke up the next morning, twisted in my sheets and not recognizing my own bed for a moment, I couldn't recall what vegetable had accompanied the duck. Or the char. I no longer even knew whether the chocolate soufflé had been served with Chantilly cream or whipped cream. Maybe chocolate sauce. Or mango, for all I could remember.

Robert had been like a computer virus. He'd wiped my memory clean of all but him.

The phone rang. I reached for it, noticing for the first time that the sun was high in the sky outside my window, and a hot summery day was in full bloom. I'd long overslept.

"You left your handkerchief in my taxi."

"I don't have a handkerchief."

"Couldn't you pretend you do? What other excuse do I have to renew our acquaintance so soon after last night?"

"As if you need an excuse. Besides, you have called just in time to save my life."

Robert laughed. It made my whole body smile.

"I would do anything to save your life. What do you suggest?"

"Tell me: What vegetables came with the duck and the char last night?"

No answer.

"Well?"

"I cannot even remember the duck and the char."

I was afraid that I'd be able to concentrate on nothing but Robert today. Instead, every part of me was invigorated. I fell in love with the elevator, noticing for the first time its pattern of scratches inside the door. How lovely. And the newsroom: what an expanse, what a gift of freedom its open space offered.

I was whistling as I strode to my desk, dropped my purse on it, and gave Sherele a whirl in her chair. Before she had a chance to react, my phone rang and the caller ID told me it was Lily.

"Hi, Mama. Where were you so late last night?"

"I went to New York. Did you call? You didn't leave a message."

"New York?!" Lily blurted, in unison with Sherele.

I held up one hand to signal Sherele to wait and continued with Lily on the phone while the quizzical Sherele slid closer.

"I got a last-minute reservation at Jean-Georges and couldn't pass it up."

"Did you fly in that storm?" Sherele and Lily chimed in unison once again.

"I took a taxi."

"A taxi!" They both echoed me, but with more feeling.

"Who'd you dine with?" Lily got that in before Sherele had a chance.

"I dined with the taxi driver."

"Oh, Mama," Lily said with disgust in her voice.

"Hey, girlfriend," Sherele said, with a big grin and a thumbs-up.

"A young one," I added, stirring the pot.

"How young?" Two voices again.

"Thirties, I'd guess."

Lily sounded outraged. "You know, you could get yourself in real trouble, Mama."

Sherele sounded tickled. "You know, you could find yourself some mighty interesting trouble with a young taxi driver."

Sherele's conversation was more to my taste this morning. I told Lily that I was just fine, everybody had behaved utterly correctly, and I'd have to get back to her later.

After I had a chance to relive my New York interlude, with Sherele rejoicing in harmony, I settled down to write up my notes. Every detail flooded back, each bite and every heightened glance. I also recorded my discussion with Robert on restaurant scams. I'd been bogged down in details, and it had been the catalyst for a broader perspective.

I felt good. I felt feminine and confident and smart.

I could laugh at my failure with the twitchy Mr. Ottavio Rossi.

I could even face him in order to interview him

about the shady restaurant experiences he'd been hinting to me. At last I had the courage to track him down.

That turned out to be less easy than I'd anticipated. His kitchen design firm didn't know where he had gone and had no interest in trying to find out. I'd have to find him through my restaurant contacts.

I'm not totally comfortable with my daughter dating a waiter, but in this case it was useful. Brian didn't know Ottavio, but he suggested I try Machiavelli, as it had been hiring a lot of waiters at the time Ottavio had gotten his job. Of course, I didn't tell him the nature of my connection with Ottavio.

Nor did I tell Machiavelli who I was or what I wanted with Ottavio when I called there in search of him. The maître d' must not have arrived yet; the man who answered the phone sounded like the effusive waiter who'd plied Sherele and me with *Prosecco* and prosciutto. This time I used his enthusiasm to my advantage.

"No, darlin', we've never had a Rossi here. Can't anyone else help you?" he responded sympathetically.

"No, I need Mr. Rossi himself, and it is very important. I know that he is a waiter in an Italian restaurant. Do you think any other waiter there might know him? He's kind of new. Maybe you could think of another Italian restaurant that has had an opening for a waiter in the last few months."

"Well, hon, the Italian restaurants I know have been laying them off rather than taking them on. Just a minute. Giorgio has just come in. He knows all of the Italian guys in town. You just hang on and I'll ask him."

I held on, wishing now that I'd left the guy a good tip when I'd been to Machiavelli. And I was glad that Andy Mutton's exposé hadn't gotten this waiter fired.

He was back. "Giorgio says there's a waiter named Rossi at Coastline. New guy. New in town, I think."

"I'll try that. Thank you very much. I appreciate your taking the time."

"Think nothing of it. And you come see us sometime. Just ask for Andrew. I'll take good care of you. Good luck, darlin'."

Now that I was close to encountering Ottavio again, I didn't feel quite so sure of myself. I closed my eyes and slowed my breathing. I must handle this cleverly. Should I be the spurned Charlotte Sue or perhaps Chas Wheatley, who would be a stranger to him? If I was ever to encounter him in person . . . I suddenly broke into a sweat, thinking how lucky I'd been that Ottavio hadn't been on duty when I'd dined at Coastline with Homer and Sherele. How would I have explained myself? How could I have faced him? Maybe I shouldn't call him after all.

I'd hedge my bets. I'd just call and find out if he works there, then figure out later how to approach him.

The phone at Coastline rang six times without anybody answering, and I was about to hang up. I could hear it switching, as if to voice mail, then suddenly a growling voice came on the line. "Cigar lounge." The man had an accent. Italian? It wasn't a voice you'd want to meet in a dark alley.

"Is this Coastline?"

"Yes, madam. It's the cigar lounge at Coastline. Nobody's here yet."

That was a relief. I could just ask my question and not have to explain why I didn't want to talk to the man I was seeking.

"I'm sorry to call so early, but I am looking for a waiter named Mr. Rossi."

"That's me."

Wrong Rossi. Wrong voice. I was stymied once again. "Thank you, but I'm afraid it's a different Mr. Rossi I'm looking for. He's a new waiter."

"I'm new. A couple a months."

"No, it's a different new waiter. His first name is Ottavio. Ottavio Rossi."

"I tell you, that's me, lady. Ottavio Rossi."

I was dumbfounded. It's not as if Ottavio is a common name.

"Look, lady, I gotta set up for lunch. You wanna tell me why you're calling?"

"Oh, I'm sorry, I've made a mistake. I must have gotten the name wrong. Sorry to take up your time."

I hung up, bewildered.

It didn't take more than a few days to realize that Robert and I were going to find it nearly impossible to carve out time together, at least over the next couple of months. You wouldn't have known it from our blithely dropping everything for a jaunt to New York, but we both had heavily scheduled lives.

I'd already booked my dinner engagements for the following weeks, which tends to happen at the start of summer before people go away. And Robert, beginning his new job while continuing to drive the taxi until he was sure the job was going to last, found himself exhausted. Our mismatched schedules became a standing joke, though at least I wondered at times whether we were unconsciously avoiding having a long time alone together.

I'd hoped to take Robert along on my next visit to Coastline, since his enthusiasm for fine food was even greater than Homer's. But the two of us couldn't stake out a single mutual full-blown evening for weeks. Instead we met for coffee, a drink, or a quick, casual dinner, while we dreamed together about dining grandly. Food was sublimating sex, too. We talked about consumption rather than consummation.

I didn't know whether this relationship was going to go anywhere—in particular, whether it was going to go home to bed. But we were such an unexpected pairing that I was content to let it play out gradually and leave undecided whether I was going to be Robert's lover, friend, culinary guide or even mother substitute.

I tried not to compare Robert with Dave, who'd also rarely dined out with me, but for different reasons.

Dave has a physical aversion to fancy food. Ties chafe his neck, French food makes him queasy, he breaks out in a rash after he eats anything the least bit trendy—balsamic vinegar, cilantro, lemon grass. He'd rather eat the greasiest, soggiest pizza than a grilled lobster with tarragon beurre blanc. And sitting at a restaurant table for two hours makes his legs cramp. Just the guy for a restaurant critic.

How did I keep winding up with men who couldn't

or wouldn't take advantage of the *Examiner*'s dining largesse? Why did I have to dine out more with acquaintances than intimates? Couldn't I find a guy with the time and stomach for enjoying the city's restaurants with me?

Increasingly, my evenings were packed with social obligations. I was constantly preoccupied with trying to mesh my restaurant reviewing needs with my companions' geographic and dietary demands.

Summer is always the hardest season in my profession. The city began its annual meltdown, when everyone else lives on cold suppers and frozen desserts. For me, though, instead of kicking off my shoes and firing up the charcoal while sipping a gin and tonic, I have to trade bites of pappardelle and cassoulet, fill up on three-course meals, and sample heavy menus from start to finish. I'm still in a world of jackets and ties.

13

Wild mushrooms. The first bite of my appetizer rang a warning bell. That fibrous texture of the near-raw chanterelle, the watery blank taste of a morel soaked too long. No crisp edges, no woodsy aroma. I poked my fork again into the mushroom-and-scallop panfry and tried a second bite. Something was definitely wrong.

"Don't you agree, Chas?" I tuned back into the conversation at my table and nodded vigorously, as if I knew what I'd just been asked. The two couples, whose names had fled my mind, were chattering about where they'd eaten in Paris last month, reciting their menus, ingredient by ingredient. Dish-dropping, I call it. Far more tedious than name-dropping. All the while, they were enthusiastically forking up their appetizers as if Paris were right there on their plates.

"You've got to taste this lobster cake," the tall woman with the flounce of tangerine hair said, as she plopped a piece on her bread plate and passed it my way. Her burly husband–Carter, his name popped back into my head–added an oyster with truffle mousse to the plate, assuring me that it reminded him of the oysters he'd eaten in New York last week at Le Bernardin. I hoped the other couple–Douglas and Marina, I recalled with relief–would take the hint and offer me bites without my having to prod them.

Dinner with Chas Wheatley: What am I bid? I dread these charity-auction donations. I'm approached often to contribute to school auctions, opera and symphony auctions, and "body part" fund-raisers–for heart, kidney, and lung associations. They all want me to take the winning bidders along for dinner when I review a restaurant. Eventually I learned to offer some less time-consuming donation to most charities and limited my auction dinners to Lily's school–until she graduated–and hunger-relief organizations.

These dinners with strangers ultimately turn out to be interesting and sometimes fun, at least when I can get my guests to talk about themselves rather than spend the evening on how I got to be a critic and what I think of every restaurant in town. But at first I inevitably feel like a sideshow performer, and the logistics are always complicated. When people have paid hundreds of dollars to dine in your company, you feel you owe them a great meal as well as sparkling conversation. But a restaurant critic can't predict which restaurants are going to be impressive. What's more, it's awkward to explain to your guests that since you're reviewing the restaurant and the newspaper is paying for their food, you need them to order different dishes and to give you a taste of each—or to exchange tastes if they'd like. And there is always someone in the group who wants just a small green salad, no dressing, followed by a well-done filet mignon. The worst are the guests who spend the evening trying to persuade me to donate another dinner to their children's school.

So far, though, tonight seemed to be a success, at least for my guests. It had taken months to schedule a date between the two couples' travels. Then they wanted a restaurant they hadn't tried before, which made the choice difficult since they seemed to eat out even more than I do. But somehow they had missed Coastline.

All four were as excited with their appetizers as a kid with a plateful of Oreos. But to me the lobster cake and oysters bore out the disappointment of my mushrooms. Either Benny was having a really bad day or somebody else was at the stove. At least I hoped this dinner was an aberration. Benny had seemed such a promising chef.

Since he was also a shy chef who avoided dining room appearances, there would be no way to be sure whether he was here unless I asked. The entrées worried me even more. Only the desserts—which, of course, would have been made by the pastry chef rather than Benny—lived up to my expectations. By the end of the evening, I hadn't eaten much, but my guests didn't seem to notice, and I felt stuffed with descriptions of the great five-hundred-dollar meals of France. Nor did my guests notice that I was preoccupied and puzzled during the meal, since most of what the conversation required of me was smiles and nods of agreement.

Fortunately, I'd hidden my consternation from the staff and from Gianni, who was passing out cigars to his friends and flashing his dimples to the women as he kissed their hands. When he rushed over to bow good-bye to us and asked whether we'd enjoyed our dinner, my guests' effusiveness masked my mumbled, noncommittal, "It's certainly been an evening," delivered with a big smile. I considered asking whether Benny was around, but I didn't want to prolong the encounter, so I decided to call him tomorrow.

My preoccupation continued as I walked home after fending off Carter's insistence that his driver take me there. I needed a walk. Of course, I always need a walk, usually a far longer one than the twenty blocks this would involve. I didn't bother to argue with Carter that the dangers of Washington's streets are far less than the risk to a restaurant critic of not getting enough exercise as an antidote to endless rich meals. I'd learned the lesson from Miss Manners in a column years ago: I didn't give any explanation, I just said, "No, thank you."

Anyway, no mugger in his right mind would venture out into such a Washington night. During the day, the summer sun had heated the streets until tar was oozing and sticking to pedestrians' shoes, and long after nightfall the hot rubbery smell still stung my nostrils. The air felt like the back end of an air conditioner, a lazy current so smothery you wouldn't pay the compliment of calling it a breeze.

I headed home to Seventh Street by way of

Pennsylvania Avenue, in hopes that the broad streets and monumental white buildings would lend an illusion of coolness. Sure enough, in the moonlight the White House looked like a vanilla ice-cream cake. I walked down the middle of the barricaded avenue—I always find it a kick to walk in the street, even when it is permissible. Heading along the east side of the White House, I thought I was alone until I heard Mozart playing softly, then caught a whiff of rank body odor as a bicycle rolled slowly past me. The cycle was a home on wheels, weighted down by boxes lashed to front and back, packed tightly with clothes and whatnot.

By the time I reached the end of the block, the bike was propped against the spiky, black iron fence, and its rumpled owner was fishing peanuts out of the box that was wired to the handlebars. One for him, one for the squirrel; he doled them out evenhandedly. Here was one of our poorest citizens, feeding the president's squirrels.

I nodded, and he did, too. "Hot enough for you?" Even the homeless keep the tradition of the standard Washington summertime greeting.

Once the cyclist's Mozart faded, the thick air along Pennsylvania Avenue was so empty that I could hear my heartbeat from inside my head. I felt as if I were walking through gravy. I tried to think cool thoughts. The Washington Monument off to my right; a popsicle, coconut-flavored. The Willard Hotel on my left: an all-white sundae, draped in marshmallow, with whipped cream curlicues. Up ahead, Freedom Plaza, its fountain spraying cool droplets into the night sky.

The noise picked up at Ninth Street. The old *Evening Star* building, grandly etched and carved in dignified, timeworn white stone, emitted bursts of color and sound as the last revelers at Planet Hollywood pranced out of its doors.

I could see the Capitol ahead of me clearly now, its dome like double-decker scoops of vanilla. And then I was at my corner, where the twin towers of the fanciful little building that houses the National Council of Negro Women tonight looked like upended twin strawberry cones in the palest pink.

Daydreams or no, sweat was trickling into my ears and down the back of my neck.

What a waste of an evening, I grumbled to myself. All right, raising hundreds of dollars for a soup kitchen is worth a few hours of my time, and I did hear a rather full list of what's being served in Paris this month. But for me the main point of the evening was to evaluate the new chef, so if he wasn't there, I had nothing to show for it. And if he was, I'd have to rethink my opinion of this chef who had impressed me so much.

If you want a quiet place to work, try the newsroom of a morning paper before ten A.M. People who try to reach reporters in the morning chide us that we keep bankers' hours.

I wish it were true. Banks in my neighborhood close at three P.M., and even the most accommodating one only stays open until six. If I saw a reporter leaving the *Examiner* at three P.M., I'd figure she was on assignment or going to lunch, either of which could also be true if she was leaving as early as six. The newsroom is inevitably full at seven, and plenty of those reporters and editors who arrived in the morning are still around at eight or nine P.M.

That's one reason I seldom go to dinner with colleagues—they eat too late. Sherele is a rare exception: She'll sometimes dine with me before the theater. And if she doesn't have a play to review, her hours are her own. But the rest are on too different a schedule for my requirements.

I arrived at the *Examiner* early on the morning after my Coastline dinner—not because I wanted quiet, but because I wanted to get in a good walk before the city began its daily summer meltdown. The direct route is only eight blocks, but once I detour to see what's flowering on the Mall or around the Capitol, I can stretch my walk a mile or two. By the time I reached the *Examiner*, even though it was only nine A.M., my red cotton-knit dress was splotched with purple sweat marks and clinging to my thighs, which are not a part of me I'm eager to have outlined.

I was jolted out of my reverie by the smell of the picketers in front of the building. Their signs took me by surprise. They were taxi drivers protesting the *Examiner*'s series on substandard vehicles and inept drivers. Either these demonstrators had decided to parade through the night to avoid the midday sun, or they'd been sleeping in their cabs to save commuting time, I guessed from the look and the reek of them.

At first I looked for Robert before I realized he'd have no part of this. None of the demonstrators was remotely like him. None was the least bit groomed; every one needed a shave, a haircut, a steam iron, and a fresh pair of socks. These drivers looked like their ramshackle cabs—the ones Robert complains about bitterly whenever we stumble onto the subject.

No wonder I walk.

Everyone who works at the *Examiner* must have been trying to beat the heat. Thanks to the commuters who wanted to avoid stifling rush-hour traffic and the city dwellers whose room air conditioners were no match for the three-digit daily highs, the newsroom was as full as I've ever seen it. And for once the air-conditioning—which on some days is so cold that the telephone operators sneak electric heaters under their desks—was just right. With everyone at a comfortable temperature, facing plenty of hours in which to get work done, the mood was energetic.

The swarm of taxi drivers out front had headed my thoughts in Robert's direction. Now the unexpectedly crowded newsroom threw a switch in my head. Dave appeared, full-size and nearly real.

"Hey, babe. How was last night?" He swung his long legs off the trash can he used as a footstool and stood up, towering over me by nearly a foot. "Did you give them their money's worth?" Dave's craggy face held its familiar lopsided grin as he leaned down and gave my shoulder a squeeze.

I stood beside his empty chair and let the play inside my head run on.

"The restaurant was a bust," I told Dave, as he pulled up a chair for me from one of the few empty desks. He settled his lean frame back into its slouch and propped up his feet again.

"I thought you loved Coastline," he said, ruffling his lanky toffee-colored hair and looking at me as if he'd rather be running his fingers through mine.

"It was off. The food was definitely off. Now I've got to find out why." I fingered a long, limp strand of my own hair. A poor substitute for stroking his.

"Too bad. You should've joined me and the guys for a late pizza. Pepperoni and sausage. It was great. I saved some. Took it home. Maybe you'd like to come by for a slice tonight."

"No, I've got to get to another restaurant. If it's not too late, maybe I'll stop by after dinner." Unlike Robert, who ended his workday late and started early, Dave usually spent his evenings at home and rarely came to work before ten.

"Tell you what," said this voice resonating in my head. "The weatherman's giving us a break this weekend. A cool front's coming. So I'm going to wrap a tie around my neck Saturday night and go to any restaurant you choose. I'm also determined to drink some wine." Dave is strictly a beer guy. "I mean it, Chas. I'm even setting aside all day Sunday to recover."

That's the man of my dreams.

As I pulled out my desk chair and closed down my daydream, I knew the answer to the question I hadn't asked myself about Robert. I'd been trying too hard. I'd wanted to want him. Despite his sweet, adorable ways, his sexy eyes and the way he walked, his lively mind and responsive tastebuds, I wasn't even faintly in love with him. I was just trying my damnedest to have a crush on him.

Maybe he'd be relieved.

I vowed to arrange a grand dinner with Robert no matter how much juggling it would take to do so. We had to talk. At the same time, I'd have to resolve last night's mystery.

I left my number on Robert's pager, then dialed Coastline. "May I please speak to the chef?"

"Which chef?"

"Benny."

"Sorry, he's not here. Who's calling?"

"This is Chas Wheatley. When do you expect him?"

"Oh, Miss Wheatley. Can somebody else help you? Benny is out of town for a few days. His father died."

"I'm sorry to hear that. Who's this?"

"This is Giuliano. I'm the one who waited on you the first time you dined here. I'm sure you wouldn't remember me, but I used to work with Brian at La Raison d'Etre."

"Of course I remember you. And Brian has told me what a good friend you've been to him. Thanks for the information, Giuliano. I'm on a fairly tight deadline, so I'd be grateful if you'd ask Benny to call me as soon as possible after he returns. Please give him my sympathy, too."

"I'll tell him the minute he comes back. And I'll look forward to serving you again."

I hung up and reevaluated. Now I'd have to postpone my next visit to Coastline until after I heard from Benny. And I'd wanted to take Robert there.

Benny's being away for a few days turned out to my advantage after all. Robert, too, had a death in the family. He sounded like a lost boy—not so far from the truth, I admitted to myself. And I wanted to mother him when I heard the sadness and the strain in his voice. His anxiety about taking off time from his new job and from his driving was a mere flea bite against the grief of losing his middle sister. He was steeling himself, as well, to tell his father. I comforted Robert as best I could and promised him a restorative dinner at Coastline when he returned.

14

Washington is infamous for its suffocating hazy summer days. It's even worse, though, when the haze turns to a downpour and the heat doesn't subside. The rain feels almost like steam. On such days, the water doesn't so much cleanse the streets as stir up their stench. The moisture makes everyone's skin feel waxy, as if the whole sky needs water softeners. Washington turns into a fetid jungle.

And the unruly Potomac River floods with the slightest provocation. Overcemented low-lying areas remind us once again that they were originally swamps. At traffic circles and on suburban highways, cars plow through momentary lakes, throwing up walls of water on either side.

The city was drowning and sweating and belching water. I had to do my waiting and pacing indoors.

A week later, neither Robert nor Benny had returned.

One man after another was moving out of my reach.

It was ironic, then, that I found myself going to Sunday lunch at Ari's house. My ex-husband had always felt out of my reach when I was married to him, and only after we divorced and he found a new love, Paul, had I been able to grow close to him.

That had taken years, and it was all due to Lily. At first I competed with Ari for her loyalty, but as she turned into a fiercely independent teenager, I realized that Ari could be my greatest ally in my relationship with Lily. Nobody else but Ari cared about her as much as I did, and I could keep doubly in touch with her life if Ari and I exchanged information. Even Paul turned out to be an asset to my parenting. His flamboyant, cheeky affection drew Lily out from even her most secretive times. His was a voice she trusted, and I learned to appreciate his instinctive good sense. I was sorry Paul wasn't going to be at the lunch, even if his absence meant more of Lily's attention for Ari and me.

This get-together was arranged at Lily's bidding. She'd been too busy lately to see either of us, so she figured that if I met her at Ari's she could get two parents for the time of one. That suited me, since I don't often enough have time to see Ari, either. And I love lunching at his house. Ari is one of the most revered chefs on any continent and has been for nearly half a century since he was a precocious *stagiaire* in France's top kitchens. His catering kitchen turns out more exquisite and consistent food than any restaurant in town, and he always has leftovers. He also dishes up the juiciest restaurant gossip.

In Lily's honor, he'd assembled a small vegetarian

buffet, heavy on the wit and light on the calories. In recognition of the summer heat, there was a brilliant salad of reversed colors–golden beets and blood oranges. A clear aspic looked like ice, tingled with tomato essence, and held suspended cubes of white mozzarella and tiny green leaves of basil. It was even more refreshing than the classic Italian tomato-basil-mozzarella salad, and it owed its character to a liquid distillation of tomato that Ari had been working on for years.

I was on my second helping of corn-peppercorn custard and savoring the way the fresh corn sweetness bounced against the faint heat of the black and red pepper. The talk was as light and spicy as the lunch. Lily and I were competing to invent names for this wonderful dish when Ari, who had been even more quiet than usual, interrupted in a dark voice that stopped us short.

"Many chefs are angry with you, Chas." The way he plunged right in made me realize he'd been sitting on this statement for a long time.

"Chefs have always been angry with me, as you well know. Show me a critic who doesn't make chefs angry, and I'll show you a shill for the industry." I tried to sound bantering, but I was defensive.

Lily was so astonished at Ari's attack that she spoke up in my defense. "Mama never says anything to make a chef angry except when he deserves it, and you know it, Papa."

I couldn't remember her siding with me against him before. But I didn't want to repay Ari's hospitality by stepping between him and his daughter. Besides, Ari hardly ever makes rash statements, so I realized he must have had a good reason to blurt out such a complaint.

"Who's angry? About what?" I managed to stifle my defensive tone.

"I don't care that they are angry at you," Ari stammered. "Or, I mean, I do care. But I don't mean that you should temper your writing in order to avoid making chefs angry with you." Ari is known for his dignity or lassitude, depending on who's observing.

Uncharacteristically, he rearranged platters as he talked and snatched my plate like a busboy being paid by the pound. "I am worried. What I have been hearing is something different from the usual. Even the good chefs are expressing displeasure. And some are sounding more like thugs than professionals."

"Tell me what they are saying."

"That's even more worrisome. They are being careful in my presence. As soon as they see me, they stop talking. It is their tone that makes me uneasy."

"They should worry more about their customers than about me."

"I agree. But restaurants are big business these days. People will go to unimaginable lengths to protect a billion-dollar enterprise. And while they might shrug off a story about their serving instant mashed potatoes or frozen *boeuf bourguignonne*, they will not be so complaisant about an accusation of breaking the law."

"I appreciate the warning, Ari. And believe me, you're not the first to suggest I need to be careful. But in the newspaper world, this is mild stuff. Done all the time. The *Examiner* won't let me get into trouble."

I didn't feel quite as confident of the protective instincts of the paper as I was pretending to be. In fact, I made a mental note to talk to the paper's lawyer tomorrow. I didn't want to show my vulnerability to Ari, though. It was time to change the subject.

"At the moment, my greatest danger is in not having a restaurant to review. I'm getting really frustrated waiting for Benny Martinez to return to Coastline so I can write my column on it."

"Has he taken a vacation at this time of year? I'm surprised he would do that, since it is a heavy tourist season, and, even more important, he is new in the kitchen. Gianni Marchelli must be getting soft if he permits Benny a vacation now."

"It's not a vacation," Lily chimed in. She'd been hearing about Coastline endlessly from me.

"No," I explained. "Benny was called away on an emergency. He's absent from the kitchen because his father died."

"That would be a very long absence," Ari said, sitting down at last. "Benny's father died when he was a small boy."

I paced and fumed until eleven A.M. on Monday morning, the earliest I could hope to find Gianni at Coastline.

"Is Benny there?" I tried the receptionist one more time.

"No, he's not. Who's calling?"

"It's Chas Wheatley from the *Examiner*. Can you tell me where I might reach him?"

"Hello, Ms. Wheatley. Can I help you? Benny has gone home because his father died, but unfortunately nobody here knows how to get in touch with him. He is apparently still needed there by his mother, but he will be back before long."

"I'd like to speak to Gianni, please."

"I'll see if he's in. Please hold."

"Chas, my dear. How are you? When will we see you again? We have some fresh razor clams you must try. I will save some just for you if you will tell me when I can expect you."

"No, thank you, Gianni."

"Oh, I know that you do not like to get special treatment. But these clams are so wonderful, you must taste some, and they need not have to do with anything you write. Just a little vacation for an hour to taste something extraordinary."

I adore razor clams.

"Gianni, I need to talk to you about Benny."

"Isn't it a pity? A sad time for a young man. And just when he was feeling comfortable in the kitchen."

"Forget it, Gianni. I know his father died when he was a kid. Tell me where Benny really is."

"Oh, I see. Let me transfer to the phone in my office. Don't go away, Chas. I want to talk to you about this."

Gianni put me on hold, and I set up a new header on my computer, ready to take notes on whatever secrets Gianni was about to divulge.

"Are you there?" Gianni was back on the line. "I know I should have told you earlier, Chas, but I was too devastated. And I wanted to figure out what I was going to do next before I discussed it with you."

"Gianni, this has played havoc with my schedule. When is Benny coming back? Obviously I can't write a review with the material I have, and you must be eager, too, to have your previous negative review updated."

"This is very hard for me, Chas, but I just have to tell you right out. Benny is not coming back."

"He's not coming back? What happened? And why has your staff been telling me he'd be back any day?"

"Everyone is too ashamed. I had to fire him."

"Fire him?" I was just repeating Gianni. I guess I had to hear all this twice for it to sink in. "Benny was the best chef you've had."

"I know. How well I know it. I felt I was stabbing my own back. But I had no choice. He was abusive to the salad girl."

Hadn't I heard this story before? Coastline's first chef had been fired for sexual harassment. What's in the water there? I sagged with sorrow for Gianni, for all he had tried to build at Coastline, for the customers who weren't going to get to taste Benny's cooking. Benny had hardly seemed the type.

"Tell me about it." I was once again grateful for my quiet keyboard, which allowed me to transcribe Gianni's words without him being reminded that I was doing it.

"There's nothing much to tell. The salad girl, Denise, was something of a troublemaker. Maybe she provoked it. But late in the service one evening—the night before you were here, in fact—she and Benny got into an argument. They were still fighting when the rest of the kitchen staff went home. You might even say she seemed to be staying on just to fight with him. But there was no doubt that Benny was very angry. The next morning she called me and was extremely upset. She said Benny had hit her. Blacked her eye. She was going to press charges."

"You already went through something like that once," I said, encouraging him to elaborate.

"Did I ever. I knew the restaurant couldn't survive another legal charge against us. I had no choice. I had to promise Denise I would fire Benny immediately. I tried everything I could to calm her down. She finally agreed to take the charge no further. I had to pay her off with a two-week vacation. She said she wanted to go back home to her mother and father to recuperate and get her head together. I even gave her plane fare."

I felt terrible for Gianni. And for the salad girl. Even for Benny.

"How are things going with her now?"

"She hasn't come back. I think she used the money to head for a cooler climate."

Gianni had been doubly screwed. So had I.

"Why didn't you tell me? You knew I was about to review your restaurant. You could have at least saved me one visit. And you didn't even tell me when I was there, as if I wouldn't notice."

"I'm sorry, Chas. I knew you would notice. You're too good not to. But to be honest, maybe I sort of hoped you wouldn't." Gianni paused. Instead of stepping in, I kept quiet, forcing him to talk more than he might have otherwise. It's a standard reporter trick. "You came the very night after I fired him. I hadn't yet absorbed it. I just felt terrible. I'd had such great hopes for Benny and things were going so beautifully. For a while I just went along trying not to think about it. I almost convinced myself that Benny had really left for a family emergency and would be back."

"What about the staff? Why have they been lying to me?"

"I think they must have been trying to protect Benny. Not make it public. Everybody liked Benny."

Giuliano's story was different. After begging the waiter's home number from Lily's boyfriend, Brian, I confronted him about lying to me and saying Benny would be back soon. When I heard Giuliano's reason I could hardly blame the guy. He said Gianni had promised the staff a substantial bonus if Coastline got a good review from me. Everyone had agreed to pretend nothing had changed, in hopes that I'd give up waiting for Benny and write the review on the basis of what I already had. Giuliano was full of apologies and excuses: The kitchen was just as good without Benny, he told me wishfully. I knew better and I hoped that in his private moments Giuliano did, too.

Somebody on the staff must have been looking beyond his own bottom line, because word got to Benny that I was asking questions and getting answers. He called me to add his.

"Miss Wheatley, I am sorry to take your valuable time, but I would like to tell you from my side what has happened. I am not working at Coastline anymore. I think you know that."

"I wish you'd called me sooner, Benny. I've been trying to chase you down for weeks."

"I am very sorry. You have been so kind to me. I wanted to tell you, but I could not." Benny sounded two or three decades older than the nearly electric young man I'd talked with at Coastline.

"Were you away?"

"No, I had to honor the deal I had with Mr. Marchelli."

"After he fired you? What kind of a deal is it to be fired? Did he promise not to tell about your attacking the woman?"

"I did not do that! It is not true!" The old fire returned to his voice.

"If it isn't true, why didn't you fight back? Why did you just leave?"

"I could do nothing. I had no way to fight. Nobody would believe me. Nobody could prove that I did not hit her if she was going to say that I did. I was not in a court of law. People will always believe such a thing when a woman says so."

"That's not true. People here are innocent until proven guilty."

"Only in the courts, not in people's minds. And courts cost money." Now Benny's voice sounded very young. Scared, maybe.

"Did you confront the woman? What about her black eye?"

"Miss Chas, I have not seen her again. I have had no chance. I tried to find her to talk to her but I don't know where she went." His voice cracked. "I did not hit her. You have no reason to believe me, but I just wanted to tell you anyway. I would not hit a woman. Denise and I were friends. We had arguments; it was almost her way of friendship, to tease and yell and make a fuss. It happened many times. But we always came back to joking and being friends. When I left that evening, she was very funny and once again friendly. I don't know what happened."

Benny sounded natural, not rehearsed. His words rushed out with feeling, with all the emphasis in the right places. I started taking notes.

"Tell me about it from the beginning."

Denise was a bad-tempered woman, Benny claimed; everyone thought so. But Benny liked her, maybe because he saw that nobody else liked her and he felt sorry for her. He was nice to her even when she was surly and stubborn, and he had learned to joke her out of a bad mood. Gradually they became friends.

On the night of their last argument, Denise came in as nervous as a caged lion. She took more cigarette breaks than ever before, and she wasn't paying careful attention to the plates she arranged. Benny tried to improve her mood, but instead she succeeded in getting him to lose his temper.

"We screamed a lot that night." His voice was scratchy with embarrassment.

"And everybody heard," I urged him on.

"Yes, everybody heard. But what they did not hear was when we stopped fighting and became friends again. Like every other time. Maybe the difference was that all the other times we became friends again while everyone else was there. This time Denise stayed late, and everyone else was gone but she was still there."

"Was that unusual? For her to stay late?"

"I think so. I don't remember her staying that late before. I guess she was upset. Wanted to make up before she left."

"Did you usually stay late?"

"I was always the last to leave. Except for Mr. Marchelli sometimes. I liked to be the one who locked up. Then I could be sure the kitchen was ready for tomorrow." Benny took a deep breath, as if to swallow his feelings about this kitchen where he'd been promoted to the equivalent of a gold medal, then had it snatched away. He went on hesitantly. "A kitchen worker like me has no power, no job security, no union to support him when he has a problem. You can see why I could not fight this accusation. I don't even want to do that now. I just want to try to find another job far away and go quietly. That is why I called you."

"What could I do about it? I wish I could help, but I'm not in the position to find you another job."

"Please don't think I would ask such a thing. You have already been a very great help to me by liking my food. I am calling you because you are a very important person and a very nice person. I want to ask you please to not write this bad thing about me. If people don't know about it, I hope I can find another new job."

"How will you do that without references?"

"Mr. Marchelli has given me a reference."

That surprised me. Gianni was taking a chance. I liked him better for that.

"And how will your family live until you get another job?" I wasn't sure I wanted to know the answer to this. Why was I getting sucked in?

Benny hemmed and hawed at this one. "Mr. Marchelli has helped me with that, too."

"He gave you severance?" I was astonished.

"Not exactly. He gave me ten thousand dollars if I

would not tell you that I was gone from the restaurant."

I'd always wondered what would be the street price of a good review.

I couldn't promise Benny that I—or somebody else at the paper—would not write about his dismissal. But I did promise to keep him informed and to give him a chance to talk to anyone at the *Examiner* who might be writing about him. He wasn't happy with this compromise, but I pointed out that it gave him hope and assured him fairness.

He had one more piece of business. "How did you discover that I was gone?"

"I could taste it."

"I'm sorry, I don't think I understood what you said."

"I went to Coastline the night after you left. I could taste the difference."

"I hoped that was what I heard you say. Oh, Ms. Wheatley, I feel much better. I have been so unhappy and afraid. I have thought that maybe I would never be a chef again. Hearing that you have taken so much notice of my food makes me think that I can try again to achieve such a position."

I hoped it would be at a restaurant I'd have a chance to review. I never let politics get in the way of a great meal.

Nor did I ever let my taste buds get in the way of my politics. I was curious about Denise now that I'd heard two conflicting stories about her fight with Benny. Despite my ducking the question with him, the fact was that nobody else at the paper was likely to pay more than cursory attention to this story. Some reporter would get a statement from Gianni, another from Benny, and note that Denise was unavailable for comment. A firing wasn't worth a lot of time, except to me now that I'd gotten involved. Thus, unless I followed up on Denise myself, I might never find out the real story.

I didn't want to enlist Gianni or Benny in my investigation. The only person I knew who could possibly help me find Denise was Giuliano, the waiter who'd lied to me. Now that I'd caught him in his lie, he owed me something to make amends. Information would do.

"Do you have any idea where I might find Denise? I don't even know her last name." How much of a threat could I sound if my investigative capabilities hadn't gotten me as far as her last name?

"Smith."

That was going to be a big help.

"Do you know where she lives? Does she have a husband? A family?"

"Sorry, I can't be much assistance there. The office has her address, but she hasn't been at her home since the incident in question. I've heard the accountant telling Gianni that. She's kind of a loner—husband died in jail years ago, no kids, parents in some little midwestern town."

"That's a start. Do you have any idea where? Or what her maiden name was?"

"Now that you mention it, I do know that. She made a big joke out of being the white-bread cousin of Benny Martinez because her maiden name was Martin. It was kind of a bond between them."

Martin. Almost as distinctive as Smith.

"What else? Did they talk mothers' or fathers' names? Hometowns?"

"You know, Chas, you're good at this. I didn't think I knew anything at all about Denise. But your questions make me remember."

"Just doing my job, Giuliano. You know what it's like, doing a job that looks easy but takes a lot of experience to do well," I said, practically gagging on my blatant attempt to butter him up, not to mention encourage him to see me as all-knowing.

"You can say that again. People think that all it takes to be a waiter is the ability to stand on your feet for a few hours and carry a tray."

I didn't want to get too far off the track. "You have to develop good rapport with the kitchen staff, for one thing. And I know that's not easy, especially with a salad person like Denise."

"Exactly. She was a challenge, that one."

"What part of the midwest did you say she was from?"

"Ohio. That was it. Benny kept mixing it up with Iowa."

"Great, Giuliano. You've got quite a memory. Any idea what town? Or her parents' first names?"

"Her dad's is easy. Benjamin. That's what made their names so funny. Benny Martinez, Benjamin Martin. They talked about the coincidence every time they made up from a fight."

Now I was getting somewhere. I entered the name in my computer in all caps, boldface. "As I said, you've got an amazing memory." Slather it on, Chas. "I wish you'd heard what town she was from. I'm sure you could dredge it up for me if you'd ever heard it."

"I'm sure it came up sometime. Let me think. Not Cleveland. Not Columbus. Someplace smaller. A town I never heard of in Ohio. But I'd heard of it someplace else."

"Athens?"

"No, someplace else in the United States."

"Springfield?"

"No. Wait a minute. Southern. I know, Virginia."

"Virginia, Ohio?"

"No, a town with the same name as one in Virginia. Near Norfolk. I've got it: Portsmouth."

I knew Portsmouth. It's a town on the Kentucky border that has all the energy of a deflated balloon and a population whose average age appears to be eighty-five. It has a café called K & M that closes about eight P.M., but if you arrive in time, you'll find homemade pies and some of the best dinner rolls the midwest has ever produced. I figured that in a town that looked this empty, the phone directory couldn't have many Benjamin Martins.

It didn't. Only two, and one was the son of the other. One was also more deaf than the other, so I got my information from the brother of Denise Martin.

Yes, she'd been living in Washington after her husband was transformed from incarcerated to deceased. In Portsmouth, Ohio, the words "jailed" and "dead" apparently have no more social acceptance than curse words.

Benjamin-the-Younger also seemed to recall that Denise had been working in restaurants–she'd always been "good with a Brillo pad and a dish towel" was the way he explained her career choice. He didn't exactly know what she had been doing in those restaurants where she'd been working and had no idea of the names of any of them. Most important, she wasn't back home in Portsmouth. Hadn't been back in years, said Benjamin, with certainty.

Might she have stopped by to see her parents when he didn't know about it?

"Hardly," he said. "My bedroom window looks right over their kitchen and bedrooms; bathroom, too. We also share a backyard. There ain't nothin' going on over there that I don't know about."

I was beginning to get a picture of why Denise left Portsmouth in the first place.

"When was the last time you or your parents heard from her?"

Benjamin paused and gave that some thought.

"It's been some years now, miss. Two or three, I'd guess."

"Do you know anybody else she might go to visit? Other relatives? Friends? Anyplace she'd be likely to go on a vacation?"

"I'm afraid I couldn't help you with that. Denise is the kind of person who won't go anywhere if she can help it. Never could get her out of the house even, without practically setting it on fire. She liked to stay where she was. It sure surprised all of us when she got herself up and went off to Washington, D.C."

I thanked Benjamin and gave him my number, asking him to please let me know if he or his parents heard from Denise. He never even asked why I wanted to know.

15

The sun had come out at last. A soggy Washington lay sparkling under its punishing glare. As if the city fathers were waging a war to end summer, the air-conditioning at the Municipal Center was cranked up so high that Homer Jones wished his vichyssoise was hot leek-and-potato soup. No matter. The turkey sandwich—the bird rubbed with plenty of spices and garlic, fresh from the oven so it hadn't turned stiff and gummy-tasting in a refrigerator—reminded him of Thanksgiving. He'd had the counterman at the Bread Line add some pieces of skin, too, along with arugula and the house-made mayonnaise. Usually Homer ordered his turkey on a ciabatta roll, but this time he'd asked for a baguette. More crust, more chew to help siphon off the tension.

Today's unidentified homicide victim—the special of the day, Homer had begun tagging these nuisances—was a woman. It's rare to find a woman who's totally unidentifiable; if nothing else, someone usually comes looking for a missing woman before long. But that wasn't the half of what had Homer big-time worried. The shit about to hit the fan was where she was found.

The weeklong rains had flooded the Tidal Basin, that little picture-perfect, softly rippling pond surrounded by cherry trees and anchored by the Jefferson Memorial. Usually it's Washington's most romantic tourist spot. Not at the moment, though. All along its rim, when the high tide had receded, a ragged edge of debris had been deposited in its wake. Under the world-famous cherry trees, hundreds of small, dead fish sparkled among the empty Fritos bags, ice-cream wrappers, even a mangled osprey and a child's orange life jacket. Plus a boiled-looking bloated arm attached at one end to a tangle of branches on shore and at the other end to a still-submerged torso of a young woman.

Homer shuddered to think what tomorrow's newspaper headlines and video footage were going to do to the rest of the tourist season. Maybe even to next spring's cherry blossom festival. Australian Broadcasting had already arrived; could the Japanese be far behind? Thank goodness the park police were going to bear some of the brunt of this. That had its own headaches, though. Coordinating the investigation with them could prove to be a bother, and if a couple of congressmen decided to grandstand on this case, it would be pure frustration.

Homer swiped up the last of the mayonnaise from the sandwich wrapper and started his paperwork.

DECEDENT'S NAME (Last, First, Middle):
unknown
SEX: female
RACE: unknown
AGE: unknown
HOME ADDRESS: unknown
POSSIBLE MANNER OF DEATH: homicide
ADDRESS AND LOCATION OF DEATH: Tidal Basin
FOUND DEAD TIME: 5:00 A.M.

Once again, Homer had to leave much of the form blank. No next of kin. No occupation. He couldn't say yet whether the decedent was an alcoholic or a drug addict. As so often before, no wallet, no purse, no papers or personal effects at all. Just a mess of waterlogged flesh that had been a feeding ground for fish for longer than Homer cared to contemplate.

Homer could only hope that the woman had been fingerprinted at some time in her life or had been reported missing to one of the local police districts. If he got a lead, he could track down dental records, but that was unlikely with no wallet or papers on her. Even putting her description on the Teletype and circulating photos wasn't going be of much help, given the body's condition. Homer's strongest hope was that the publicity would flush out somebody who knew her, though the newspapers surely weren't going to show her face.

As Homer spotted a stray sliver of turkey on his desk and popped it in his mouth, his satisfaction was spoiled by thought of the downside of the publicity. Once again the homicide department was going to be ridiculed as the gang that couldn't shoot straight, the investigators who not only couldn't find the murderer but couldn't even figure out who the victim was.

I couldn't believe Homer wanted a hot soup in Washington in the summer, but there he was, urging the waiter to see if the chef would whip him up a bowl of her oyster stew.

We were at Georgetown's beautiful old 1789 restaurant, because it was Wednesday. The last time I'd offered Homer and Sherele their choice of dining places in honor of his birthday, Homer had requested 1789. It was a Tuesday, though, and that's chef Ris Lacoste's day off. Today Homer reminded me of the rain check I'd promised him and pointed out that this was definitely not a Tuesday.

When Homer arrived, I was glad he'd chosen 1789. He looked as if he needed its quiet and gentle ministering. His linen-weave tan suit was elegant, his shirt the color of cream of celery soup was an inspired match, and his tie could have passed for a Dior, even though I knew it wasn't. His eyes, though, appeared shadowed and dull, and he was fidgeting with the silverware.

The waiter wore a mournful look as he returned to the table to report on the soup order. The chef would be glad to cooperate, he ventured hesitantly, as if he were expecting Homer to dispatch him to jail before he could make his case. The problem was that oysters were not in season.

"I'll have scallops! I'll have clams! I'll have lobster! I'll have any damn seafood you can scrape up in your kitchen. But I want it made just like your oyster stew, with chopped walnuts and celery and those bits of crispy prosciutto in it." The waiter looked relieved, but just for a moment, until Homer continued his rant. "And be sure it's hot!"

The waiter's shoulders rounded in his tuxedo jacket, and he muttered a pained "yessir" as he turned away and headed for the kitchen.

Sherele was embarrassed. "Perhaps you should have asked the waiter to bring you a dog or small child to kick," she blurted to Homer. Then she looked ashamed and tried to make amends by explaining to me, "The reason for Homer's jackboots treatment of the waiter has nothing to do with the waiter, of course. Homer's just a bear because his job is stressing him out."

I seldom saw Homer and Sherele lose patience with each other. I threw Homer what I hoped was a sympathetic glance, leaned back in my chair and examined the colonial molding, the etchings of early Washington, the tiny brass oil lamps with their vanilla silk shades.

"An expensive restaurant such as this should be prepared to meet its customers' needs. That's the obligation a restaurant takes on." Homer defended his rudeness.

"The same thing might be said about a lover," Sherele countered. "You live as if taking an evening off is a crime. Nobody expects you to be able to identify every victim who's stripped of IDs and dumped in a back alley. You've still got to eat, you've still got to sleep, you've still got to spend a little quality time with your woman. Not to mention that vacation you keep postponing."

"Look, sweetheart, that vacation problem wasn't my fault. The first time, I got sucked into the Starbucks case, the second time I had to follow up that lead on the canal murder."

"The first time might be an accident, but the second time begins to look like carelessness." Sherele was trying to defuse the moment with humor. She took Homer's hand.

"Where's that from?" I asked Sherele.

"'The Importance of Being Earnest.'" Both of them answered me. In fact, all three did. The waiter had quietly approached the table with a steaming bowl of soup.

"Your lobster stew, sir," he said, as he placed it in front of Homer. "And three spoons, in case the ladies would like to taste it."

Homer lifted his spoon in one hand, stroked his tie with the other, and leaned over to inhale the steam. He dipped in the spoon and brought it to his mouth, then thought better of it and dipped again, careful this time to scoop up a little of each ingredient: celery, walnut, ham, and lobster. I hardly noticed my crab cake as the waiter set it in front of me I was so caught up in Homer's pursuit of pleasure.

After two more spoonfuls, Homer's face glowed like chocolate that's just begun to melt. And so he had. "There's nothing like great food to put the world right," he said, with the first smile of the evening.

Sherele had a look of forgiveness on her face.

So did the waiter.

Abruptly, Homer realized that the poor berated waiter was still standing at his side. He reached his hand out to shake the waiter's, which really took the hapless man aback.

"Sir, I owe you an apology. I hope you don't have many customers as boorish as me. I can only thank you for putting up with me so graciously rather than socking me in the jaw."

"I haven't had to resort to that yet, sir," the waiter replied, tentatively meeting Homer's hand halfway. Then he nodded and edged away, as if unwilling to turn his back on this madman.

Homer was overflowing with apologies as he spooned his soup, and still more of them when Sherele reminded him that he ought to save a taste for me, since I was reviewing this restaurant.

By the time we were halfway through our bottle of crisp, straw yellow Sancerre and our entrées, and I'd offered around tastes of my pine-nut–crusted chicken to exchange for a chunk of Sherele's salmon with Persian spices and Homer's veal chop, we were close and comfortable friends again, sharing office gossip along with the food.

Homer was even ready to talk about what had been bothering him. He explained how he was dreading the *Post* and the *Examiner* tomorrow, not to mention tonight's late news, because some of the media were bound to use the woman-under-the-cherry-trees story as an example of police incompetence. This was going to be one more log on the fire the media had been building against the District government. From potholes to murders, the city was being portrayed as decaying into ashes. Homer was part of a group of local leaders intent on making the city work better and demanding that the media recognize the improvements. This highly visible and likely unsolvable crime would be a setback.

"The best I can hope is that the publicity will bring someone forward who can identify her."

"I'm sure that's going to happen eventually, honey. What have you got so far?" Sherele overflowed with sympathy once Homer had turned in his jackboots.

"Just a woman. Nothing special to distinguish her. Sort of young, thirties or somewhere in there if I had to make a guess. Ordinary clothes, what was left of them. Stabbed once. Probably taken by surprise and didn't get to fight back. Face battered as well as bloated, though, especially around the eyes. Been dead for weeks."

I suddenly didn't know what to do with my mouthful of wine. I couldn't speak and I couldn't swallow. It was the mention of eyes. I'd been thinking of black eyes every day since Gianni'd told me about firing Benny because he'd punched Denise in the eye and nobody knew where she was. My stomach churned and I had to struggle to keep everything from coming up while I willed my wine to go down.

"Sounds gruesome," Sherele said absently, distracted by my obvious distress. "You all right, Chas?"

I got my internal traffic sorted out and took a deep breath. "I just had a weird thought. . . . No, it probably doesn't make sense . . . pretty far-fetched. . . ."

Homer was gnawing enthusiastically on his veal bone. I've always been impressed by Homer's ability to appreciate food in any situation. He's known to enjoy the classiest lunches no matter how gory his day. So I was flattered when he interrupted his pursuit of clingy morsels to rescue me from my stuttering.

"Out with it, Chas. Nothing can be so far-fetched or ridiculous that I'm not willing to consider it. I'm at a dead end here. So to speak."

He put down the bone, then picked it up again and turned it over in hopes of having missed a stray bit.

"I'd agree," said Sherele, nodding toward the bone, "you are at a dead end."

Homer put the bone down, looking sheepish. Time for me to provide diversion to head off another skirmish between these two testy lovers.

"I know a woman, probably the right age, who might be missing."

"Missing? For how long? How tall is she? What color hair? What does she look like?"

"I don't really know. But I could find out. The thing is, she might not really be missing. It's just that she got into sort of a fight. In a restaurant. A couple of weeks ago. Nobody's seen her since the following morning."

Homer had me pinned to the back of my chair with his eyes. The implications of what I'd just said began to dawn on me. I stiffened as if I were about to be interrogated. What was I doing? I'd turned the handle on a door I didn't want to open.

"She might not really be missing? What does that mean?" Sherele was drawn into the impending inquisition.

"She might have just gone somewhere. On vacation or something." I wanted to back down, have them forget I'd said anything about this. With both of them staring at me, though, and both of them silent, I reluctantly continued. My old interviewing trick was working against me. I had to fill the silence. "It's just that nobody here knows where she is. She hasn't shown up at work. And her family, who live in Ohio, haven't heard from her. Though they're not usually in touch anyway, so it probably doesn't mean anything."

Homer took out his notebook. "What's her name? You got an address? Any contacts? It can't hurt to poke into this a little. God knows I've got nothing better to do with my time on this case."

I explained about Denise and her fight with Benny, and her going off on vacation but so far not returning.

In my retelling, the possibilities settled heavily on my mind. I lost my appetite. But I still had a job to do. I ate my dessert. With Sherele. Homer didn't even stay for the chocolate terrine.

* * *

It's disturbing enough to think about strangers who have died violent deaths. To consider the battering and stabbing of someone you know, even someone you know of but haven't met, is a fearful prospect. After a night of dreams I wanted to forget, I was glad the next morning that I had a diversion.

I was attending a school for waiters.

It turned out to be prudent that I'd registered in my mother's name so nobody knew I was a restaurant critic. I'd skipped the classes on dress and grooming, on approaching the diner, taking the order, serving and removing plates and wine service. I'd waited for the session of most particular interest to me—and the one the teacher would least like a reporter to attend. It was on increasing your tips.

"An enterprising waiter can double the check after the entrée," said the teacher, who was, despite the morning hour, dressed in black tie, with his black shoes at a high gloss and black hair ridged with comb marks that made it look like corduroy.

The students, the men slouching and inattentive and the women trading bottles of nail polish, sat up straighter and picked up their pens at this news.

"First, of course, there's dessert. If you haven't already reminded your guests to order their soufflé at the beginning of the meal, give them another chance now. Desserts that are made to order are big profit items for you—since they are priced considerably higher than the other desserts—unless there are people waiting for a second seating. Another advantage is that soufflés take a long time, so they give you time to sell something to your guests for them to enjoy in the interim. Suggest a dessert wine while they are waiting. If they aren't responsive to that idea, it's a good time to point out that they seem to need another bottle of water. Perhaps they'd like to taste a small sorbet or maybe a little ice cream while their dessert is being prepared. Pre-desserts are a very popular item these days."

Pre-desserts? The same diners who insist on no-fat salad dressings and vegetables without butter are expected to embrace the idea of a dessert before dessert?

Now that he had their full attention, the teacher wandered among the students, offering nonverbal grooming tips as he spoke. He handed one a comb, pointed to the untied shoe of another, even tugged the shoulder of one woman's blouse to cover her bra strap.

"Don't take a no for coffee. You didn't get any takers the first time around? Present them with more choices: espresso, cappuccino, decaf espresso, decaf cappuccino. You've got to wear them down. Make it tiresome for them to keep saying no. Café *diablo*, Irish coffee. Every single sale adds another dollar or two to your tip."

The students were writing down every word.

"After-dinner drinks!" He paused. Looked around. Made sure he had everyone's eyes on him. "They are the easiest money you will ever make in your life, unless you're good at picking horses."

Pens were waiting.

"Just keep in mind that there is a liqueur for every taste. Your job is to promote it. Here's where it is important to know your diner. Is he a conventional, conservative type, who started with shrimp cocktail and went on to filet mignon, medium well? Or was he drawn to the farm-raised tilapia with three sauces? You know his taste by now, so just ratchet it up a notch. You go through the usuals, the brandy and the Kahlúa and the Grand Marnier, then get more specific when you see the slightest twitch of interest. If he brightens at brandy, suggest your VSOP, your Napoleon, your very special Henry-the-whatever. If he fancies himself a connoisseur, go into your Armagnacs. Too highfalutin for his taste? Tell him about your old rums, or the aged bourbon that is so special it's like a brandy. Don't forget the ladies. Sell them those delicate sweet sherries and ports, or a crème-de-menthe drink to refresh the mouth. Most important, always offer a refill—with the bottle in your hand and tipped toward the glass so it seems almost rude to say no. Just remember, when the entrée plates are cleared, this is not the time to start saying good-bye to your diners; this is the time to start doubling your take."

The students were all smiling as if they'd just been given a raise.

"And now your homework."

Their faces fell.

"I want you to do a little research. It will help you set your goals, to fix in your mind that you should never give away for free anything you can sell. You will each pick a restaurant from the list I have here, and you will find out as much as you can from it about those extras that make all the difference in your pocket. Bottled water: How much does the restaurant charge for it? How many bottles does it sell a day? Does it have any breads that come at a price–garlic bread, an à la carte bread basket? How many of those does it sell, and how much do they cost?"

A hand shot up. The teacher nodded.

"I've got a friend in Miami. A waiter. He says that all the really sharp restaurants there add the tip onto the bill automatically. What do you think about that?"

The teacher rubbed his hands along the lapels of his jacket as if savoring the fabric. "It's the best thing that ever happened to the profession. And Miami is the edge of the wedge."

"What's so good about it?"

"First, it puts a floor on your tips. No more cheapskates shaving the tip down because their bill is so high they think you're being overpaid. No tourists who figure that if ten percent is enough in their hometown café, it's enough in the big city. But most important, there's that bonanza when the diner forgets that the tip's been included and he adds another tip on top of it. One more good reason to push those after-dinner drinks: They soften the diner's thought processes."

The waiter school turned out to be useful for me on two counts. It added a different angle to the material I'd been gathering on sleazy restaurant practices, and it had allowed me to postpone obsessing about Benny and Denise while I waited for Homer to come up with some hard facts.

The problem demanding my immediate attention was that my file on restaurant scams had grown far beyond a column's worth, or even a series of columns.

It was getting to be enough for a book. I was almost making it my beat.

That's why, after I wrote up my notes from the waiter school, I went in search of Helen. I was losing my perspective.

Helen is the only person among the *Examiner*'s management who seems to know that we employees have more to our lives than scoops and deadlines. She also excels at talking us through reporting problems, writer's block, or any sort of journalistic dead end. Sometimes the entrance to her office looks like a soup kitchen line of the bedraggled, sad, and needy. Today the crowd was light: just me.

"Set the tricks and swindles aside for a while," she suggested, sitting on the edge of her desk so there would be no barrier between us. "Turn your thoughts to something else so the material can settle and sort itself in the back of your mind. Write about someplace you like. Or maybe focus on a different kind of problem for a while."

"That sounds like the right approach to me, but I've already finished writing up Jean-Georges. I'm not sure what I should do next."

"I'll bet you do. Perhaps you just don't want to do it." She said it in such a sympathetic way that I didn't feel berated. I knew she was right.

"You mean Benny Martinez."

"Exactly. I know that you are afraid of getting it wrong. Or injuring this chef you admire so much. But you mustn't miss the opportunity to tell the readers what they should know. It's good that you are reluctant to do this story. Your concerns will just assure that you write it all the more fairly."

"Why me and not Investigative?"

"Because it is, above all, a food story. No investigative reporter knows the restaurant world as you do. You understand what makes this important."

"How do I make sure that I get it right?" I wouldn't admit any possibility of inadequacy to any editor except Helen. Only she could be trusted not to file it away to shoot me down in some future discussion.

"That's easy. Get some help. We have all these crack investigative reporters here; take one to lunch. Ask Dawn."

My face must have looked as if I'd just cut open a durian, an Asian fruit that smells like a tropical cesspool.

"Okay, it doesn't have to be Dawn. There are plenty of others."

She paused to think.

"Not at the moment, though. Vince is on vacation . . . oh, hell, everyone is on vacation. Summer is such a drain."

She stood up and walked around her desk, then sat behind it. She was getting down to business. "What you really should do is remind yourself that this is professional and not personal, and call Dave."

"You know I can't do that."

"At some point, Chas, you are going to have to go back to working with the man. Unless you or he leaves the paper, you'd best get back on a collegial footing with him."

Helen's a softie, but she is wise enough to gently but firmly demand the best from us. Her encouraging me to reestablish contact with Dave was purposeful.

I just wasn't sure whether its purpose was to get me the best tutor in the business or to get me back with the best lover of my life.

My reason for not asking Dawn for help wasn't that she'd made a play for Dave when she first came to the paper back when our romance was secret. Well, that was one reason, but not the most important one. The more serious one was that Dawn is a thief. She steals ideas and fences them as her own stories. She was one of the causes of Dave's frustration with his job. Every time he'd get onto a really good story, she'd scoop him. It was as if she had his computer password and a wiretap on his thoughts.

That narrowed the field of available investigative reporters down to Dave. What was giving me trouble was that there was nothing I wanted more than to talk to Dave. In my experience, such obsessions were not to be trusted as a guide to action.

I dialed his number. Not in California—I didn't even have that one, and I couldn't face asking anyone for it. I called his extension across the room and waited for his voice mail to pick up. I left a message in what I hoped was a warmly businesslike tone, telling Dave that Helen suggested I call him to ask his advice on a story I was writing.

I hung up and wiped my sweaty hands on my pants, took two deep breaths, and knocked my cup of coffee across my computer keyboard.

No good was going to come out of trying to get any serious tasks done, I warned myself, as I cleaned up the mess. I might as well pass the time some other way until he called. I'd spend the interim cleaning the unanswered and unfiled mail from the bin on my desk.

A half hour later, my desktop was suspiciously clean. I'd convinced myself that none of the mail needed any answer beyond a "thanks for your note" scribble at the bottom of the original letter or on an *Examiner* postcard. I could barely sit still, especially once I realized it wasn't even noon yet, and given the time difference, Dave wouldn't check his voice mail for at least an hour. Or maybe not until his noon lunch break, three hours later here.

Whenever I'm desperate to waste time, I pick up the phone. Lily was my best bet for this particular hour. I didn't tell her I'd already put in a call to Dave. I tested the waters first, complaining that Helen had pressured me to call him.

"Mama, you'll have to see him every day when he returns to the newsroom, unless you're willing to look for a new job." Lily sounded just like Helen.

"I don't want him to think I'm chasing him," I said.

"No woman who's chasing a man wants him to think she's chasing him," Lily countered.

"I'm not chasing him! That's the point." Nobody could put me on the defensive faster than Lily.

"That's the point I really want to make. I think you should chase him."

"Oh, Lily."

"Just listen to me, Mama, even if I am just your daughter. I know you as well as anybody in the world does, because I'm an awful lot like you." That was an unprecedented admission from Lily. It gave me a jingly little feeling of happiness—and as she'd calculated, it put me in a more receptive mood for what she was saying.

"Of course you don't like the idea of chasing a man," she continued, confident that she had my sympathetic ear by now. "Don't forget, though, that before you left, you did chase him. You chased him away. Now it is time to think about chasing him back."

I didn't exactly disagree. Maybe I was looking for permission.

I muttered a few "mmm"s as I thought over what Lily was saying. Even added an "uh-huh."

Since she is so much like me, she began to hedge her bets, back down a little. "You'll be able to tell how he feels about it, Mama, and get hints about whether he wants to start things up again. Just take it in small steps. See how it develops."

"And what if it develops that I've made a fool of myself?"

"That's not possible. You could never make a fool of yourself. And Dave doesn't have a mean cell in him. He'll let you know whether he hopes to come back as your boyfriend or as your colleague."

"You're right. Which is what I'd expect, since you're so much like me," I joked.

"And like you, I can't stand not knowing the end of the story. You'll feel much, much better establishing now what your relationship with him is supposed to be when he gets back."

"Lily, I love you."

"Same here, Mama. But there is one more thing I've been wanting to tell you."

"Sure."

"It's about the story you're writing. You seem to have decided that the chef was unfairly treated, and you haven't even talked to the woman involved. All too often complaining women are dismissed as troublemakers. I realize you think this chef is talented and a nice guy, but that doesn't mean that he couldn't hit a woman. Some of the nicest guys in the world do."

Lily was right. I had prejudged.

16

I skipped lunch. Too much to do at the office, I told myself. Waiting to see if Dave would call, I avoided admitting to myself.

"I didn't think you'd be there," Dave said at one-fifteen, which was when the judge called a break in his trial.

"Are you disappointed?"

"That's not what I meant. It's just that it's your lunchtime."

"Had you hoped to just talk to my voice mail?" Why was I doing this? I didn't seem able to talk to Dave without a whine or an accusation.

"No, I'm glad it's the real you. At least I was. I thought you'd be out, but I just called in for my messages, and I didn't want to wait to call you."

"I'm not being very nice to you, am I?"

"For someone who left me a message asking for a favor, you're certainly not."

I fervently wished I could see Dave's face as he said this. I couldn't tell from his voice whether this was said with a smile and a wink or was dead earnest. Even e-mail allows little smiley faces to signal a joke. I decided to risk taking it as a good-natured tease.

"That's probably because I gave up lunch so I wouldn't miss your call. You know how mean I get when I'm hungry."

"Can't say I have much recollection of your being mean. Guess you never had time to get hungry when I was around."

As if Dave could hear me blush, or maybe because he didn't want to risk my contradicting him, he jumped in again before I could answer.

"What I really want to know, Chas, is how you're doing?" That old familiar caressing voice.

"I'm doing fine, more or less."

"I've been thinking with regret about our last conversation. I guess I wanted to see if I could make you jealous. What I never got around to, though, was giving you a chance to make me jealous. So tell me, are you seeing anyone special?"

I hadn't expected Dave to plunge right into our personal lives. I hadn't expected Dave to say anything he was saying. I squelched an inclination to tell him that of course I was dating—the kind of suggestive response he'd given me in our last conversation. Habits of self-destructiveness are tenacious, but I caught myself in time. It would be a shame to keep on reacting to old hurts rather than to the conversation of the moment. Dave had already volunteered that he'd been eager to return my call, that he'd wanted to talk to me, that he didn't think I was a mean person, that he was sorry he'd tried to make me jealous, and that he was capable of being jealous about me. What could I possibly have to complain about in all that?

"There is nobody special in my life. There's not even anybody not special in my life at the moment," I announced, wishing I'd resisted the hint of "at the moment."

"At the moment?" Dave, ever the investigative reporter, was inevitably looking for nuances.

"What I meant was that I just don't feel very interested in developing that part of my life for now."

"I know what you mean. I went out with a lot of women when I first got here."

My breath got caught in a little sound halfway between a sob and a moan. I covered it by clearing my throat and adding an "umm hmm."

"That didn't last long, though," he continued. "I got bored. I just didn't care enough to continue to make the effort. I hope you know what I mean."

I hoped so, too. "Are you trying to tell me, Dave Zeeger, that I'm a spoiler?" I was smiling into the blind phone, but my heart was pounding from my brazenness.

"We were a good team. That doesn't come along so often."

"Probably not."

"The real question is whether it ever comes back."

Here I was, sitting in the middle of the newsroom at lunch hour, open to everyone's view, and people walking by, nodding the hellos and good-byes of lunch hour, and I wanted to put my head on my desk and cry. Hope, regret, joy, fear. I wanted to sob and howl and mourn and beg. I wanted Dave back, and I was terrified to let him know but equally anxious about wasting an opportunity that might not return.

"I don't know yet."

How much do you want it? I really wanted to ask.

"I'm sorry. I'm out of line. Oh, hell, Chas, I've got to get back to the courtroom in a minute."

"I haven't gotten to ask you about my story. Look, before you go, I promised Helen I'd get your advice on this thing I'm working on. A chef's been fired for hitting a woman, and he says he was paid off to keep quiet about it and that he didn't do it."

"What does she say?"

"I don't know. I can't find her."

"What have you tried?"

I told him about tracking down Denise's parents.

"Good job. There's not a lot I could tell you that you haven't already figured out. I'd say you should just keep following your leads."

"She might have been murdered."

"Murdered? This is getting beyond your standard restaurant review, isn't it? Have you talked to Homer Jones?"

"Yes, it was his unidentified victim that made me think about Denise."

"I saw those stories. Nasty journalism, and pretty embarrassing for Homer, I'd say. Homer's being put through hell. If you've identified his body, he's going to be one grateful homicide detective. Still, I'm surprised that the paper sees it as your story."

"It's not. At least the murder isn't. The question is whether I should get involved in the story of the chef being fired and the charge of his assaulting Denise, especially since I can't get Denise's side of it. Maybe I should just wait until I find her. Or until that body is identified, in case it's her."

"No, you don't want to risk being scooped. You've got to go with what you have. Hey, they're calling me in. I've got to go. But I want to talk to you about this. As soon as you're back from dinner, phone me at home tonight and we'll go over this."

I didn't want to waste a day before I started pinning down the details, so I spent the afternoon imagining what Dave would tell me I needed to do, and I did it. I felt cheered on by his compliments about my finding Denise's family and looked forward to impressing him tonight with more of my reporter instincts.

I had the facts. I just hadn't sorted out which they were. Benny had been fired, confirmed. Benny had attacked Denise, not confirmed. Benny had been offered ten thousand dollars to keep his firing a secret from me, not confirmed. Denise was missing, more or less confirmed. Denise was dead—no, that was a possibility with no basis outside of my own imagination.

I needed to talk to three people: Gianni, Benny, and Denise. I'd start with the easiest to find, Gianni. He was always in his restaurant.

"Chas, my sweet, when are you coming to visit us again? We have everything back on track. Everyone here is eager to show you that Coastline is at its best."

"Have you decided on a new chef?"

"I'm not sure that I need a new chef. The kitchen staff wishes to try to run things as they are, and I am going to give them the chance."

Visions of watery mushrooms and insipid lobster

cake inhibited me from making an immediate response.

"Chas, are you there?"

"Sorry, Gianni. Someone just interrupted me. What were you saying? Keeping the staff as is?"

"Do you think it is a good idea?"

"You know I can't comment on that," I said, hoping my voice sounded friendly. "But I'll bet it will be a relief, after the expenses of Benny leaving."

"What kind of expenses are you referring to?" An unfriendly cold steel edge made deep cuts in Gianni's silky tone.

"The money you gave Benny."

"Oh, that was just the pay that was due him for the week."

"Benny earned ten thousand dollars a week? I'm in the wrong end of the food business."

"Ten thousand? Nothing like that. You know how people exaggerate. Somebody's added an extra zero. Where are you getting your information?"

"Are you denying that you gave Benny ten thousand dollars when he left?"

"I definitely and absolutely am. I think I have a reputation for being generous, but not for being crazy. I hope you're not going to print such a thing, Chas, or I'm going to have people hounding me night and day to hire them. Besides, I'm sure you wouldn't like to be caught with your numbers way off base."

"Okay, I got your message. Just one more thing. Have you heard anything from Denise yet?"

"Not a word. I confess I did slip her a little money, just so she could take a bit of a vacation to recover from her unfortunate experience. Apparently, the money has taken her farther than I thought it could. My guess is that she used it to set herself up somewhere new, and we won't hear from her again."

"Let me know if you do, will you?"

"For you, my dear, anything."

Benny was harder to find. I started backward on my Rolodex, which of course meant I was bound to find my first lead among the Bs: Boucheron, Ari, my ex-husband.

Despite his real or imaginary ten-thousand-dollar windfall, Benny had been looking for fill-in work until he could land a steady job, which might take some time and require him to move to another city. Ari's catering company was usually in need of more hands than he ever had the presence to hire, so it had evolved into an informal temp agency. Ari had Benny whisking beurre blanc at that very moment.

"Why don't you come over?" Ari suggested, after I told him I needed to interview Benny. I knew my ex well enough that I recognized his invitation as a signal that he thought I'd get further pumping Benny in person than on the phone.

That was fine with me. I can eat beurre blanc by the spoonful.

The dish Ari was experimenting with had the kind of exquisite simplicity that's nearly impossible to find: every ingredient local and at the height of its season, tasting clearly of itself. So hard to accomplish except in a home with a dedicated cook and a vegetable garden. Thin slices of rockfish from the Chesapeake Bay—wild, not farmed—were seared in a hot nonstick pan, then turned upside down onto a hot plate so that the residual heat cooked the bottom just until it lost its transparency. The fish was filmed with beurre blanc that had a little diced tomato to lend color and additional acidity, and it was served with noodles so sheer you could read a menu through them, tossed with tiny, sweet fresh peas and a little more beurre blanc. The trick is to be able to do this perfectly for a party of a hundred or more.

I was reduced to dipping my bread in the leftover beurre blanc when I finally slipped my first serious question into the conversation.

"Benny, your sauce is perfect. In fact, it's so good that I'm finding it hard to get down to work. But I need to ask you some questions."

Benny smiled, but his mouth quivered at the edges. He looked uncertain.

"Spoon her a little more of the sauce, Benny. That's Chas's idea of dessert," Ari said, probably to give Benny something to do while I barraged him.

Benny brought the saucepan to the table and ladled enough to cover my plate. I tried to look not just grateful but reassuring.

"Why do you need to ask me questions? You're not going to write about me, are you?" Benny's smile was losing its battle. He looked just plain anxious.

"I have to write about the changes at Coastline," I said, skirting the direct admission that I was writing about him. "I didn't say I wouldn't write about it; I said I would let you know if I *was* writing about it. And I want to ask you more questions specifically in order to be absolutely fair to you." Even to my own ears I was protesting too much.

"There is nothing fair about this," Benny said miserably.

"There might be. At least I can make sure people know the truth. First of all, I need to hear once again exactly what happened between you and Denise, who was there when it happened, and any details you can give me that might help me to verify your story."

"I've got to go and make some phone calls," Ari said, saving Benny the embarrassment of having a third person hear the gory details. "You've worked a long, hard day, Benny. Why don't you sit down and have a beer," he added, as he handed a bottle to Benny and pulled out a chair next to me.

Benny took a long swallow and hunched over the table, eyeing me warily as he told me once again about the argument with Denise.

"She was in a very nervous mood that night. Right from the time she came in. She took many cigarette breaks. And bathroom breaks. In fact, she was away from the kitchen more times than she should be. And she was not working well. Her plates, they looked sloppy."

That jibed with what Benny had told me before, though he hadn't mentioned bathroom breaks. I hoped that signaled he was feeling more comfortable with me.

"At what point did you begin to argue?"

"It started slowly. I probably was looking at her in an angry way and frowning at her plates. I didn't want to start something, so I kept quiet at first. Then it became too much. She was slowing down the service. I asked her what was wrong with her, and she said to me, in a sort of mean way, that nothing was wrong. Then I took the plate she'd just finished and put it in front of her face and told her that yes, something was wrong, that plate was wrong."

Benny stopped for another long pull on the beer, then continued.

"She started yelling. I started yelling. Everyone in the kitchen kind of moved away, like they were giving us room to fight. Then the maître d' came in and told us to shut up, that people could hear us in the dining room."

"Did that stop the argument?"

"It stopped the yelling. I felt very ashamed, and I didn't say anything anymore. I'd been so angry that I even forgot about the kitchen windows that connect us to the dining room. At least we were in the back, where the customers couldn't see us."

"What about Denise?"

"She walked out. I thought she had left for the evening, so I asked one of the other girls—excuse me, women—to take over her work. That's hard to do, but she was very nice about it and worked very hard until Denise came back."

"She came back to work?"

"Yes, it was a long time later. A half hour, an hour, I don't know. But she looked calmer. Still sort of mean, though. She didn't say anything, just kind of shoved the other woman aside to make room for herself and kept looking at me in a funny way as if she'd stuck pins in a voodoo doll or planted a bomb in my car or something."

"So you were afraid she'd done something dangerous to you."

"No, not exactly. I wasn't afraid. I just thought she

looked a little strange. You know, like you see in the movies when somebody has set a trap or something. But I knew Denise was only mean on the outside. Underneath that, she liked me."

"But the fight started up again?"

"It was right at the end of the service. I don't even know what started it. Maybe I looked critical of something she was doing. She always complains that I'm too critical. Anyway, before I knew it, we were yelling at each other again. I stopped it this time. I said that we both had to shut up because the people out there could hear us. I was also worried that as the kitchen cleared out, people could look through the window and see us, too."

"Of course! Why didn't I think of that! If you hit Denise, even after everyone else had left the kitchen, someone in the dining room might have seen you."

"I thought about that, too. The cleanup crew is sometimes still hanging around until the very end. But Denise stayed very late, as if she didn't want to stop arguing with me. She kept saying bad things to me until after everyone left. I told her that she should go home. I didn't need any more fighting. She wouldn't leave and she didn't stop trying to make me angry. She even lit up a cigarette in the kitchen, saying it was too hot to smoke outside."

"At what point did she leave?"

"It was after everyone was gone. I checked the dining room and the offices. I told her that everyone had left and she had to leave, too, so I could lock up. She just sat down and started crying."

"Crying? You didn't tell me that before."

"I felt a little embarrassed to tell you. I felt very bad

for her. I told her that maybe it was a bad time of the month for her, and she should go home and lie down and she'd feel better in the morning.

"I guess maybe I was right because she told me she felt better already and hoped I would forgive her. She'd been under a lot of tension but she'd make it up to me. She even said she'd like to take me out to dinner next Sunday night."

"Had she ever invited you to dinner before?"

"No. But one time when I caught her sneaking a couple of steaks out of the kitchen she offered to cook one for me at home."

"Did you accept?"

"I told her I couldn't be bribed with a steak or anything else, but I'd put the steaks back in the walk-in and wouldn't tell the boss unless she did it again."

"So you both left?"

"She left first. I still had a few things to do before I left."

"And when did you see her again?"

"Never."

"Didn't you ever hear from her again, either?"

"No, nothing."

I told Benny about my calling Denise's family. He couldn't add anything to what her brother had told me. No friends, no acquaintances outside the Coastline kitchen that he knew of. One more dead end.

"A last question, if you don't mind." I screwed up my courage to confront Benny about the money, and finally just blurted it out. "Gianni says that he gave you one thousand dollars, not ten thousand dollars."

"You told him what I told you?" Benny was agitated. He bounced up from his chair and paced across the kitchen. He turned and looked at me. "How could you tell him that? I trusted you. You can't write that!"

"You didn't tell me it was off the record."

"I didn't give you permission to write it. I just told you as a friend."

"I'm not a friend, Benny, I'm a reporter." I felt miserable. I had been playing by the rules, but a guy in Benny's position doesn't always know what the rules are. That's one of the hardest things about being a reporter. I hate receiving information that people don't want me to know and then having to make it public. It's even worse when people think that because I'm friendly to them, my being a reporter doesn't count.

Benny seemed distraught. "I had an agreement with Mr. Marchelli. He paid me that money so that I wouldn't tell you that I was gone from the restaurant."

"You kept the agreement. You didn't tell me you'd left; I already knew it. And I didn't say that you told me. I didn't even say where I heard about the money. I just told him I heard that your leaving cost him ten thousand dollars."

"What did he say to that?"

"He said that I had my figures wrong, that it was one thousand dollars and that it was salary that was owed to you."

"I'll go with that."

"What do you mean? Are you denying that you got ten thousand dollars? You made it up?"

"Let's just leave it that whatever Mr. Marchelli says is right. Except that I did not hit the woman."

"These things can be proved. I can track down the check."

"He paid me in cash."

"Ten thousand dollars in cash? I can find where you deposited it."

"I haven't deposited it."

"Benny, I hope you're not walking around with ten thousand dollars in your pocket or hidden under your mattress."

Ari returned with an uncanny sense of timing. He took one look at us poised at opposite ends of the kitchen and stood next to me, putting his hand on my head as if giving me a blessing.

"One thing you should know about Chas," he said to Benny, "she always writes fairly and honestly. You don't have to worry because her articles never hurt anybody who doesn't deserve to be hurt."

Benny did not look one bit relieved.

Ari then turned to me and said, "I've never met a man more honest than Benny, and I am not speaking just of his cooking."

Now Benny looked relieved.

As for me, I was glad to be able to leave on a cordial note, so I thanked Benny profusely for his time and his honesty. And his beurre blanc.

As Ari showed me to the door, I turned to Benny with one last question. "You know that waiter, the one in the cigar lounge, the one named Ottavio Rossi?"

"Yes."

"It's the strangest thing. I met a waiter with the same name, but he was a different man."

"You must mean the first Rossi," Benny said.

"What do you mean, the first Rossi? There are two?"

"There were. This guy named Rossi came to work, but I think there was some mistake. He was the wrong man or something. So he left, and the other Rossi took his place."

"And both were named Ottavio?"

"Is that an unusual name?"

For my story on Benny, I felt I was leaving with even less information than I had had when I arrived. But at least Ottavio had become a puzzle again rather than a dead end.

Trying to sort out my information back at my office, I was grateful that I'd already written this week's column. I was far from ready to write about Benny's firing. I needed more time to mull over what I knew and fill in what I didn't know. And I certainly needed Dave's help to work out what I could fairly say in print.

It's a mistake ever to consider journalism a contemplative profession. The daily need to fill pages means there's a constant race to tag information and print it before it fades into oblivion or—even worse—some competitor runs it first. Maybe race is too simple a metaphor. Much as I hate the way the guys who run the *Examiner* routinely describe the world through sports, I sometimes see journalism as a baseball game—pitching, hitting, striking out, stealing bases, running, tagging are all parts of the process—but it's a game conducted at high speed, as if baseball operated against a clock. To make it more complicated, the teams play against themselves as well as each other.

Bull Stannard had just switched sides on me.

"Wheatley, I want that Coastline story for your column today."

"Today? I've already got a column today. Besides, Coastline's not ready."

"Make it ready."

"Bull, nobody's breathing down our necks on this. My sources aren't going anywhere else. I promise you, if we wait until next week, it will be a much better story."

"If I wanted a much better story, I'd give it to Dawn. You're not an investigative reporter; she is. You're a restaurant columnist, and that's why you have this little item. It's about restaurants, and people want to know who is or isn't cooking in them. Don't try to make Pulitzer material out of it. Just write the damn column."

I wrote the damn column.

I made it simple. I told people Benny wasn't cooking at Coastline anymore. Before that, of course, I had to explain who Benny was, how long he'd been there, and why he'd come to be chef. That filled up most of my allocated space anyway. I included little of the scandal, merely a couple of sentences recalling that the previous chef had been fired because of a harassment charge (which the *Examiner* had reported at the time). I wrote that Gianni Marchelli claimed he'd had to fire Benny because a woman—the same woman as before—had complained that Benny had assaulted her. I stated that the woman was unavailable for comment and noted that Benny denied the accusation. I finished by quoting Benny about why he hadn't fought the charge. Mayhem in the kitchen had been transformed into a few dry, matter-of-fact sentences.

Helen switched around a few words, asked me to clarify a point about the previous chef, and pronounced the column acceptable. I didn't agree with her, but to say so would not be in my best interests.

Bull is a crusading editor when the subject interests him. Restaurants do not. Any news connected with restaurants is entertainment—or advertising revenue—including all those credit card and pricing scams I'd been digging up for months. I realized that I might have been considering that investigation as hot news, but he saw it as filling column space. He'd ordered a specified number of inches of scandal to be delivered on a particular date. I was the catalog and he was the shopper.

I must have been scowling as I left for dinner. When I passed by Dawn's desk, she looked up with a smile. It froze in place while her eyes narrowed in response to mine. She looked like a Cheshire cat. A skinny one.

17

I was comforted that Dave would understand exactly what I'd been up against in Bull's demanding I do the column for tomorrow's paper. Dave would probably even suggest some further digging I could do on the case and how to sell Bull on my following up. Dave wasn't one to waste a morsel of exclusive information.

It was midnight when I dialed his phone number. I got that little electronic tune signaling that the number I'd dialed was not in service, so I tried again. Same response.

I'd forgotten that Dave had moved since I'd last recorded his number. What kind of reporter was I? I couldn't even track down a fellow reporter. Or the guy who was the major obsession in my life.

I wracked my brain to think of a way to find where Dave was living, but there was nobody at the *Examiner*'s phones so late at night who'd be able to help me. I couldn't wake up anybody on the newsroom staff for such a request. I'd have to wait until morning to get in touch. In the meantime, I left a message on his voice mail. Maybe he'd check it before he went to bed. Then I could explain what happened before he saw my story.

"You're a wimp, Wheatley."

I'd already showered, dressed, and ground my coffee beans, and I was drinking my espresso, but for Dave in California it was the crack of dawn when he called me. Maybe he routinely reads my column as soon as he wakes up, I speculated with an excited jolt. He wouldn't have been expecting my story on Benny to run today.

"What are you doing up so early?" In my momentary fluster, I inhaled so deeply that my espresso made me nearly woozy with its aroma. On second thought, that wasn't coffee euphoria.

"Don't try to change the subject." Dave sounded distinctly more sober. "That was a stupid, namby-pamby little story you did. When are you going to start writing like a grown-up?"

My face felt tight and hot; my eyes burned damply. "Who are you to talk about grown-ups? If you're so good at staring down Bull Stannard, how come you're hiding out in California?"

Did I really say that? Where did that thought come from? Some self-destructive little munitions plant hidden in my brain, no doubt. It exploded right on target.

"That's what you think? You think it's Bull I'm hiding from? Look, Chas, the last person in the world

I'm afraid of is Bull Stannard, and you of all people should know that."

My anger had been repositioned and aimed at a more appropriate target: myself. "I'm sorry, Dave. You're absolutely right, and I knew that. It's just that you said exactly what I've been saying to myself all night and all morning. I couldn't stand hearing it out loud."

"No, I'm the one who should be apologizing. I shouldn't have come on so strong. I know Bull's name is no accident. And that he makes it all the harder for women to stand up to him. I was just disappointed to see this story underplayed, when I knew that with a little time you could have pinned down enough for it to make a splash. Why didn't you call me? I would have helped you to deal with Bull."

"I did try to call you." Now I wished all the more that I'd gone to the effort of paging him before I'd finished my column. "But I only had your old number. It would have been too late anyway. I had to get it in for early deadline, since it was my weekly column."

"I didn't understand that, either. You couldn't talk Bull into letting you follow it longer? It could have been page one."

"He said that it if it were page-one material, he'd have given it to Dawn."

"The bastard. He was just jerking your chain. Dirty way to make you back down, if you ask me."

The rest of the conversation didn't get into declarations of revived love and renewed commitment, but it was decidedly friendlier than most we'd had since

Dave had left for California. I had more I wanted to ask him about investigating Benny's firing, but I decided that could wait. I wanted to reestablish the personal side of our contact—how he was doing in California, what he was doing with his free moments, whether he'd found any non-California pizza.

Nor did I repeat my question about what he was doing up and reading my column so early. I didn't want to risk any answer less exhilarating than the one I imagined.

Lily called as soon as I sat down at my desk and turned on my computer. The moment was unprecedentedly early for her. Did everyone wake up early once a week and read my column in order to be the first to tell me what I'd done wrong?

"You can be so unsympathetic to women sometimes, Mama."

I have never been able to figure out why young women set themselves up as protectors of the gender against us old ones. We're the ones who fought the feminist battle and handed over the spoils to them.

"How was I unsympathetic this time?"

"Ganging up on Denise like that."

"Denise? Do you know Denise?"

"No, I only know what you wrote in your column today. You made it sound as if she's a troublemaker, complaining about harassment from one chef and then abuse from another."

"But she did. I just reported what she charged. I didn't judge it or comment on it. After all, she did get two chefs fired."

"You could have at least presented her side of the story."

"I tried to. Didn't you read that she was unavailable for comment?"

"Then you shouldn't have written the column until she was available for comment."

"I couldn't agree with you more."

Lily didn't necessarily want me to agree with her. She treats our relationship as if arguments are more interesting than conversations. Nevertheless, I was delighted to find that the people I love get up early to read my column. I didn't want to comment on that, since it would almost certainly assure that she would throw it away unread next week, but I did thank her for calling and told her about how the column came about. As I expected, she redirected her outrage to Bull, who had pitted one professional woman (me) against another (Dawn) in order to screw a third (Denise). She ended the conversation seeing us both on the same side of the unending war.

Even Homer had read my column.

"I can tell you why Miss Martin was unavailable for comment," he boasted, even before he said hello or told me who was calling.

"Who is this?"

I knew by then, but it didn't hurt to teach Homer a bit of humility.

"Hell, Chas, you know who this is." He sounded cheerful, though.

"Now that I hear you cursing, I surely know. How are you, Homer? You sound as if you've caught up on a little sleep."

"Wouldn't say that, but I am feeling distinctly more human and competent this morning. Thanks to you, I might add."

"What did I do for you? Everyone else is chewing me out. It's nice to hear from someone who has something positive to say."

"It's Denise Martin. We've positively identified her."

Where was my brain? I hadn't really listened to Homer's conversational opener. I mentally flipped back to it now.

"Her? You mean the body?"

"Yep. The body in the Tidal Basin. You've saved my ass on this one, Chas. Brilliant connection you made."

I felt far from brilliant, just nauseated.

"How did she die?" I'd never met the woman, but I felt weighted with a sense of loss. I'd heard about her, talked about her, tried to meet her. Now I would probably never know what actually happened between her and Benny.

"Stabbed. Beaten up around the face first. One of those all-too-rare open and shut cases."

"Shut? You've already got the murderer? Who did it?"

"Arrested Benny Martinez this morning. Bail denied. You can read all about it in your own paper tomorrow. Sherele and I have a little celebration over a planked salmon and a bottle of Beringer chardonnay planned for this evening."

Every conversation with Homer got bogged down with food. I didn't want to hear about his planked salmon at the moment. Not when he had one of the most talented chefs I knew heading for jail.

"What makes you think Benny did it? He said he and Denise were on good terms. And Ari says he's one of the most honest men he's ever known."

"Even an honest man can wield a knife or a gun if the circumstances are right."

"But even if he hit her, that's a far cry from murder. You've got to have more to go on than that to arrest a man for murder."

"I do. I've got Denise herself."

"A black eye? That doesn't tell you he murdered her."

"Give me more credit than that, Chas. Denise herself gave me the rest of the evidence I needed. A piece of a knife broken off in her chest. Benny's very own favorite chef's knife. You know how possessive a chef is about his knives."

I knew. And I felt sick.

Now the story was Dawn's. She wouldn't ordinarily stoop to writing a standard police story, but as she explained to me, this involved the bigger issue of harassment in the workplace and the passions evoked by such gender issues.

She said this as she sat on my desk—right on top of the open menus from three delis I was reviewing—and dangled those legs that I find disgustingly long and skinny and inevitably seductive to men.

Those legs would be enough reason for me to hate Dawn, but she was also probably two-thirds my age, twice as aggressive as I am, and enchanted with her own sexuality. Furthermore, she'd once tried her damnedest to come between Dave and me, though she seemed less interested in him now that he was available. What fun is a guy if he doesn't have a woman you can take him away from?

I knew exactly why Dawn had decided to dirty her manicured and purple-polished hands on this seamy murder case. She saw restaurants as glamorous. She envisioned free meals at Coastline. She might even parlay her reporting into interviews with other prominent restaurateurs who would feed her quail eggs and caviar (foie gras would be too caloric for her) while they talked, and ever afterward be eager to make a good table available to her at a moment's notice.

Now she was harvesting my Rolodex for chefs she might interview and baldly asking for my notes on Benny's firing. I kept most of the conversations with Benny to myself.

The girl is good, I had to admit to myself when Ari called me a few hours later. She'd quickly discovered that Benny had been putting in some part-time hours at Ari's catering company, and she'd hopped right over, just in time for a late lunch.

Ari was disgusted. He called me as soon as she left and complained about how little she had eaten and how she had scraped the sauce off the fish, even cut every smidgen of the fabulous buttery crust from the *pommes anna*. I savored every insulted sniff I could hear across the phone wires.

He was also disgusted with me, though. He held me responsible for Benny being arrested. And in defending myself from his accusation, I found myself shifting my arguments from Benny's innocence to Benny's guilt.

"What would you want the police to do after they found a piece of Benny's own knife in her body?"

"Where is the rest of the knife? Not attached to Benny. Anyone could have used his knife. Anyone who had access to Coastline's kitchen."

"But who had a motive besides Benny?"

"What motive did Benny have?"

"She'd gotten him fired."

"She had also brought charges against that other chef, the one Benny replaced. That's not what I'd call a motive."

"You're a chef, not a homicide detective."

"And you're a restaurant critic, not a private investigator."

Not yet. But that could change.

After Ari and I said good-bye to each other with steely politeness, I had to admit to myself that I really agreed with my ex-husband. Benny didn't strike me as a murderer, but what did I know about murderers? More important, Benny had sounded sympathetic to Denise, even while he was hurt and bewildered by her making charges against him. And most important, he didn't seem all that interested in my search for her. I've seen enough *Columbo*s and *Murder She Wrote*s to know that the murderer can't keep from obsessing about what's being discovered about the victim. Benny hadn't even called me back; I'd had to track him down at Ari's. Nor had he tried to run. He could have been in Havana by now.

The case was closed, Homer was celebrating with my best friend, and all my other friends and relatives were angry with me. Even worse, I was scheduled to make another professional visit to Coastline. With Robert.

18

Transcribed from Communication Between Senator Larry Michaels and Jamaican Coffee Consortium Lobbyist Harold James

LM: So sad for his wife and children. And a disaster for your party.

HJ: More than that. For the country.

LM: I can't imagine what would drive him to do such a thing.

HJ: They say it was a woman.

LM: From what I hear, that was nothing new. He'd already had several, and apparently even his wife had caught him before.

HJ: This time was different. He was far more secretive. Something dangerous. Someone who could be seriously hurt. Or could hurt him.

LM: Who?

HJ: I haven't been able to find out. He was very, very careful.

LM: Just give me a hint. American? Jamaican?

HJ: I mean it. I really don't know.

LM: If that's true, why did he kill himself?

HJ: Somebody apparently knew, somebody who could scare him that badly.

LM: Blackmail?

HJ: Not for money. He didn't have much of that. Information, possibly. Or favors.

Given the circumstances, I wished I could be dining anywhere but Coastline. And with my mind largely inhabited by thoughts of Dave, I wasn't too keen on dining with Robert at the moment.

Who was the wise person who said that life is a matter of getting what you want when you no longer want it?

The minute I spotted Robert poring over the menu, his eyes burning passionately with thoughts of Olympia oysters and soft-shell crabs, I realized I was being unfair. Robert looked no less endearing through the eyes of a friend than of the seducer I'd tried to be. And if I wasn't going to give him me, he'd probably be no less thrilled with Monterey spot prawns.

"Chas, my dear, I am so pleased to see you. Are you alone?" Gianni kissed me on both cheeks. I usually feel uncomfortable when a restaurateur I'm reviewing greets me this way. I think of it as a signal to anyone watching that I am going to bestow special favors on the restaurant because we are intimate friends. And like a Mafia kiss of death, it feels sinister. But Gianni does it so well.

I explained to Gianni that I was meeting the young man in the rear, and he immediately insisted on moving us to a bigger table. I resisted. And I hurried to Robert's table to avoid getting into a discussion of Benny Martinez before dinner.

Robert rose to greet me. His two-cheek kiss was more welcome to me. I'd forgotten how much I liked his bearded face and those warm eyes. Not to mention his elegant English accent.

As soon as we got rid of Gianni by sending him off for two kir royales, Robert made the evening easier for me.

"You look more delicious than anything on the menu," he started, which made me squirm even while it delighted me. The squirming part didn't escape his notice, so he took pains to put me at my ease. "I am very glad to be the friend of such a fine and beautiful woman. I hope we will always be good friends."

He said a great deal with that emphasis on the word "friends." He'd signaled that we were both operating under the same set of rules. We had adjusted the temperature of our relationship and now we could both be comfortable. I thanked him—a multilayered "thank you"; then I took it upon myself to lighten the evening.

We were starting over. Less exciting but more appropriate.

It was great fun.

We ordered all the kinds of seafood that Robert had heard of but never tasted. He compared the shrimp and scallops and oysters he'd eaten in Lebanon as a boy to those from New England and the West Coast. I saw the meal through his palate, not minding the pastiness of the scallops' flour coating or the overcooking of the shrimp. I filed those flaws away for my review and just settled back and enjoyed the adventure of dining with Robert.

His new job was absorbing long hours because he wanted to learn American business quickly, and he was constantly rushing from office to taxi with little sleep in between. He was also frequently flattened by grief over his sister. So life was a struggle for now. But he'd drop the taxi driving as soon as he felt secure in the job.

He talked about his old girlfriend. She was still an ex and not, as I'd speculated, a renewed girlfriend. He had no interest in that; instead he had his eye on a Lebanese woman who was the houseguest of a cousin of his. I told him of my conversations with Dave and my hope of our eventually getting back together. He looked both crestfallen and happy for me. Just as I was for him.

Gianni interrupted our semi-heartfelt good wishes for each other in order to invite us to the cigar room. He knew better by now than to offer me a free cognac, but he told me he'd just received a shipment of an extraordinary one he'd bought at auction for a very good price. I should try it for my readers, he suggested.

I, too, saw it as my duty.

Robert and I were shown to a leather sofa in a dark corner, before it a low table with a white cloth and yellow roses floating in a crystal bowl. Every table in the cigar room had an ashtray, of course, though the VIPs seemed to have big ones so heavy that they were hard to lift. Pretty awkward to empty, I thought, though they were expensively handsome. Gianni wasn't one to cut corners in any way that showed in the dining room.

The pre-dinner champagne, the fumé blanc with

our dinner, and now the cognac conspired with my lack of sleep to lull me to a near haze. I wanted to tuck my legs under me and rest my head on Robert's shoulder while we talked.

As he'd done on our trip to New York, Robert was reading my mind. "I wish I had taken you to bed that night," he said, not having to specify which night. He knew where my thoughts were lurking. "I miscalculated. I thought that I would be making you want me more. I didn't want the experience to be trivial, to just happen and be finished. I believed that after a time of waiting you could not easily leave me. I was wrong. At the same time, I am glad that we restrained ourselves. If I could not have you in a serious way, I would not like to lose you as a friend. And this way it will be easier to be friends, I think." I nodded, but he wasn't finished. "And it means that I will all my life keep this little yearning for you."

I liked that. This young man had already discovered the excitement in denial. The imagined experience that's more powerful than reality. The immortality of wishes.

He also was gallant enough to have shifted the nuances of the event so that it sounded as if he'd been the aggressor and I had exercised the restraint. He was generously offering me the memory of being the rejecter rather than the rejected.

I leaned over to give Robert a friendly kiss, and all hell broke loose. I knocked over his cognac, and when he reached to save it, he knocked over the bowl of roses. The water flooded the table, the ashtray, the cigar that Robert had been savoring as if it were a beloved part of some woman's body.

You would have thought we'd set fire to the table. The cigar room waiter rushed over and swept the massive ashtray from the table as if it were about to explode. He left the rest of the disarray on the sopping tablecloth while he went to dispose of the ashtray. We began mopping up the rest with our napkins. The waiter reappeared with a dry tablecloth, stripped all the debris from the table, and instead of removing the old cloth, just covered it with the new one. *Gianni wouldn't like that,* I thought. But I didn't say anything when Gianni arrived a minute later with a tall vase of roses. I'd been hoping he'd replace our cognac rather than our centerpiece. Eventually he did.

Fortunately, Robert and I were dry. And laughing.

"A warning to us," I said. "From now on we restrict ourselves to shaking hands."

"And safe subjects," Robert added, raising his new cognac to toast me.

"There are no such subjects."

"Food," Robert reminded me.

"It's not safe for me. Food is work."

"You're right. But it's safe for me."

"Exactly. So you can talk about food."

"And you'll just listen?"

"I'll try anything once."

Robert began a sly grin, but stopped himself. "So. Tonight's food. I will tell you what you thought of it. Are you with me?"

I nodded, lips sealed in an indulgent smile.

"The scallops needed a hotter skillet. Their flour coating was not cooked enough, so was a wee bit gummy rather than crackly."

The guy was good. I nodded and motioned with my hands for him to continue.

"Don't misinterpret me. I loved the meal and had a wonderful time. But I wasn't paying for it. And your enchanting company doesn't come along with everyone's dinner. So I'm trying to think objectively here. The shrimp had a truly commendable flavor. You can only find that in shrimp that have never been frozen. But much of the trouble of procuring fresh shrimp was wasted in their cooking time. It was too long."

He went on, as if my thoughts were his words. Then he summed it up so well that I was tempted to take notes. "It is not easy to find such superb ingredients. Even better, they are made to look beautiful. The recipes are wonderful, or at least almost wonderful. But there is a sloppiness. Or maybe it is a little amateurishness. A stopping short of what you would hope for each dish. The chef needs discipline."

"The chef needs to get out of jail."

I told him about Denise's murder and Benny's arrest. He asked perceptive questions about my impressions of Benny and about my feelings regarding Benny.

"You don't seem to believe he did it," Robert concluded.

"I don't. I can't quite get myself to, even though everything I know about the story points to him. The problem is, I can't bear to think of such a talented chef as a murderer. All those great meals lost to prison."

"You're not capable of such simplistic thinking, Chas. I understand that it's hard to think of anybody, particularly someone you know and like, as a murderer. I think there is more nagging you about this."

"Could be. I'm not clear about much these days. There's only one thing I am really certain of at this moment."

"What's that?"

The waiter had wandered close to our table, so I lowered my voice to a near whisper.

"That Coastline needs a new chef. And much as I hate to heap more troubles on Gianni's head, it's my job to tell the readers of the *Examiner* that."

My mention of work was a signal to us that it was time to leave. I asked for the check, adding a big tip because I felt guilty about the negative review I was about to write, and asked if I might take a menu with me. It was too large to simply sneak it into my purse, and since the staff already knew who I was, I could openly ask for one. Robert took charge of carrying it, opening it for a fond last look as we stood to leave.

Gianni came to the table when he saw us leaving. He said good-bye and that he hoped that we'd enjoyed our meal. He anxiously examined my face for the signs I'd learned to hide behind a bland smile.

As Gianni led us to the door, Robert dashed back to the table and plucked a rose from the vase. "I hope you don't mind," he said to the waiter, who was following our little parade, "but I very much want this lady to have a memento of the evening."

While Gianni walked on ahead, not noticing that we'd fallen behind, Robert took the menu from me and closed the rose in it. A dried rose pressed in a menu. Robert hadn't given up on romantic notions.

The waiter looked horrified. I know roses are expensive, but we'd just dropped a couple of hundred bucks into the restaurant's coffers, so this was nothing to make a fuss about. Nor would I expect him to be so rude as to challenge Robert on it.

"The thorns. They will prick you," the waiter said in his thick Italian accent, sounding as ominous as if we'd unearthed a land mine. "Let me take it to the kitchen and clip them off."

He'd only been trying to be helpful after all. The service at Coastline didn't need any improving.

"That's very kind, but don't bother," Robert said.

"It's no bother," insisted the waiter, as he reached for the menu with its pressed rose.

Robert held fast. "Don't worry; I can take care of it."

"Then let me put it in an envelope for you. It will be easier to carry." The waiter hadn't let go of the menu.

"Totally unnecessary. We're fine without an envelope."

"I will make sure you have the right menu." Neither man was ready to release it.

"I already checked," Robert responded with an edge of irritation. The waiter was being annoyingly obsequious.

Gianni had turned back and noticed this polite little power struggle.

"Ottavio!" he said sharply.

The waiter looked up and dropped his hands to his sides.

Robert led me out the door as if we were being pursued by yapping dogs.

Ottavio? That was *Ottavio* Ottavio? I'd forgotten about the two Ottavios, and I'd missed another chance to drop a casual question about them.

* * *

The first call the next morning was one of those weirdly intimate encounters that at some time faces every person whose name regularly appears before the public. Once you have a byline or a television presence, people act as if they know you—which they, in a way, do—while you haven't the faintest idea who they are.

I'll be in a movie line or waiting for a table in a restaurant, when I'll hear people behind me talking about me as if I'm a friend. "Chas says the Ethiopian restaurant across the street has great *injera*," they'll say. And I'll want to tell them that they've got it wrong. It was the *Post*'s critic who'd said that. "Chas likes the roast chicken here," one will boast to a friend, as if I'd just slipped him insider information. I want to remind him that I also said to ask for it with the skin-on garlic mashed potatoes instead of the frozen fries.

I don't. I value every smidgen of privacy I can get, particularly in a restaurant, where all too often my every bite and grimace is being watched.

Don't get me wrong: I love the idea that people react to my reviews as friendly advice, that they see me as a familiar rather than some disembodied authority. I thrive on the letters that tell me of the good meals their authors attribute to me, and the ones from the restaurateurs who vow they are going to name their first daughter after me.

It's just that some encounters are oddly one-sided, as if I were wearing a mask. Here's an example: I was appearing on a panel, and as I do on such occasions, I was wearing big glasses and a huge hat pulled down over my face to prevent any restaurateurs in the audience from recognizing me. Because the start was delayed, I had a long time to chat with the men on either side of me, one a famous author and the other a television executive. We shared jokes and observations, exchanged anecdotes, became fast friends. After the event, I stripped off my disguise in the ladies' room, then went outside to hail a taxi. The two men were standing at the entrance, chatting away like the friends we had all been. But they didn't recognize me and ignored my attempts to greet them as if I were a groupie intruding on their privacy.

The phone rang, and as always, I announced, "Chas Wheatley."

"Have you no shame?" A woman's voice with a foreign accent challenged rather than greeted me. I tried to remember which restaurant I'd reviewed this week. Nothing negative enough to warrant this kind of reaction. Maybe my offense was last week's review.

"Are you sure you have the right number?" I hoped to find an easy way out. These confrontations tend to go on for a long time.

She read off my number to me. "Miss W. Isn't that you?"

"Probably. But what have I done to upset you?" I tried for a lighthearted and friendly tone.

"You husband stealer!"

Maybe this was Robert's ex-girlfriend. The accent didn't sound Lebanese though. More Caribbean.

When I didn't answer right away, she escalated. "You murderer!"

That couldn't be me. "I'm sorry," I said, "but I don't know what you're talking about. Maybe you have the wrong person after all."

"Don't try to squirm out of this, miss. You won't get away with pretending nothing happened. I could always tell when he had something going on with a woman. I could always tell."

It was beginning to sound as if even the right woman would be only one of many possible home wreckers in this poor woman's life. I began to feel more sad than angry about her attack.

"Please calm down and let's talk. Tell me what makes you think I had any kind of relationship with your husband? I don't even know whom you're talking about. For a start, what's his name?"

"This time he slipped. He kept your phone number in his pocket, written inside a matchbook from one of the fancy places you made him take you. It was your name—Miss W."

"That doesn't mean a thing. So what if he had my number. Lots of men have my number, but that doesn't mean I'm sleeping with them. And it doesn't mean they're cheating on their wives." My sympathy had shifted when I'd heard she'd gone through the poor guy's pockets.

"How easy it is for you to lie. But you won't get away with it. I'll make you pay for this."

I don't like threats. They make me defensive, which makes me mean. "Listen, lady, don't take up my time with your crazy imagination. Go talk to your husband."

"I can't. He's dead."

I had almost hung up on her. "Oh, I'm sorry." That certainly put a different light on her going through his pockets. "I want to assure you, truly and sincerely, that I wasn't having an affair with your husband. I didn't even know your husband." That wasn't strictly true. Since I didn't know who her husband was, I didn't know whether or not I knew him. Such complexities were better left out of the conversation.

"And you're the reason he killed himself. I will spend the rest of my life finding ways to hurt you like you hurt me and my children."

"But I don't even know your husband's name," I wailed.

"How could you ever forget Hamilton Leslie now that you destroyed his life?"

Hamilton Leslie? Sounded familiar.

I might not have remembered the name except that Hamilton was also the first name of the *Examiner*'s former editor, so I'd commented on that to Vince Davis when he was reporting the guy's suicide. Hamilton Leslie was the head of the Jamaican Coffee Consortium, the golden boy among his country's political leaders, who had inexplicably committed suicide.

"What did Hamilton Leslie and I have in common?" I asked Vince, once I'd extricated myself from the phone call, interrupting his playing a hot game of Minesweeper on his computer.

"Now there's an interesting question. Astrological sign? A fondness for young boys? I give up. What's the joke?"

"It's not a joke. It's a serious question. I just got a strange call from Leslie's widow. She thinks he and I had a thing going on between us, and she's threatened to get back at me for his death."

"Whoa, I didn't know about you and Leslie." Vince raised one eyebrow in a leer.

"There's nothing to know. I never so much as met the guy. I never even heard of him until you told me about his suicide."

"Why does this dame think otherwise?"

"She says she found my phone number in his jacket pocket. I haven't the faintest idea how that happened. Was Mrs. Leslie considered crazy? I thought you might know about her, and whether she really could be dangerous."

"I've never heard a word against the woman. From everything I've heard, she was one of those strong and wise wives who know how to keep a good marriage with a good man going despite a little extracurricular activity on his part. They do say that his suicide had something to do with a woman, that this time it wasn't his wife who caught him, but some political enemies. Nobody seems to know who the secret lover was, but apparently she was somebody prominent, whom he'd met when he visited Washington."

"The question remains, why did he have my number on a matchbook."

"A matchbook? Wait, let me think a minute." Vince switched from Minesweeper to his story files and brought up his notes. I pulled up a chair from the next desk and slumped in it while I watched him scroll. Finally he turned to me and gave me a thumbs-up. "I think I've got it. I'd forgotten all about it, but I'm the one who gave him your number. He was one of those guys who loves good food, keeps up with all the new restaurants. You know the type."

"All too well."

"If I remember correctly, which isn't too likely at my advancing age, I mentioned to you that he intended to call. What happened was, Leslie went to a restaurant he said was so good that he wanted to tell the world about it. Or he wanted you to tell the world about it. When I was interviewing him, he asked me for your number. What sparked my memory was that he wrote it inside a matchbook from the restaurant."

"He never called me. At least I don't remember such a call. What was the restaurant?"

"I thought I might have written it down here, but I didn't. Unfortunately, my aging brain cells aren't good enough without notes. I have no idea."

"Let me know if you remember it."

Gianni might have been reading my mind. I was dawdling at my computer. On the desk, the Coastline logo stared at me from the front of its heavy leather menu. My fingers were idle but poised on the computer keys in case they decided to get to work on their own. My mind was a gridlock of thoughts: Benny's murder charge, Dave's wavering, Robert's sweet acceptance of whatever fate delivered, the strange intermingling of a Jamaican suicide and my job, and my frustration over Coastline's inconsistencies.

The latter was what I was willing my fingers to consider. When I can't sort out what I want to say in a review, sometimes ordering my fingers to start typing makes my thoughts fall in place on the computer screen. My fingers spell out what my mind doesn't want to admit, in this case the flaccid cooking that was pretending to be Benny's. Coastline, at this stage, was a dud.

"Chas, I can't let things go on the way they are,"

Gianni announced when I picked up the phone and stated my name.

For a moment, I reacted with panic. Was he, too, going to commit suicide? "Take it easy, Gianni. You're overreacting. Life can't be that bad."

It's a good thing he didn't mean suicide. My blurted clichés might have driven him right to the gun case.

What he meant was that he couldn't let things in Coastline's kitchen stay the way they were. Gianni's good sense and well-honed taste had won over his wish for an easy solution. On his own, without my having to chastise him in print, he'd concluded that he needed to hire a chef—someone of Benny's caliber, he vowed. He begged my indulgence and apologized for all the time and trouble Coastline had caused me.

"Of course I'll have to postpone my review." I stated the obvious.

"I'd like you to do more than that, Chas. I want you to take that menu I gave you and throw it in the trash. Maybe it sounds silly, but this is important to me. I can't bear to know that it even sits in your file."

"Don't worry . . ."

"No, I mean it. I am so ashamed of what I was allowing to happen. Do it now. Indulge me and I promise to make it up to you by turning this into the best restaurant in Washington," Gianni pleaded. Modesty has never been part of his charm.

It wouldn't hurt to go along with the game. I dropped the menu into the trash can. "Okay, I've done it. Now I'll be delighted to hold you to your vow to be the best."

"I can't tell you how grateful I am. But you know

me, never satisfied. Now I want you to do one more thing. I am calling to ask you to help me to become better."

That would be stepping over the line for a restaurant critic, and Gianni should know it. I started to protest, but he interrupted. "I'm not asking you to participate in the decisions. You are too honorable a journalist for me to suggest that. I just want to use you as a listening post, silent if you wish. With your permission, I would like to call you from time to time to tell you what is happening. This might even provide some information for you, maybe a little story on how hard it is to find a good chef these days."

When he put it this way, Gianni was offering me something—inside information—under the guise of asking my assistance. His old-world chivalry had found a gracious way to offer me potential scoops.

I told Gianni I'd be glad to help.

As long as we were being such cozy friends, I felt primed to ask Gianni about something that had long mystified me. I felt a little silly and hoped I wasn't revealing more than was good for me, but I could no longer resist.

"The cigar room waiter. Did I hear you call him Ottavio?"

"Yes, Ottavio. Wonderful waiter. Straight from Italy."

"What's his last name?"

"Rossi. I'm sorry, did I neglect to introduce you? I apologize for my bad manners."

"I'm kind of confused. Some time ago I met a waiter named Ottavio, but he was a different man."

Gianni's reply was slow in coming. "I don't

remember that you were here then." He sounded hesitant, as if he were searching his memory. "He was only on duty for a short time. A few days. You couldn't have met him."

"I was right? There was another waiter with exactly the same name? He worked at Coastline?"

"Can you believe such a coincidence? I couldn't believe it myself." His laugh sounded forced. A kind of "heh heh."

"So he was for real?"

"Apparently it's not so far-fetched as it sounded at first. Rossi, of course, is almost as common as Smith in Italy. And Ottavio is one of those names, like Sean or Adam in this country, that were kind of a fad in Italy back when these two men were born. Good thing the first Rossi left, though. It could have been complicated to have them both working the same shifts. If you didn't meet him here, how did you know him?"

"I don't really remember, maybe some other restaurant after he left Coastline. You know how we restaurant critics get around." My "heh heh" couldn't have sounded any more authentic than Gianni's.

"What restaurant?" Gianni asked the question as if Ottavio had left owing him money.

"I can't remember. I thought you might know."

"Naah, the guy skipped without a trace. Couldn't even find him to give him his last paycheck."

I said good-bye no less mystified, but relieved that Gianni had no hint that I'd met Ottavio through a personals ad.

As I thought back on the exchange, I saw I'd gotten more information than I'd realized at first. I'd verified that Ottavio had worked at Coastline, which meant it was the "pretty weird place" Ottavio'd referred to when he said, "If only people knew what restaurants get out of them, they'd sure watch their backs."

I also knew that Gianni was lying to me. Ottavio Rossi the first was nowhere near the age of Ottavio Rossi the second, so unless I'd misunderstood Gianni, his reasoning that they were both born when it was a fad to name your baby Ottavio made no sense. Besides, Ottavio the first wasn't Italian.

Most important, though, since I'd verified that Coastline was the weird place Ottavio had mentioned, I didn't have to find him anymore. As for my humiliating encounter when Ottavio dumped me at the deli, I could forget about it and get on with my work.

Not quite. I was faced with the disconcerting truth that I had no restaurant to review this week. I'd have to do some juggling.

My irritation with Coastline as the cause of my crisis had dissipated, though. Now I could be the first in Washington to report Coastline's new hire, and I'd have enough background on the search process that I might get an extra Table Matters column from it. I could also subtly nose around to find out why Ottavio had considered the place weird.

Last night's notes were history. Of no use for my next review. The menu, though, I might as well save as a souvenir. It smelled of the rose pressed inside it, and sentiment led me to fish it from the trash and stuff it into my briefcase. I'd add it to my home collection of menus with special memories.

* * *

With no review to write today, I pored over my lists and reorganized my dining schedule, trying to juggle the professional and social requirements of my work. The professional problem was that I had to dredge up a place I'd already visited twice so that tonight's third visit would position me with enough information to write a review tomorrow. On the social side, I'd promised Homer and Sherele a first-visit dinner tonight. Homer would be disappointed; he likes to have free rein over the menu choices rather than being limited to ordering dishes I haven't tried before. On the third visit, I'm forced to be a dictator.

"Don't you have to review Kinkead's again?" Homer chided when Sherele handed the phone to me so I could personally fill him in on the plan for the evening.

"I'm sorry, Homer, but you've been on the A list for a long time. You've got to earn some hardship points now and then if you hope to stay on it." The A list consists of not only the really good restaurants, it's those I've been to once so I'm fairly certain they are good, but haven't been to more than once, which means that my guests don't have to pass up the best dishes because I've tried them already.

It's a tricky balancing act. Somebody's got to go to the bad restaurants with me, those places I have to review because they are news, not because they are worthy. And somebody has to try the brand-new untested ones, not to mention the ones in the far suburbs, or the ones that don't take reservations and make us wait in line for a table. You'd think my friends would be grateful that I pick up the check for their dinner, or they'd at least pretend they were along for my company. But for my close friends, being a reviewer's guest becomes, well, work.

Then why don't I always take new people along? There are countless gourmet wannabes thrilled to dine anywhere with a restaurant critic who's paying the tab. But for me, taking strangers is risky. I have to be sure they will play by the rules, that they'll be willing to order what I need to taste and to share their food, to be discreet about what they say when the staff is in earshot. I have ex-friends who've returned to a restaurant on their own after we've dined there together and told the maître d' who I was in order to ingratiate themselves. Some guests forget about sharing and absentmindedly gobble up the garnishes or accompaniments before I can taste them, and then there are those who have started a new diet and can't eat anything that is relevant to my review. Some ask for their food without the sauce or with no butter. Occasionally guests embarrass me by making unwarranted complaints to the waiter about the food or service, or by announcing to the maître d' that we all loved this or that dish, whereas I don't want the restaurateur to have any idea what my review is likely to say. The biggest problem, though, is that it is wearing to dine out night after night with people you don't know well, who are more or less strangers. It's like having business dinners back-to-back, but worse. Most business dinners don't require you to take mental notes on the food and service, to observe everything that's happening in the dining room, and to taste every dish while making small talk.

How does it all add up? Being a restaurant critic is still the best job in the world.

In addition to dining free, having an excuse to try every restaurant and to taste all of its dishes, the job allows me to vent my feelings. I get to spread my joy, I'm paid to write about what most interests me, and—sometimes the greatest kick of all—to voice my complaints. When a maître d' ignores a reservation, when a waiter treats customers with disdain, when the food is delayed and cold and the cooking is mean-spirited, most people have no recourse other than leaving a stingy tip and going home to lick their wounds. What my friends envy most about my job is the opportunity for telling the world.

Stymied in my writing, I was faced with a choice of catching up on my expense account, answering the stack of letters I'd shoved to the back of my desk, or some other equally onerous housekeeping task. Instead, I decided to satisfy my curiosity and repair my reputation in one fell swoop.

I love tracking people down. This time it took only a few phone calls and hints that I was writing a story for me to find the number of the hysterical Mrs. Leslie.

"I'm Chas Wheatley, the woman you called earlier about your husband, and I want to express my deep sympathy for your loss," I started, talking as fast as I could to get to the next part before she hung up on me. "I truly have never met your husband, but I have investigated and found out why he had my telephone number in his pocket. I thought it might make you feel a little better to hear the explanation."

"I'm listening."

"You see, I'm a restaurant critic. At the *Washington*

Examiner. One of our reporters interviewed Mr. Leslie."

"I remember."

"It seems that during that trip your husband was so impressed with a restaurant where he dined that he wanted to help out the chef by getting him some publicity."

"He was always a generous man, always trying to help people," she said softly, sounding teary.

"That's what I've heard. He was quite a wonderful man; everyone says so." I paused for a moment because listening to Mrs. Leslie sob was making my eyes well up, too. "You really needn't have worried. He had my number on that matchbook only because he was going to call me and suggest I review the restaurant."

"That sounds like my husband. I'm sorry. It was a terrible thing for me to accuse you like that. I hope you will forgive me. It's just that I'm . . . sometimes I am a different person these days. I turn into a dreadful stranger. I have such horrible thoughts and I can't stop myself. I want to know who made my husband so afraid that he had to take his own life. I want to find out and to punish somebody. Such a waste of a good man; it should not go unpunished."

"Why do you think he was afraid?"

"I know my husband. I have always known that he is susceptible to women, but it is a weakness that we are able to discuss. I never have to doubt that he loves me. Even this time, he has confessed to me that he had succumbed." She'd been speaking of her husband in the present tense, but as her voice grew calmer, she switched to the past tense. "It was nothing new. It was the same as always. Except for one thing. He was ashamed because he had been involved with a married woman."

"There's more proof that I wasn't the woman. I'm not married, so it wouldn't have been me he'd been seeing." I didn't comment on the double standard of this married man finding virtue in avoiding married women.

"He would never have betrayed another marriage. He carried enough guilt for betraying ours."

"So you think that shame drove him to suicide?" I was getting caught up in the story.

"No, not that alone. He would not have abandoned me for that. He knew that I would rather have him with any dirt that clung to him than not have him at all. There was only one thing that would have driven him to leave me alone in this world."

"What would that have been?"

"Something that would hurt the party. He loved his country—but only his country—more than he loved me. I accepted that, too."

"What did his affair have to do with the country?"

"It must have been this woman. He did not know she was married at first. When he found out that she had a husband, and knew who that husband was, he was very afraid of it becoming public. He stopped it immediately. But somebody must have found out."

"Blackmail?"

"Something like that. But not for money. For something more important, something he could not afford to pay."

"And you are trying to find out why?"

"I am *going to* find out why."

I wished her well and told her I would keep my ears

open around Washington and let her know if I found out anything that would help. As we were saying good-bye, I remembered the most important reason I'd called.

"What restaurant was the matchbook from?"

"The one that had your phone number?"

"Yes."

"It is called Coastline."

"You're right. He did have good taste."

19

Steaks are not meant to be bargains. The only reason for going to a restaurant for a steak is that a restaurant has access to better meat than what's available to a home cook, and can even age it on the premises. All that warrants big bucks. The expense is all the more worthwhile because restaurants can cook a steak at a higher temperature than one usually can with a home stove, so it can be seared and browned before the interior has a chance to overcook.

I like my steaks black-and-blue, or Pittsburgh style, which means seared over such intense heat that the surface is crusty while the meat is merely warmed and still red. The only way to achieve this at home is by adapting Paul Prudhomme's notorious Cajun blackening technique: Heat an iron pan on the stove until it begins to turn white and ashy, when it's so hot that browning occurs in seconds rather than minutes. This technique is not something to try without a very good exhaust fan, or your smoke detector will screech and your neighbor's likely to call the fire department.

Even if you've got the blackening technique mastered, you'd have to do a good bit of research and cajoling to buy prime aged steaks of the quality a steak house like Morton's or this new Cityside Grill can acquire. All of which explains why a steak at nearly thirty dollars is a good value.

What about a fifteen-dollar steak? In most cases, I'd rather eat a hamburger. If it's made from good freshly ground meat and handled lightly, a burger can be thick, juicy, tender, and magnificent for half that price. A bargain steak, though, is likely to be no better than one you can cook more cheaply at home in less time than it takes you to read a menu.

Homer, who wasn't even paying for his steak, was grumbling because I'd already ordered the porterhouse and the rib eye on previous visits to Cityside. He was being restricted to the filet mignon, and he complained that it's not a flavorful enough cut for him, since it has no marbling and it's from a part of the animal that doesn't get much flavor-producing exercise. Sherele had been a good sport and volunteered to try the salmon, knowing that ordering fish at a steak house is as foolish as ordering a steak at a seafood restaurant. That left the pasta primavera—the inevitably dreary nod to vegetarians—for me. Sherele's and my greater sacrifices didn't render Homer any more gracious.

"Why not the roast beef?" Homer couldn't drop the subject.

"I've already tried it."

"You probably tried a rare cut. You've got to tell

your readers how the outside cut is, too, you know."

I could sympathize. To cook a prime rib at home that's as good as at a steak house, you'd have to be hosting a whole dinner party or expect to have leftovers for a week. Much as Homer is devoted to cooking at home, he probably never finds the opportunity to rustle up a rib roast. It's too inefficient to buy a whole expensive prime rib for one or two people, even if he could find steak house-quality meat.

I hoped to cheer Homer by splurging on a good red wine. Even that wasn't working. The first of the '90 Bordeaux I ordered was sold out. The waiter apologized and recommended a wine that didn't interest me. I surveyed the list again, only to find that the Silver Oak and Ridge cabernets were also out of stock. The waiter was painfully embarrassed and kept trying to suggest other wines, but I wanted to make my own choice. I decided to splurge even more on the '91 Antinori Solaia. Gone. By now I was suspicious. I gave the waiter a list of wines and asked him to let me know which were available. As I expected, few existed except on paper. This was one of those fake wine lists, composed to look impressive. Usually restaurants can get away with the facade by training their waiters to be aggressive in recommending wines they know are on hand and steering customers away from the others by disparaging them. I'm the kind of customer they dread.

Once I had Homer settled in with his filet—which was exactly rare enough for him—and a Hess cabernet, his scowl lines disappeared. It was time to talk to him about Benny.

He, too, wanted to talk about Benny, but Benny the chef, not Benny the murderer.

"What difference does it make when the chef is not in the kitchen? After all, the great French chefs travel all over the world publicizing their restaurants and cookbooks. And America's top chefs do the same even more. They're always cooking at the James Beard House in New York and charity dinners in Dallas or Miami. Some of them run restaurants in Tokyo and London as well. Isn't it true that all the major chefs in LA and Chicago also have branches in Las Vegas?" Homer paused to cut another soft, pink chunk of meat while I nodded, my mouth full. "What does a chef actually do in a restaurant? Surely he doesn't cook every dish."

I put down my fork. I'd had enough of the far-too-healthy-tasting pasta. "There are degrees of supervision, and some chefs are better than others at training and managing their kitchen staffs so that they can replicate the chef's ideas. Take Benny, for instance. He's young and new at supervising a kitchen. While Wolfgang Puck has enough experience and talent and long relationships with protégés that he can successfully handle restaurants in Los Angeles and Spagos in several countries, Benny is just getting started at developing his style and transmitting it to his staff. He's at a stage where it's crucial to build momentum. That's why it's a particular loss to have him locked up when he's obviously not a danger to society and probably didn't do it anyway."

I was a little heavy-handed, I admit it. Homer wasn't amused. Whether it was on purpose or absentminded revenge, he ate the last bites of his filet without saving me a taste. That was a wasted thirty dollars for the *Examiner*. I was now as angry as Homer.

"Next time you're going to be assigned to order the pasta primavera, my friend," I threatened. I felt the world was conspiring against my doing my job today.

Sherele, as always, came to my rescue. Unnoticed by me, she had reached over and cut herself a piece of Homer's steak earlier, and it rested intact on her plate, hidden from my view by the hillock of hash browns. She forked it over to me with a complicitous grin.

"'All's well that ends well,'" she said, as lame a theatrical quote as I've heard from Sherele. She was caught between being embarrassed for Homer and feeling defensive of him.

I admitted to myself that I wasn't going to get anywhere by nagging about Benny, so I opted for salvaging the evening. I decided to give in to Homer and talk about restaurants.

He loved it.

"How did you know the lobster bisque was going to be factory-made?" Homer warmed to my change of heart.

"The secret is to look at the menu as a whole. Did you find lobster anywhere else on the menu? No. And there's no way a restaurant is going to buy lobsters just to make bisque with them." I stopped for a bite of the steak. Homer had finished his and was wiping his plate with a piece of bread. I didn't want him to make plans for mine. "The place to order lobster bisque is where the kitchen uses fresh lobster meat as an ingredient—not just whole steamed lobsters, either. Chefs make bisque as a way to use the extra bits of lobster meat and to get some mileage out of the shells by boiling them for the stock."

"No wonder I've eaten so much bad lobster bisque in my day." Homer had torn off a second piece of bread for scrubbing his already squeaky-clean plate. He eyed Sherele's hash browns. "And what about the potato skins? You said they were likely to be good here."

"The same rule holds. If there are no other fresh potatoes evident on the menu, the kitchen isn't going to have leftover skins lying around, so it will serve frozen ones, much like frozen french fries. But this steak house serves mashed potatoes and hash browns, and lots of them. It's going to have plenty of skins left to turn into cost-free appetizers." Since I'd finished my bit of steak, I held up my nearly full plate of pasta and offered it to Homer. "You still hungry?"

He shuddered. "Not for that."

"I'm sorry about the filet."

"He didn't like it a bit, as you can see," Sherele said.

Homer's piece of bread stopped its roaming. He looked embarrassed. "I guess it was pretty good. I'd forgotten why it is that so many people order a filet, even people with their own teeth."

"I think Homer's trying to say, 'Thank you.'" Sherele took the lead.

"I am indeed. Not just for the steak, which I'd unfairly bad-mouthed, but for the good company. A fine evening."

"You're welcome. I might even consider moving you up to the C list if you continue to clean your plate."

Homer reached over and kissed my hand. "I have so much more to thank you for, too, my dear benefactor. I can't tell you how you've improved my life with your intuition about that Tidal Basin body. Our identifying Denise is all due to you." His fingers felt a little greasy, but hand kisses are rare enough that I wasn't inclined to be picky.

"Given what a hard time I'm having reviewing restaurants, maybe I should look into a job in the homicide department."

"We sure could use another body."

Sherele laughed. "I thought you already had too many of those."

"You know what I mean, Sherele. A warm body."

"You see Chas as a warm body?" Sherele asked, with a leer. That girl wasn't going to cut him an inch of slack tonight.

"Hey, lovebirds, let's think about dessert." Their teasing was making me feel lonely for someone to tease.

Chocolate will always shut Sherele up.

It wasn't until Homer was scraping up the dregs of Sherele's chocolate crème brûlée that he returned to the subject of his work, but I could see it had been waiting to reappear.

"The one I'd really love to resolve is the happy murder. I'd give anything to identify that one."

I was signing my credit card receipt, in my fake name as usual. I'd tuned out while I was calculating the tip, so it took me a moment to replay his words in my head and react to them.

"Happy? What kind of murder is a happy murder?"

"That's what I called it. The guy in the Georgetown Safeway Dumpster."

"I missed that one," I said.

"You were too busy celebrating your new column,"

Sherele explained. "As I recall, it happened around the same time."

"That long ago? I must have been mightily preoccupied to miss a story on a murder in Georgetown. Why was everyone so happy about it?"

"It's not that anybody was happy about the murder. It's just a way I have, my little shorthand for keeping our countless unsolved murders straight. This one particularly sticks in my mind because the guy was more or less my age, and not an addict or drunkard; and even though he had no taste, he had enough self-respect to be wearing a jacket and tie. It's rare that we can't identify the body of a guy who seems basically okay except that he's dead."

"Dead but happy?" I asked. I still didn't understand his shorthand.

"Homer, you're talking to yourself. Explain why you call it the happy murder. I've sort of wondered myself," Sherele prompted. She was searching under the table for her purse, apparently impatient to leave.

"Excuse me. I thought I'd mentioned it. I called this the happy murder because the guy was strangled with his own tie. One of those stupid yellow happy-face ties."

I'd reached for my purse, too, and at those words dropped it upside down. I sat frozen as Sherele and Homer leaped to retrieve my rolling coins and runaway lipstick.

It was a long night. Homer had wanted me to go down to his office with him to review what I knew about Ottavio, but I balked. If I was backed into revealing how I'd met Ottavio Rossi, I didn't want it to be in a roomful of policemen. Sherele undoubtedly noticed I was skirting that issue, and to my relief she kept her mouth shut except to suggest we all go to her apartment. Homer clung stubbornly to the idea of going downtown, but Sherele presented the best of arguments: She had a bottle of homemade corn whiskey she'd brought back from a family reunion in Georgia. An old Travis tradition.

"How come I didn't hear about this before?" Homer asked, meaning the liquor, not Ottavio.

"Didn't know if it was legal," Sherele admitted.

"It's not."

"Illegal to bring in, or illegal to drink?" I wanted to know.

"Probably illegal even to smell," Homer said. He turned to Sherele. "Your place it is."

Moonshine wasn't all Sherele had to tempt us. A two-inch-thick chunk of steak, even followed by chocolate, doesn't keep Homer's appetite quiet for long, and Sherele and I had eaten little of our fish and pasta. We were all primed for the cheese straws and benne wafers she had stashed in an old fruitcake tin. Nibbling a handful, I rooted through her refrigerator and found an old favorite I hadn't seen in years, real in-season tomato aspic.

I'd hated tomato aspic until after my freshman year of college, when I traveled through the South on summer vacation. Until then I'd thought of aspic as old people's Jell-O. But that was because I'd only tasted it made with canned tomato juice. The very thought of that metallic gelatin makes me shiver. Sherele, though, makes her aspic the right way, which is to wait until tomatoes are in season. She peels and sieves three or four of them, mixes a little of their juice with an envelope of unflavored gelatin, then stirs the softened gelatin into half of the puree, which she brings to a boil. When the gelatin is well dissolved in the hot tomato puree, she stirs in the rest and seasons it well with salt, pepper, Worcestershire, and lemon juice or a touch of vinegar. Maybe a dash of Tabasco. Some people add chopped celery leaves and parsley, but Sherele is a purist. Chilled in an antique jelly mold and presented on a bed of bibb lettuce, her aspic makes you feel cool and refreshed just to look at it. Such an aspic far outclasses gazpacho, if you ask me.

It arrived at the table just in time to divert Homer from his unanswered question about how I'd met Mr. Happy-face-necktie, Ottavio Rossi. While Homer dug into his plateful of cool red shimmer, I used a technique I'd learned on talk shows. Instead of answering his question, I responded with only what I wanted to say. I explained that I knew little about the guy except that he was divorced and fairly new to town. And he'd been a waiter at Coastline.

I was hoping I could give Homer enough information that he wouldn't need me to reveal that the classified advertising department that handled the personals ads could track Ottavio down. As we talked, I had an inspiration. I remembered the name of Ottavio's kitchen design firm, and I came up with a story that I'd been interviewing him about restaurant kitchens.

That solved my problem. Now Homer had a lead he could pursue even if Coastline didn't know enough about Ottavio to help trace his family. And my connection with the possibly dead man seemed natural.

My next puzzle was to figure out how long after I'd met Ottavio this unidentified man was found dead.

I didn't like the answer: The next morning. He'd been murdered the very day I'd met Ottavio, not long after I'd "finished my interview," as I'd depicted the encounter to Homer. To myself, of course, I was wondering, had Ottavio really brushed me off as I'd supposed, or had he been actually intending to feed his parking meter and return to me, but been waylaid by a strangler?

As I was falling asleep that night, I replayed the scene with Ottavio in my head: the beige-on-beige empty deli, the smirking waiter, the espresso that tasted of old, unwashed aluminum. I felt my burning cheeks as the waiter watched me leave by myself and recalled my surprise at the radiant sky as I walked out the door. I remembered feeling old and so angry that I kicked at a crumpled napkin on the sidewalk.

His napkin.

Had the murderer spotted me?

20

"You got any more friends you haven't seen for a while?"

Homer called to tell me the good news, that once more I'd been a critical connection in one of his unsolved murders. Ottavio's former boss in the architectural firm had every bit of information Homer had needed, and Ottavio's ex-wife—widow, now, I guess—had actually been sad to hear that the guy had died, even though she'd been angry about his disappearing without keeping up his child-support payments and she was the beneficiary of his rather generous insurance policy.

I was sad, too. In death, the rough edges tend to disappear and we give the departed every benefit of our doubt. On the other hand, I was drying my tears retroactively, even now glad to be able to reinterpret our meeting without the humiliation of Ottavio dumping me. Added to the mix of emotions: I was scared. A murder had been committed almost under my nose.

I couldn't tell Homer that.

Nor could I tell Dave why I was so interested in Ottavio, since the official story was that I'd been interviewing him for a story on restaurant kitchens, rather than auditioning him for a romance.

Dave and I were talking fairly regularly now, at least as regularly as seemly for two "friends" living three time zones apart and working long and unpredictable hours. If we'd been admittedly a couple again, we could have made more obvious efforts to keep in touch. But we were both wary and afraid to seem pushy—at least I was, and I hoped that was the reason for Dave's inconsistency.

I didn't tell Dave—or Homer, of course—how nervous it made me to be so close to two murders. Or three, if you count that strange Jamaican suicide. I'd been able to explain away the suicide and Denise's murder as being only incidentally connected with me, since I'd never met either of the victims. Ottavio was another matter. I not only knew him, but might have been the last person (more accurately, the last non-murderer) to see him alive. I couldn't get him out of my thoughts. I had a ghost to exorcise, and I was driven to prove to myself that Ottavio's murder had nothing to do with me.

As an investigative reporter, Dave played according to strict rules. Pin down at least two sources for everything. Get your informants on the record. He thought such serious stuff as murder should be left to the police and experienced crime reporters.

In all, Dave would worry over my getting involved, and he couldn't help much at a distance, so when I talked to him I downplayed my concern to sound like mere curiosity.

Homer, in the manner of homicide detectives everywhere, would ridicule my worry and insist I leave everything up to him. Solving murders was his job, he'd remind me (while not hesitating at all to usurp my job by commenting on every dish and every nuance of service at the restaurants I was reviewing). When I'd made the tiniest suggestion to him about the investigation, he'd "little lady'd" me and delivered a speech about how you've got to take these things slowly. When I reminded him of the obvious–that all three deaths had something to do with Coastline–Homer gave me a supercilious look and said, "Chas, honey, you can't arrest a restaurant for murder."

I couldn't even talk to Sherele about my obsession. Like Dave, she'd worry. Thus she might be driven to tell all to Homer, trading my secrets for my safety. That could hamper me, of course. And most important, if I wanted Sherele and Homer to keep me informed of how the investigation was going, I'd have to pretend only the mildest interest, mostly couched in terms of how hard it must be on Homer.

There was only one person I was close to who wouldn't worry about my snooping around the circumstances of Ottavio's murder. That, of course, was Lily. Daughters consider their mothers invincible. Life is more convenient that way. For Lily, as for me, the natural order of things dictates that I worry about her rather than vice versa. So she'd be my best possible coconspirator. We even had a family tradition: Lily had helped me—knowingly and inadvertently—solve a murder before. And I'm a strong believer in continuing family rituals.

Our relationship has long been peculiar in that we don't do what most mothers and daughters do together. We don't shop much, not even for groceries. We don't go to hairdressers. We don't play bridge. Lily has no interest in the long walks I take, and I don't have evenings free for theater, movies, or even TV. What we do together is dine. We'd been talking about trying to find some new mother-daughter activity, and here it was. Crime solving.

Lily jumped at the idea.

I broached it on the phone with Sherele sitting at the next desk, which made for a pretty stilted conversation, in a sort of family code. Sherele seemed safely occupied with a phone interview, but the girl not only has eyes in the back of her head, she has two sets of ears. She's the only person I know who can talk and listen at the same time. I was taking no chance that she'd pick up clues to Lily and me planning a search for the murderer.

From my end of the conversation, I tried to make it sound at first as if Lily and I were talking about Ari, Brian, anybody but the man Homer had confirmed was the dead Ottavio Rossi. I was letting Lily do most of the talking, and I was steering her with yes's and no's.

Once she'd figured out what I was proposing, she carried the ball. "We start with an advantage, as I see it. Women can get away with appearing innocent, and a restaurant critic isn't expected to be interested in anything much but the sauces and wine service."

"I couldn't agree more, Lily. That's why this is the perfect job for you." I jotted a note to myself to mention to Sherele that Lily had been approached about a music library job, which I'd just invented.

"Of course, the simplest conclusion is that Benny murdered Denise and Ottavio. Not that we have any idea why Benny'd want to get rid of a waiter who'd just come to the restaurant."

"There could be some problems with those qualifications. You definitely need more work in that area. And don't forget that other job we talked about."

"The Jamaican suicide?"

"That's the one."

"I'm not so sure that is more than a coincidence. I don't see why a suicide should be connected with a couple of murders just because the man ate in the same restaurant. Half of Washington has eaten at Coastline. I'll bet you could find a bunch of deaths if you tracked down everyone on the reservations list."

Lily has a tendency to complicate my life (and hers) at any opportunity. Once again I found myself weeding through her complaints to seize the important issue. "You don't need to apply everywhere at once, my dear. All it takes is one job at a time to build a career."

"Huh? I've lost you. You mean we only have to solve one murder in order to be detectives?"

"No, that's not quite the kind of career I had in mind."

"I'll try again. You mean we only have to solve one murder."

"At a time."

"I get it. You figure solving one will unravel the others."

"Yes, I knew your skills would point you in the right direction."

Sherele hung up her phone and leaned over to me, interrupting my conversation. "Lily's got a new job?"

I wiggled my hand to show that it was iffy.

Sherele grabbed for the phone, but I slid my chair back to keep it out of her reach for a crucial moment. "Sherele wants to congratulate you on your new job offer," I quickly said into the receiver, hoping Lily's quick mind would come up with a legitimate-sounding job in a hurry.

"Hi, sweetie," Sherele said into the phone. "Has the National Symphony finally called you?"

I couldn't hear what Lily was saying, but I could see by Sherele's face that she'd come up with something creative.

"Marching band? I wouldn't have thought you'd be interested in teaching a marching band." Sherele looked puzzled.

Then she brightened. "Just for a weekend? Yes, it does sound like a change of pace that could be fun."

Gianni's lips felt cold when he kissed me on both cheeks. Understandably, he was confused and nervous to see me at his restaurant after I'd assured him I wouldn't be reviewing him yet. And I felt a little guilty about making him so nervous. I also felt uncomfortable putting an unnecessary dinner at Coastline on my expense account, though I reasoned that my connection with these murders was all because of my job, so the expenses for investigating them could be justified . . . somehow. The point of our being here was for Lily to see Coastline so we could brainstorm with a mutual frame of reference.

Lily thought the food was good, since she didn't know how wonderful it could be and maybe would be again. In any case, she seemed to enjoy the evening. In no small part that was because I let her order whatever she liked. I had no need to evaluate specific dishes, so if Lily chose to eat only a plain mesclun salad and a platter of smoked salmon, it was fine with me, for once.

Even I ate lightly. Clams on the half shell don't require a chef, and while oysters aren't at their best in summer's months without an *R*, Maryland's cherrystone clams are plump and sweet and nearly the match of any oyster. Instead of an entrée, I ordered a second appetizer of cold, steamed seafood with a sauce rémoulade. Unlike most of the three-course restaurant meals I'm usually forced to eat even in the summer, this perfectly suited my appetite and the sweltering heat.

So we had a satisfying evening. Not that we saw anything that might be a clue. We were careful to keep our voices low and switch to innocuous gossip when any staff approached our table, but in truth we didn't have secrets to keep anyway. Dinner was just dinner. Gianni continued to wear a slight wrinkle between his eyebrows as he passed by our table from time to time, but he left us alone.

If Gianni knew Ottavio was dead, he had no reason to suspect that I did, too, or at least I hoped he didn't. And obviously he didn't know of my connection with the Jamaican suicide, tenuous as that connection was. So the only part of this murder spree that I could openly mention was Denise.

With so little to go on, I didn't want to waste any opportunity, so I looked for a way to casually bring up the murder with someone—anyone—on the staff.

Gianni came through for me.

After dinner, he approached the table to ask how everything was and to tell Lily how pleased he was that I had chosen to introduce her to his restaurant.

"As I do for many of my first-time customers, I would like to buy you an after-dinner drink. And a cigar, if you indulge in such things."

Lily hates cigarettes, as classical musicians tend to do, but to my surprise she accepted Gianni's offer of a cigar. "We had a cigar club in college, a group of women," she explained to Gianni and me.

As soon as Lily's cigar was lit and her Clear Creek pear brandy was poured (I was drinking Armagnac), Gianni was called away, but he promised he'd be back shortly.

"I must get to know this charming and wise young woman," he'd said as he left. Lily and I grimaced at each other behind his back, and I mimed opening a notebook and taking notes. It might turn out to be a useful evening after all.

Once Gianni was out of earshot, Lily shook her head as if clearing her ears after a swim, and said, "That's much better."

"What's better?"

"The music. I mean, no music."

"I hadn't noticed."

"Oh, Mama, how could you have missed it? I didn't think I could stand another minute of that watery new wave background noise in the dining room. It sounds like the moving walkways at O'Hare Airport. All tinkly and electronic. Thank God for silence."

"Your being a musician still amazes me. Obviously you didn't get your talent from me or your father. We're both oblivious."

"Maybe my senses have become acute because you've always fed me so well." Lily took a sip of her clear brandy and, with a sigh of contentment, leaned back on her sofa and stretched her arms above her head. "This is quite a luxurious little cigar room, isn't it?"

"Money well invested, apparently. Everyone who's anyone comes here; it always seems to be full."

Lily had turned and was examining the wall, tracing a finger down the silk paneling. "Wow! They certainly spared no expense. That feels like Sonex."

"What's that? It looks like Thai silk to me."

"Not the fabric, what's behind it. Sonex is a top-grade acoustic padding. You can feel its pattern beneath the silk. The best sound studios use it on their walls."

"No wonder there's such an air of privacy here. You can't even hear the conversation at the next table."

Feeling secure to talk freely, we turned the conversation to the Coastline murders, as we now thought of them. It was a subject we exhausted pretty quickly. I didn't have anything to tell Lily except that before he'd died, Ottavio had mentioned some dirty secrets about Coastline, but that I hadn't yet figured out what he'd meant. I'd jotted down some notes but must have misfiled them.

"They'll turn up, I guarantee," I said, in hopes that

the promise would force my mind to remember where I'd stuck them.

In my experience, just saying what floats through my head on a subject, and even exaggerating it, helps my mind to make connections, often while I'm sleeping. Thus, my purpose for the evening was to seed our minds with random thoughts that might sprout overnight.

In the meantime, we might as well finish family business.

"Ari said you're making the reservation for his birthday dinner next week. You'd better call soon. The Caribbean Cafe tends to be crowded on weekends."

"I'll do it tomorrow. I'm really glad you're going to be a part of Dad's birthday," Lily said. "It was so awful all those years you and he were fighting."

"I agree. Life is much nicer with Ari as a friend. And I think it's sweet that he keeps choosing that Caribbean restaurant for his birthday dinner."

"Now that you mention it, I've always wondered why. He's hardly the conch fritter type."

"It's nostalgia. We had our first vacation together in Jamaica. We had such a wonderful time that I think he does this as a gesture to our friendship. Of course, I almost died–"

"Died? You never told me about that, Mama."

"I haven't told anyone about it, I suppose. It was so frightening that I forced it out of my mind for years. It would have been pretty ironic for me to have missed out on being a food critic because I died young of a food toxin."

"I thought your iron stomach could handle any food."

"That's true, almost. Fortunately, the one food that affects me violently is utterly unavailable. You just don't find fresh akee outside of Jamaica."

"What's akee?"

"Do you remember that Harry Belafonte song about 'akee, rice, salt fish are nice . . . '?"

"'Jamaica Farewell.'"

"Right. Well, akee is a strange Jamaican fruit—originally from Africa—that looks and tastes sort of like scrambled eggs. It's delicious, but to me it's deadly."

"That scrambled-egg stuff. We've had that before. Didn't Dad get it one year at the Caribbean Cafe? I'd forgotten the name. I remember you making me taste it, though, and you tasted it yourself."

"The akee you get here is canned, and that is nearly impossible to find. My problem is only with fresh akee, which they hardly serve even in Jamaica anymore. The canned kind is perfectly safe. But with the fresh, if it is the least bit unripe or not properly cooked, it can make you queasy, sick, or, as nearly happened in my case, kill you. I was just lucky that the hospital knew how to handle it, and that it was the first bout for me. I was warned that a second encounter could be fatal. I didn't think I'd ever want to taste akee again, but once I knew it was safe when it's canned, I couldn't resist trying it. It is so subtle and fascinating."

"As I always said, Mama, you've got guts."

Lily saluted me with her pear brandy and I returned the salute with my Armagnac. Then she puffed on her cigar, for which I had no response.

"Have you had a true Havana before?" Gianni slid onto the sofa next to Lily.

"My first," Lily said with a contented smile. "Not my last, I hope."

"A lovely young woman like you will have men plying you with Cuban cigars all your life," Gianni said, as he pulled out his own cigar and rolled it under his nose.

"This is a magnificent room." Lily nodded her thanks and returned the compliment, instinctively knowing what would please this proud and elegant restaurateur.

"Gianni, I can't get Denise out of my mind." It was getting late, so I interrupted to get us started on the real purpose of the evening. I launched the subject in a non-directive way, wanting to see where Gianni would lead it.

"I, too, can't get over it. Has your friend Homer Jones made any progress in finding the murderer?" Gianni turned the spotlight of his attention on me. He has an intimate smile and sympathetic eyes that feel like warming lamps.

"Homer thinks he's already found him. Don't you believe Benny is the murderer?"

"I cannot imagine that young man doing such a thing. It is too out of character." With Gianni focused on me, I noticed, Lily was appraising him. I could see her taking mental notes.

"It had to be someone from Coastline. The knife was from this kitchen. And Benny did have that fight with Denise."

"The more I think about it, the more I realize that she provoked it. I think I was too hasty in firing Benny."

While this struck me as good news, it also made me feel smothered by a great weighty cloud. If Gianni had realized this earlier, had not acted in haste, maybe Benny would still be cooking in this kitchen. Maybe Denise would not be dead. I could see my reaction mirrored in Lily's face.

But what about Ottavio?

"Who else could have done it? Who else from here?" I assumed Gianni had some other idea if he was ready to exonerate Benny.

"Nobody from here. I'm sure of that. Many people have access to our kitchen. Delivery men, customers, inspectors."

He was flailing around blindly. He had no more idea who else could have murdered Denise than I did. Or he wasn't being candid. In either case, he showed himself as only being self-serving when he revealed his real agenda: "I'm thinking of hiring Benny back."

"How can you? He's been denied bail."

"I'm working on that."

I was astonished. And impressed. Gianni would be taking a big public relations risk if he rehired a suspected murderer. Whether his plan was motivated by a drive to improve Coastline's food or to achieve justice for Benny, my sympathies were with his cause.

Lily and I walked a while, arms entwined, neither of us ready to give up the evening without feeling we'd accomplished something.

"Gianni looked as if he was about to throw up when he saw you walk in," Lily observed.

"No surprise there. I'd told him I wouldn't be reviewing the place until after he'd hired a new chef." The smell of melted tar from the sunstroked streets was giving me a headache.

"We don't have the foggiest idea what we're doing, do we?" Lily, too, was wilting in the stifling night air.

"We found out that Gianni doesn't think Benny's a murderer."

"No, we found out that Gianni would even hire a murderer if it would benefit his restaurant. He doesn't have any evidence of Benny's innocence."

"You don't like Gianni, do you?"

"Too slick. A high-class greaser."

"So you think Benny's guilty just because Gianni wants him to be innocent?"

"Not exactly. I don't know what to think. Did Benny kill Denise? Did he also kill Ottavio? It sounds as if he hardly knew the guy. Maybe the Jamaican guy killed them both. Maybe the new Ottavio killed the old one because he didn't like sharing his name. Nothing connects. How can we solve a murder without any clues?"

Our lovely evening had turned depressing. Playing detective hadn't been such a good idea after all.

21

I'm not the kind of person who can put up with nothing happening. In the midst of inactivity I have a messy tendency to stir events and try to bring them to a boil. So for a week I invented transparent excuses to call Homer, only to hear that he was more involved with new murders than with old. He was so busy that Sherele talked with him even less than I, which meant she was no good as an informant, either.

Gianni called me a couple of times, but it was unclear whether he was pumping me or I was pumping him. Neither of us found an ounce of enlightenment in the conversations.

I was bored.

So was Lily, apparently more so. Once she saw that the hunt wasn't fun anymore, she dropped it altogether. I was on my own. I was adrift.

I was ready for diversion, so ready that I agreed to do a good deed for Robert. Ordinarily, the idea of visiting somebody's father in a nursing home would suggest all kinds of excuses to me. In addition to the usual reasons a normal person might beg off, I hate being paraded as Ms. Restaurant Critic. It makes me feel like a trained animal, a seal playing a tune on a row of horns, or a monkey bowing and tipping his hat on cue.

Robert had told his father about me—in one of his father's more lucid moments, I presumed—and his father had expressed a great desire to make my acquaintance and talk about the restaurants of pre-nouvelle cuisine France. That's how Robert reported it, adding his own great apologies for imposing on me and his assurances that I need not acquiesce if the event sounded distasteful or if I was too busy.

The more Robert apologized and repeated that he would understand if I couldn't do it, the more I felt I should say yes. Even so, I would have turned him down politely and with an unassailable excuse if I hadn't been in such need of diversion.

The state I was in, I'd accept any invitation.

Robert was pitifully grateful. Even so, he added, "Might I presume to add one more small request?"

I was tempted to say no just to be perverse, since I was immediately regretting my decision. But I held my tongue.

His request turned out to be indeed small. Robert asked if I would bring along my copy of Jean-Georges's menu. His father was eager to see an example of today's grand menu presentations.

In my nervousness about what Robert, his father, and I might have to talk about, I packed up whatever other menus I could find in my apartment along with the one from Jean-Georges. Food could always carry the conversation.

Robert, too, seemed nervous when he picked me up in his taxi. I didn't make things easier when I automatically opened the passenger side's back door and started to climb in. Unthinkingly, I was acting out of habit. It was a taxi, after all. I tried to pretend it was a joke, but I could see that Robert was hurt, only pretending to believe me.

"You're really wonderful to do this." Robert started apologizing again once I'd settled myself and my bulging tote bag next to him. "I talked to my father before I left, and I think we're in luck. He sounded lucid."

"How long do these good periods last?"

"Sometimes a whole day, sometimes an hour. All too often they are just a fleeting glimpse of what his mind was. We don't have to stay long. But I want him to at least be able to remember that you were there."

I wished I hadn't dressed up quite so much. The tapping of my high heels on the bare floor of the nursing home hallway echoed like a rebuke to the slow *kerplunks* of the walkers and the swish of soft slippers. As we walked past the dining room, I noticed it was bravely decorated with posters and silk flowers, yet it still looked as medicinal as the corridors smelled.

Mr. Said's room, though, was saturated with the smell of roses. It had also been transformed by carpets and weavings from waiting-room beige to prime-of-life red and orange. Every surface was crowded with ornaments in etched brass, silver filigree, or wood mosaic. My eyes were invited to leap from dresser to desk to tabletop. Even the bed had been covered to look like a sofa, with a half-dozen pillows strewn along it. In the center of the room was a low trestle table laid with a cloth out of the *Arabian Nights*, woven with gold and silver threads on a cloud pink background. It was decorated with small quiches and puff pastries at one end, tiny fruit tarts and baklava at the other, each positioned as carefully as a jewel on a bracelet. Robert's father presided over a silver teapot with a spout as long and graceful as a swan's neck. Somehow France and Lebanon had found their way to this nursing-home table.

"I am Samir Said. Welcome to my home, such as it is. Please call me Samir." Robert's father reached across the narrow table, not to shake my hand, but to kiss it. "Forgive me for not standing to greet you." Only then did I notice that he was in a wheelchair.

Robert leaned over to kiss his father on both cheeks, French-style. My eyes darted from father to son to try to detect any likeness between them. None was immediately apparent, since Samir's features bulged into pouches under the eyes and sagged in fleshy cheeks and layers of chins. It was only when he spoke and gestured that I heard the refinement of Robert's accent, saw the familiar grace of my friend's hands and the dignity of his posture.

In Samir's own none-too-spacious nursing-home quarters, which he hadn't left in years, this courtly man was wearing a necktie—very old, very wide, and very likely a Hermès. I was glad, after all, that I'd dressed up.

Samir motioned us to chairs, probably extras borrowed from neighbors because otherwise he'd never have been able to move around the room. He poured us tea, and the rosewater aroma was overlaid with mint.

We all sampled the pastries, Samir and I taking seconds. I wondered aloud how he'd found such exquisite tidbits. They didn't come from any French or Middle Eastern bakery I knew.

"The niece of my cousin makes them. My mother's cook had taught her mother's cook. Nowadays one must bake for oneself, so it is fortunate she learned before she left the old country."

Our forks had handles that felt like plastic but looked like folk art, elongated heads of black birds with red beaks and combs. Samir explained those, too. They were indeed traditional yet updated folk art, from a Lebanese town that had not long ago been bombed out of existence. In the aftermath, these handmade plastic utensils had become more valuable than any sterling silver.

Samir went on to introduce me to the objects around the room, clearly enjoying drawing me into family history. Robert sat quietly, looking contented as his father spun tales. While I wasn't sure whether Samir was recounting the past or sinking back into it, I, too, was enjoying the lore. Even if Samir was retreating from the present into a senile version of reality, he was charming me. I was lulled by his memories of Lebanon.

"Did you bring me the menu?" His question out of the blue startled me. He hadn't lost touch with the moment after all.

"I brought you several," I said, lifting my tote bag as Robert moved the tea-time utensils aside.

Samir took the Jean-Georges menu from the top of the pile and opened it. He ran his hands slowly across the pages as if he could taste the dishes through his fingers.

"Tell me what spices were on the duck," he demanded. "What vegetables were served? How were they cooked?"

Robert must have been used to this. He remembered details I'd forgotten from our meal. Or maybe Samir had asked these questions of him countless times already.

After the Jean-Georges menu had been picked clean, Samir had an appetite for more. He approached the next menu, from Coastline. As he opened it, the pressed rose fell out and slid to his lap. Samir laid down the menu gently, as if it were ancient and fragile, and he reached for the rose.

He looked puzzled as he lifted it from his lap, cradling it by the flattened and withered bud. He rubbed the flower with his forefinger and thumb, then began to pull it apart.

I wanted to grab my rose, protect it from his childish destruction. How dare he destroy my memento? Then I reminded myself that this was a sadly deranged old man who didn't mean any harm. My rose wasn't such a big sacrifice, and Samir couldn't help himself.

"Who are you?" He bellowed, his face purple with anger and his voice startling me so that I grabbed my purse and nearly leapt from my chair to flee. Robert's hand on my arm restrained me.

"It's all right, Father. She's my friend. She's come to visit you."

Samir was shredding the flower and peering closely at a piece of it. Robert's voice hadn't placated him at all.

"Who sent you? How did you find me?"

Robert moved to his father's side, patted his shoulder, and reached for the hands that were clutching that bit of the flower. Suddenly his face looked just like his father's, a thinner and younger version of the purple outrage.

"Chas, how could you?"

They were both madmen. I stood up, backing away and ready to run.

"Who got you to plant this?" He held up a shiny bit of metal about the size of my watch battery.

That stopped me. "Plant what? What is that?"

"A bug. A microphone. What did you hope to get out of my father?"

Samir was breathing hard, his chest heaving. I was afraid he was going to die. I no longer had the nerve to leave. Confused and frightened as I was, I couldn't be so cruel as to abandon Robert at such a moment.

Besides, now I was curious.

"Where did you get that? In the rose? Is it really a microphone? Why would anyone want to tape us here? Let me see it." My words tumbled out as I grabbed the tiny thing from Robert's hand.

Samir, for all his aging brain, showed a more agile mind than mine or Robert's. He'd heard the stupefaction in my voice and quickly reassessed me.

"Both of you, please sit down. I beg your forgiveness for my outburst. We must regain our calm and learn what has happened here." Samir's voice was so soothing that it slid me right back into a chair. Robert, too.

Samir held out his hand and I meekly put the little metal gadget in it. "Now, Madam Wheatley, please tell me how you acquired this"—he paused and turned the miniature microphone in his hand—"contaminated flower."

"Why, Robert gave it to me."

Samir looked darkly at his son, and Robert started to sputter.

"Of course, it wasn't his to give," I added. Both father and son were glowering at me by now, so I decided to stop the tease and, as they say, cut to the chase. "It must have been in that flower when Robert plucked it from the centerpiece and gave it to me as a keepsake. I didn't notice it; I just pressed the rose in that menu and left it there."

Robert, relieved of suspicion, joined me in telling the rest of the story. "It undoubtedly was in the flower when I took it. That means it was part of our centerpiece at Coastline."

"In the cigar room," I added.

"But it wasn't there from the beginning. Not when we were seated." Robert closed his eyes as he tried to recall the scene.

"You're right." The moment was beginning to come back to me. "Remember, we spilled something. All over the table. They had to give us a new tablecloth and everything."

"That's when they put these flowers on the table," Robert said, his voice growing excited. "Don't you recall how we thought it was a bit much that they brought a new centerpiece, when we were about to leave before long?"

I, too, was increasingly excited as details popped

into my head. "There was that funny, awkward moment when they tried to take the rose from you. To cut off the thorns, wasn't it? You two almost came to a wrestling match. And there was something else that's beginning to make sense. My daughter pointed out to me that they used some kind of outlandishly expensive acoustical tile on the walls of the cigar room. Do you think that's why?"

Samir had heard enough. "They must have been very worried about your finding this little gadget. I'm sure they fervently hoped you would never again open this menu and reexamine your souvenir."

Robert and I were smiling to each other, reevaluating that scene when I had insisted on keeping my eavesdropping rose. How frustrated they must have been. Then I had an alarming thought. "Can they still hear us?"

Samir held up his hands to stop me midthought. "No, no. This is a very inexpensive little bugging device. A room bug. Its range is certainly not more than a mile. It is meant to be temporary and disposable. It was probably an emergency measure after you spilled water on your table and shorted out their more serious eavesdropping equipment. The important question is, what did they want to find out from you?"

Terrible thoughts were forming in my head, multiplying at such a rapid rate I felt about to explode.

I was ready to leave. I had so much to do, to think about. But Samir would not hear of it.

"What are you going to do with this little surprise?"

"The way I see it, I have to turn the information

over to the police, I must definitely tell the editor of the *Examiner*, and . . ." I paused, knowing I shouldn't tell Samir what else I had in mind.

"You want to confront the proprietor of the restaurant." He finished my thought for me. "You are thinking rashly, my dear. If you set the discovery in motion by going to the authorities immediately, you will lose the opportunity to quietly look into this little listening operation and could possibly lose your life. All because you young people have no patience."

Young people? I'm nearly fifty. Flattery, as usual, got my attention. "It's not a matter of patience," I said, noticing I was using a higher—younger?—voice. "It is a matter of public duty and of responsibility to my newspaper. And I have a friend on the police force. I couldn't betray him by withholding this, and he will make sure it is thoroughly investigated."

"Feh. Public duty? The police will, as you Americans say, screw it up. Surely an organization with such eavesdropping capability has provided itself with paid informants among the police. It may even have police headquarters bugged. By the time your police are ready to raid this cigar room, it will be as clean as a bone left by a pack of wild dogs. Furthermore, you would be doing your policeman friend a favor by waiting until you have more proof before you bring this to him. He won't be able to fend off demands that this be turned over to the FBI, and once the feds get hold of it, your friend will be assigned the janitorial duties and the FBI will get the credit."

He had a point. Many evenings I'd commiserated with Homer about the FBI snatching his cases and him being turned into an errand boy on their behalf. Nor could I forget Linda Tripp and how the federal investigators had sent her to spy on Monica Lewinsky, then made a media circus out of the material.

Samir clinched my cooperation when he reminded me that the FBI would undoubtedly also force me to cooperate, whether or not my paper approved. I had visions of those contempt-of-court jail sentences and of rival newspapers gleefully reporting my embarrassing search for romance in the personals ads—one of those commonplaces that are perfectly reasonable except when they're made public.

Keeping my discovery about Coastline from my editors was another matter.

"I'm a reporter. I must—"

"Of course you must. But there is no hurry for your 'must.' As for your newspaper, I know newspapers. Most investigative reporters are hand-fed by such people as those who planted these bugs. They write only sanitized exposés."

I thought of Dawn and felt my bile rise. "I'll insist I have to work on the story, too."

"Forgive me, Chas. I do not mean to underestimate you, for I know you to be a very fine writer. Yet no matter how competent you are, your newspaper sees your talents as suited to soft news, not hard news. Your editors will not entrust anything that could be Pulitzer material to a food critic. They may pretend to include you on this, but you will find yourself assigned to counting the forks in a quiet corner while the news reporters head off to the ball to confront Prince Charming."

How did he know so much about American newsrooms?

"You're forgetting one important factor. This could be dangerous, and I'm not equipped to deal with this kind of danger."

"I am equipped. Forgive my lapse of modesty, but I have everything you might need and can very quickly teach you exactly what you must know. And I am not talking about your bringing down a spying mission all by yourself. I would agree that the dangerous and complicated parts must be left to the authorities. I'm urging you to bide your time just a little bit and uncover just enough evidence to make sure these reptiles can't slip beneath their stones and hide from their proper fate. You will merely take the process one step further. And should you need the FBI, I have the contacts and the credibility to have the top talent at your side instantly."

He sounded a mite self-aggrandizing, but I didn't have anything to lose by listening to the next step. "What do you propose for me to do?"

"I will tell you over dinner."

Robert broke in to defend me at this point. "I'm sorry, Father, but Chas has a dinner appointment already." He knew about Ari's birthday celebration and that I couldn't miss it.

"What time?" Samir addressed the question to me.

"Eight o'clock."

"That's fine. Dinner here is at five-thirty, which is right about now. You'll have plenty of time. Just a minute and I'll tell you what's on the menu." He backed up his wheelchair as far as it would go and swiveled it like a kid on a skateboard until he could reach a carpet-covered shelf.

"But we've just eaten. And I'll have to eat again."

Samir had pulled a small black plastic box from a large mosaic one. He turned some dials and shushed us so he could hear it.

"Haven't those cordon bleus thawed yet? Shove some of them into the microwave and run hot water over the rest. You can dry them out under the broiler. These instants are going to get cold, and I don't want to have to heat them again. Besides, the board is going to have my head if I serve late one more time this week." The voice crackled a bit, but you could hear it almost as well as if you were in the kitchen.

"You see," Samir said with a laugh that rippled his chins, "you won't have to worry about spoiling your appetite. It sounds like wet chicken cordon bleu and instant mashed potatoes."

He turned a dial and the voices disappeared, replaced by a dreadful sound like a large animal being choked.

"Our timing is excellent. Mrs. Greene is sound asleep. If we hurry, we can claim her window table."

After Samir had gone to such trouble on our behalf, Robert and I could do nothing but accompany him to dinner.

Samir insisted I take the chair facing the window, with its view of a cement terrace punctuated every few feet by small dirt squares with rose bushes tied to green stakes. Robert parked his father's wheelchair on my right and sat at my left as Samir placed a polished rosewood box on the table. He plucked jar after jar from it, examining each and offering it to me to smell and approve. Sumac. Lemon pickle. Dijon mustard. Anchovy sauce. Herbes de Provence. Hoisin.

Zaatar. Samir had a world-class array of flavor enhancers as his daily dinner companion. I nodded at the sumac; I adore this lemony, reddish brown Middle Eastern spice powder. With it we could pretend that the soggy chicken breasts were chicken *tabak*, those small whole birds flattened with a brick as they're grilled.

"Tell him about the murders," Robert prodded, as his father carefully unfolded his chicken breast and extracted its slice of ham, which he set aside. He cut the remaining cheese-sticky chicken into fastidious slices and fanned them out on the plate, sprinkling them evenly with sumac. Robert and I had waved away our servings of chicken and were nibbling saltines from the bread basket.

"Here's another reason I'm nervous about taking on this project on my own. There have been two murders, both probably connected with Coastline. And a suicide that in some tenuous way might relate to the restaurant."

"This is interesting." Samir looked at me with his fork poised in front of his mouth.

I must have looked skeptical. Or appalled.

"Not the chicken," he hastened to correct my misperception. "Murder and spying are old friends, you know."

I told him about the two Ottavio Rossis—though not how I'd met my Ottavio. I explained Benny's firing and the subsequent discovery of Denise's murder. That took me through three packets of saltines.

Robert took over and related my telephone encounter with Mrs. Leslie and the Coastline matchbook she'd found in her dead husband's pocket. I was surprised at how accurately Robert remembered the details. Listening to him, I made connections that I'd ignored when I ran them through my own mind. Discrete facts now added up. Hamilton Leslie committed suicide not because of any mortal disease or problems at home, not because he was in financial trouble. From what I could piece together, he was being blackmailed over a politically explosive affair. He was being blackmailed after a trip to Coastline.

Adding murder to our stew didn't seem to faze Samir at all. "We have several goals here," he said, having finished his orange sherbet and sugar cookies, and sprinkled mint leaves from one of his jars into a pot of hot water. While his fragrant tea was steeping, he sat back with his hands clasped over his stomach, a kind of Semitic Buddha.

I noted his use of "we." I was acquiring more partners every day.

Samir outlined "our" goals. "Of course we want to bring the murderer or murderers to justice. We certainly want to strip away the cover of any spying operation, at least any that's not ours. We also might as well use this opportunity to enhance your status as a journalist."

"I'm more concerned about my role as a citizen."

"You Americans are such sentimentalists."

"How do you propose we accomplish all this, Father?" Robert, too, was assuming a role as part of "we."

"Do you know how bread makers handle a watery dough?"

Robert and I looked at each other, obviously both thinking that Samir's day had been dementia-free longer than we could have hoped, and he'd slipped back into its grasp.

"Don't think I can't see your 'poor crazy old man' looks. My question has a point. And a meaningful answer. The secret to coping with a watery dough is to use more water. Most people would flour their hands to handle such a dough, but that would make it stick. A professional knows that you wet your hands. Fight water with water."

The last thing I expected from this day was to learn a cooking tip. I was delighted.

Robert was impatient. "So?"

"We will fight bugs with bugs."

I was relieved he hadn't suggested we fight murders with murders.

By the time we took Samir back to his room, I was running late for my dinner with Ari and Lily, and Samir seemed to have used his last ounce of mental energy to outline our plan. He was calling me Mrs. Greene, and apologizing for having dropped her doll in the lake.

"He's remembering a family vacation when he was about six years old," Robert explained, as we hurried to his taxi. "It was his sister's doll. Sometimes he's fifteen again or is back in the army. I've learned to just take him as he is and be whoever he thinks I am at the moment. It's not often he has such a long clearheaded spell as we saw today."

I hoped Samir had been clearheaded when he'd outlined his plan of action for us. Even more, I prayed that I wasn't demented to give a try to the plan of a broken-down ex-spy just because I admired his ability to turn an institutional diet into a feast. But I was curious as to whether his clever and diabolically simple plan would work, and I didn't see that I had much to lose by postponing blowing the whistle by a couple of days.

22

Ari and Lily were already drinking rum punches by the time I arrived at the Caribbean Cafe. I kissed them both, wished Ari a happy birthday, and sat down before I noticed the centerpiece, a bowl of artfully arranged birds of paradise. I shivered and beckoned the waiter.

"Would you please remove the flowers. I think we can talk better without them."

"Certainly, madam. I'm sorry if they displease you." He hurried away with them before I was even tempted to explain.

Lily and Ari looked at each other and shrugged their shoulders, as if to say, "You never know what a critic's going to criticize."

I'd decided on the way over not to tell them about the bugging or my plan for revealing it, at least not yet. Ari, being a chef, is so tied into the restaurant community that I didn't want to risk his dropping hints. He's a bad actor; his feelings inevitably show on his face. Lily is probably an adept liar, but I didn't want to tempt her to rash action or to give her cause for worrying about me.

I steered the discussion to Ari's birthday and our celebrations over the years, glossing over the fact that for several years after our divorce we never dreamed we would ever celebrate anything together again. Over conch fritters and hot meat patties we talked of Lily's job search and chewed over the usual chef gossip. I felt distracted but was able to keep up my end of the conversation until Lily mentioned the murders.

I didn't think I could talk naturally about them at the moment, so I excused myself and went to the ladies' room, hoping that subject would run itself down in my absence. I needed a few moments to tame my racing thoughts, so I sat in the john, closed my eyes, and took deep, slow breaths—not a choice environment for meditation, but the only one available to me under the circumstances.

When I returned, Lily was chatting about conch with the waiter, a round-shouldered young man who didn't know what to do with his hands when he wasn't carrying a tray. He hoped to go to cooking school one day, he told her, after he boasted about the conch being fresh and bragged that the kitchen went to such lengths to get top-notch ingredients that it had a farm in Pennsylvania supply newly laid eggs.

"I'll be right back with your entrées," he promised as soon as I'd seated myself and he'd draped my napkin over my lap.

Talk of murder had been swept away by talk of food. Ari had been impressed with the conch fritters and even more so to hear that a restaurant serving so few dishes that included eggs would go to the trouble to find farm-fresh ones.

"Those eggs will show their stuff in Mama's akee soufflé," Lily reminded him.

"I'd heard that this chef was determined to improve the quality of the food here. He's dreaming of a nomination for a James Beard Award. I would say that those first courses indicated that he's improved his chances," Ari said. He knows I won't comment on the James Beard Awards, since I'm one of the regional panelists, so he wasn't looking for a response from me.

A marvelous prickly, spicy smell diverted me anyway. I turned my head to see the waiter arriving with Lily's jerk chicken and my akee soufflé. "I'll bring your fish right away, sir," he said, as he placed his aromatic burden on the table.

My soufflé smelled wonderful, though far more subtle than Lily's browned and glistening pepper-marinated jerk chicken.

"Go ahead. Don't let it get cold," Ari said.

Lily dug right in. I didn't blame her. The fragrance was irresistible. But since it was Ari's birthday, I couldn't get myself to start without him. Instead, I spooned out some of my golden eggy puff of akee and put it on a bread plate for Ari to taste.

He looked joyous as he absorbed the nuances of his first bite. "The best ever. It is remarkable how far this chef has come in the year since we've been here."

I dug my fork in, but just then the waiter arrived with Ari's fish, a show-stopping mosaic of white flesh, yellow-gold mango, and red peppers.

"My father loves the akee soufflé," Lily told the waiter, as he set down the plate.

"Doesn't your mother love it?" he asked, trying to sound playful but instead showing his anxiety. I had no immediate answer, since I was about to take my first bite. He squared his shoulders and announced, "For the first time ever, the chef received a shipment of fresh akee."

I dropped my fork in my lap, spattering soufflé across my skirt. Lily looked as if the table had just burst into flames, and she knocked over her chair as she leapt up to wrest the fork from my hand. Ari moves more slowly, so my first bite was safely in my lap by the time he slid the soufflé away from me and set it at the far end of the table.

"Did I do something wrong?" The waiter looked as if he might cry.

Lily and I spoke at the same time.

"You almost poisoned my mother," she accused.

"You did just fine," I said. "Just a little sensitivity problem. Thank you for alerting us."

By then the maître d' had rushed over, grabbing napkins as he came, and covered every offending surface with clean linen.

None of us could eat after this close call. Ari called for the check and reassured the stricken waiter that nothing was his fault. I took the check from Ari and insisted on paying. Not only was tonight his birthday, but the party had been spoiled by me.

"What a terrible coincidence, after we just talked about akee poisoning at Coastline," Lily said, as we left the Caribbean Cafe. "What if the waiter hadn't mentioned that the akee was fresh?" She shuddered.

I was thinking even darker thoughts.

As soon as I got home, I called the Caribbean Cafe and asked for the chef.

"Miss Wheatley, I'm so very upset that you could not finish your dinner. Was something wrong with the food?"

"No, just a little sensitivity problem. You couldn't have known about it. Nothing to do with your restaurant, of course. Your food was fine. Delicious, in fact. I called to apologize for leaving so abruptly."

"No apology is necessary. Rather, I am very grateful for you to explain this to me. I will tell the waiter, who has been upset that maybe he offended you in some way."

"Certainly not. He was entirely competent. He was telling us about all the fresh, new ingredients you have been acquiring. Fascinating. And impressive. I was wondering how you found fresh akee. I haven't come across it in years."

"I haven't, either. It was a wonderful coincidence. I have been spreading the word that I'm looking for sources of fresh tropical ingredients, and Mr. Marchelli–you know Gianni Marchelli–called to tell me that he had come across fresh akee. He knew I would be very happy to get some. He even arranged to have it shipped by Federal Express so I would get it at its freshest. He's an extraordinary man, you know."

I know. Extraordinary.

At home, without Samir and Robert to seduce me with their confidence, I was having doubts about carrying out our plan. Gianni obviously had taped me telling Lily about my akee sensitivity and knew we were going to dine at the Caribbean Cafe. If I hadn't discovered his spy paraphernalia I never would have made the connection—or believed it was more than coincidence.

I now had the advantage of knowing. But Gianni had a far greater advantage: He was willing to kill.

This situation was too big for me to tackle. Samir had been convincing, but he was, after all, an old man with a wandering mind. I'd been rash to even consider investigating Coastline's eavesdropping operation without backup. I called Homer.

I didn't want to call him at work; Samir had spooked me about spies and leaks so that I was afraid of someone intercepting my message. And once I got the voice mail at his home, I felt reluctant to leave a message there. He must be at Sherele's.

He wasn't there, either. Or they were indisposed.

Belatedly realizing how late it was, I decided against calling Homer's pager. I'd talk to him in the morning.

Meditation didn't work. I was too jumpy to sit still, much less to clear my mind. Sleep was out of the question.

I tried to call Dave. As his phone began to ring, I thought better of it. I hung up. Dave might have helpful advice for me, but my telling him what I knew could bring him trouble. I wasn't ready to let the *Examiner* in on what I knew until I'd clearly established it as *my* story. I didn't really need Dave until the next stage anyway.

Even though I'd decided to tell Homer about the microphone, I could still play along with Samir's idea. I'd looked at it from all sides and felt sure it was risk-free. We'd be in a public place, acting totally normally. The only danger would be that our procedure might not work. In that case, nothing would be gained, but nothing lost except our time and effort. Nobody would ever know what we'd attempted.

On the other hand, if our plan worked, the *Examiner*'s editors would hail my success and run with it. They might for a moment be furious with me for acting on my own and not immediately turning my information over to them, but I am just a restaurant critic, misguidedly trying to do my job. What could I be expected to know about how a real–i.e., investigative–reporter operates? I could plead innocence. Dave would have no such excuse. He'd have to play by the rules because he's acknowledged to know the rules. I'd have to get through this alone, at least for tonight.

Narrowing my own options renewed my sense of control over the situation. I was taking charge, even if in the smallest of ways. That was enough to let me drift into dreamless, uninterrupted sleep.

Robert was supposed to let me know when he had the equipment ready. At work the next morning, I waited for him to call as anxiously as if I were a teenager hoping for a date to the prom. There'd be no point calling him, since he was squeezing the preparations in between meetings at his consulting firm.

I sat drumming my fingers and watching the clock, impatient to call Homer. It seemed disloyal to do so before I explained to Robert that I'd changed my mind. "Patience," I heard Samir's voice in my head. "We must do things in their proper order."

Work was the most sensible distraction. Getting

some done would not only pass the time, it would put me in a better mood—my editors, too. I'd been avoiding my restaurant-scam story, and its impending deadline was adding to my tension. While I always procrastinate on a big project once the research is done and it's time to organize my thoughts for writing, this week I'd found more excuses than usual.

I had stored my notes and rough drafts on my computer in several parts, most in my personal directory, accessible only with my password. A couple of sections—rough drafts and their notes—were in the public directory, where I'd transferred them temporarily so that Helen and Bull could see them. I had slugged them with deceptive and innocuous names, of course, so that they wouldn't pique the curiosity of prying eyes. I had a bothersome tendency to forget the names myself, so I kept a list on paper, which by now was so full of deletions and new entries that I was having trouble reading it. I needed to reorganize my notes and lists. Maybe later.

While it had been several days, maybe even a week or two since I'd looked at my scam notes, I recalled that the two major sections were still in the public directory. My editors had finished with them, so I decided to review their suggestions and return the notes to my private files.

I must have been wrong. None were in my public directory, unless I'd mistaken their slugs. I checked my list, squinted over my scrawls and smudges. As best I could decipher, their slugs were as I recalled: MENU SPELLINGS and DIET PLAN. I realized I must have already switched them to my private directory. If my memory was this bad before fifty, I lectured myself, what would it be by the time I was sixty?

I couldn't find the notes in my private file, either. I typed their slugs in a search command and scoured the entire newsroom system. No luck. Could I have deleted them? Unthinkable.

Thoroughly diverted from Robert, I pulled a notepad from my drawer and started jotting down what I could remember about those two files. I felt flushed and nauseated as the list grew. Interviews. Juicy quotes. Word-for-word confessions. Statistics. Names of complainants. Verifications of material in other folders.

I sent messages to Helen and Bull asking whether they had moved my files to their private directories. Both messaged me back that they hadn't. That was a surprisingly fast response for Bull; days could go by before he responded to a computer message. I pressed my luck and sent them both notes asking whether they had made a copy of these files. Again, two immediate responses, nearly identical: "Don't worry. No copies have been made." They were concerned about secrecy, while I was worried whether the information had disappeared.

Robert reminded me of his existence, which I'd temporarily forgotten. As soon as I picked up the phone he said, clearly in a hurry, that we might have to postpone our plan. His father had lapsed back into his own world just short of finishing his part. He must have been exhausted after our visit yesterday. The nurse had promised Robert she'd call him as soon as his father had a lucid moment, so Robert had borrowed a cell phone and would reconnect with me as soon as he heard the news. We could reschedule quickly after one more conversation with Samir.

Robert hung up before I remembered to tell him about the akee poisoning I'd barely avoided and my decision to call Homer. I tried to call him back, but got his voice mail. I should have at least asked him for the cell-phone number.

I couldn't be so unfair as to just to leave Robert a message that I was going to risk dismantling our scheme by calling in the cops. Well, since the launching was delayed, I could afford to wait before I tracked down Homer.

The moment was inconvenient anyway. I didn't want a long talk with Homer right now. My thoughts were obsessed with finding my missing notes. Without them, my scam story could be down the drain. My only alternatives would be to postpone it until I could fill in the holes, assuming I could get my sources on the record again, or to weaken it by leaving out the most damaging of the details I'd gathered. All the hot stuff was in these sections. After all my months of work, either alternative was unacceptable.

I was too keyed up to act rationally. I tried closing my eyes and taking slow, deep breaths. I sneaked a peek at my watch every two minutes. The third time, I gave up and focused on my screen.

XXX

I'd been so dumb. If my files had been somehow deleted, they'd be in the purge files. Directory XXX on my screen. I called it up and scrolled through, my eyes racing ahead and my fingers forcing them back by scrolling backward every time I found myself skipping.

Nothing showed up. No such slugs, nothing dumped from my electronic basket.

Then the depressing thought hit me. Purged files are kept in the system for only three days. Then they are killed from the mainframe. Gone forever. It had been far longer than three days since I'd seen these slugs.

I countered with a hopeful thought. Maybe they hadn't been deleted but I'd accidentally strung my stories together or something. While I dreaded the prospect, I started calling up every story I had, one by one, scrolling through from beginning to end.

A waste of time.

I even looked through Andy Mutton's files, remembering how he'd scooped me on that bill hiking at Machiavelli. I wouldn't put it past him to tamper with my files. I skimmed every one of his stories, but none was pertinent.

One of the advantages of working for corporations these days is that most of them have computer departments where you can get technical assistance at any time. The *Examiner*'s had a bonus: The people who staff the computer desk don't ask questions, since what you need help on might involve secrets. I called Edie, my favorite of the geeks, and asked her if there was a desk I could use and a phone. I set my phone to forward calls to that number, in case Robert tried to reach me, and I headed downstairs.

On the way, Andy's empty place in the food section drew me as if fragrant brownies were baking in his desk. Nobody was around. I flipped through the file folders in his side drawers, but nothing looked familiar. I didn't know what I was looking for, just kept an open mind and wandered through his papers. Finally I opened the narrow center drawer, crammed with ballpoint pens and half-eaten food samples. Andy actually likes the garish fat-free granola bars and Olestra chips that come in the mail for food editors. He also likes cigars, I was reminded by a gummy-tipped, half-smoked cigar I found. It still had its band. Gianni's favorite.

In the computer labyrinth, Edie, with a quick stroking of her keyboard, called up all of Andy's private files once I'd invented a credible emergency to explain why I needed the information. The fact that he and I both work in food lent credence to my tale of someone accidentally transferring a story to the wrong basket.

I didn't find any evidence of my stories in his domain or among the recently purged stories, but after questioning Edie further I learned to my horror and relief that the computer department actually stores all purges for a year. The three-day disappearance is one of those carefully fostered myths, along with the privacy of our private files.

While I didn't immediately solve the problem of my missing notes, I was calmed by the assurance that if they'd been purged, they would be just as retrievable tomorrow or next week as they were the day they were deleted. Edie even promised to look for them in her spare time. Thus, when Robert called and said he was ready, I felt it was safe to leave my search for tomorrow.

I explained to Robert that I planned to tell Homer about the bug we'd found, and to my surprise he didn't protest. In fact, he said that he thought it was a good idea. Since Homer and I were friends, it would look suspicious if I avoided telling him, Robert said, though he disagreed with my reasoning that we'd be safer with the police as backup.

"You can't be any safer than confronting Gianni in his own restaurant," he explained. "Not only is it public, but no animal soils his own lair. Given that Gianni will want to keep all suspicion away from himself, Coastline is the safest place you could be. We'll just make sure that your colleagues know that you are spending the evening at Coastline."

I put in a call to Homer. I left messages on his pager and on Sherele's answering machine, telling them that I had some interesting news for Homer and that after I'd gone home to change, I'd be at Coastline.

I could imagine Gianni's face if he got a call for me at his restaurant from Homer.

Of course, I didn't tell Gianni I was coming. I wanted to, but I knew that would be out of character. So I resisted when Gianni called me as soon as I returned to my desk.

After my close call with akee poisoning, I'd been expecting him to call, and I was steeled for it. I forced my voice to sound warm and friendly, tried not to think of poisons or electronic bugs, but to congratulate him on having hired a new pastry chef—his excuse for phoning.

"This will make the work easier for Benny when he comes back," Gianni said, his voice dripping in an attempt to impersonate the Mother Teresa of the restaurant world.

After work I stopped at Chocolate Moose, the lavishly witty gift shop on the corner of Eighteenth and M Streets, and purchased the supplies I'd promised to bring for our escapade. Once home, I dressed in a low-cut black slip of a thing that Lily had insisted I buy. "No waiter will even notice your reaction to the food when you're wearing this dress," she'd observed. And she'd been right. It's nice to find at my age that I can still be distracting, and tonight I especially wanted to be.

Robert picked me up in his taxi. It hadn't escaped me that even though he declared this caper was totally safe, he wouldn't let me walk to the restaurant. It crossed my mind that Coastline's valet could plant something in the car while we were dining, and the same thought must have occurred to him. He parked at a restaurant around the corner, where he apparently knew the parking attendant.

"Chas, how nice to see you," Gianni lied as he kissed me on both cheeks. "You look magnificent. Under what name have you reserved tonight?" You've got to give the guy credit. He was as smooth as an '82 Petrus. And even though he wished me dead, his eyes lingered appreciatively on my décolletage.

"We don't have a reservation, Gianni. Tonight is Robert's birthday, and some friends have insisted on cooking him dinner. I've brought him for a drink and a pre-dinner cigar, if you don't mind." Robert drew a Havana from the pocket of his vanilla linen suit, as if to verify my story.

"A present from my father," Robert explained to Gianni.

"Excellent. My congratulations. Would you like to check your briefcase?" I declined. "Then please follow me." Gianni led us past Ottavio and showed us to the very table where we'd pilfered the rose. Perfect.

For once, I didn't care about the food, wasn't interested in the quality of the service or the wine list. I was not a critic tonight but a counterspy. How strange. What fun.

Robert and I kept up an innocuous conversation while we watched the activities around us with fresh eyes. Patterns emerged. Gianni would usher a group of VIPs to Ottavio, who then showed them to a table in the cigar room, one of those with a large green ashtray. Gianni would hang around until Ottavio returned to the desk, and they'd have a short conference. Customers who were not VIPs would be brought to the room by a hostess or a captain, not Gianni. No conference would be necessary.

Robert excused himself to go to the men's room. While Ottavio watched him go, I slipped two small boxes, one filled with Chocolate Moose treasures, from my briefcase to my purse. Robert had already had his way with them in the taxi, so they were ready to go.

Robert passed by the entrance to the cigar room as if he were headed toward the bar. He gave me a nod as he passed. I waited for a moment until Ottavio returned from seating a couple, then raised my hand and beckoned Ottavio to my table.

"Might you have a small thing, maybe a petit four, on which you could put a candle for my friend's birthday? Just a little something, for a joke?"

"I'll see what I can do." Ottavio smiled conspiratorially and hurried from the dining room.

Robert sidled in, stopping by the host's stand, as if checking the reservations book. He looked around the room to make sure nobody else was watching and slipped his hand from his pocket to underneath the stand's ledge. If any cleaning crew ever turned out to be so thorough, it would discover a wad of chewed gum stuck to the underside.

Robert was long back in place by the time Ottavio returned with a beaming smile and a small piece of cake illuminated by a sparkler. Thank goodness he didn't sing.

"Happy birthday, sir," he said, as he set it before Robert with a bow.

"How did you know?" Robert asked. That was overplaying it, since I'd announced his birthday to Gianni when we arrived. Ottavio didn't seem to notice.

The next part was going to be harder. I excused myself from Robert, heading for the ladies' room. I wedged a chair under the doorknob while I did my business, then removed the chair but prolonged my visit because I could hear someone in the hallway. I reapplied my lipstick, adjusted my pantyhose, took a few deep, slow breaths with my eyes closed, and wished as I opened the door and peeked out.

The hall was empty. I slipped farther along it to a closed door I knew to be Gianni's office and tried the handle. Unlocked. Again I looked and listened, then slipped into the room and out of it an instant later. Now, when Gianni returned to his desk, he'd find a beautifully crafted malachite box, a box too lovely to discard and just right for storing a few extra cigars to keep within reach of the phone. Wealthy customers were always currying restaurateurs' favors with such baubles.

Even if Gianni didn't keep the box on his desk indefinitely, he'd keep it around until he'd emptied it of his favorite sweets, Bissinger's chocolate-covered fresh raspberries, available in town only from Chocolate Moose and merely for a few days a year. The malachite box was Samir's brilliant idea. Since the cool stone would make it seem unnecessary to refrigerate the chocolates, Gianni would be more inclined to keep them on his desk.

"We loved our anniversary dinner," read the card on the box. No signature.

Since I'd interviewed Gianni for a story on Bissinger's chocolates last year, I and every one of my readers knew that he would savor one and only one each day until they were gone. Only Robert and I would know that the delicate-looking box would transmit every conversation from Gianni's desk directly to our tape recorder.

Completing my task undetected was such a relief that I nearly kissed Robert when I sat down next to him. Ottavio must have been wondering what I'd been doing in the ladies' room to leave me so excited.

I sat back with an enormous sigh. My next breath caught in my throat. "Oh." A wave of inspiration blew through me.

"What?"

"I never did get to tell you about my notes, the ones for my restaurant-scandal story."

Robert looked puzzled. Why would I talk about something real, much less secretive, in this wired dining room?

I gave him a wink and continued, improvising as I went.

"You know that story I've been working on for months? Well, a big chunk of my material is missing."

Robert looked concerned. "Really?" Then he caught himself and closed his mouth, leaving this scene to me.

"I don't know what happened. I just can't find them on my computer. I must have misfiled them or something. Hit the wrong button maybe." I gave him a poke to make him respond.

"How terrible."

"I was pretty upset. There was lots of juicy stuff in those files, and I was so worried about it being leaked that I threw away all the paper notes once I'd transferred the material to the computer. You know what a terrible memory I have, so with my notes gone there's no way I'd have enough for a story. I've lost my best research. About this restaurant, too."

Robert's upper lip was glistening with sweat. He must not have liked being thrown this curve ball with no warning. "About this restaurant?"

"Yes, but it's not as bad as I'd thought at first."

"What, the restaurant?"

I should have rehearsed him. But I'd only just had the idea. I plunged on. "No, losing my notes. While I was in the ladies' room, the most amazing thing happened." That would explain my giddy mood on returning to the dining room.

Robert gave me a mock leer and went along with the game. "What happened? If you aren't too embarrassed tell me."

I ignored his little joke. I was on a roll. "I suddenly remembered that I had printed out a copy of those notes. I wasn't planning to make any copies because I was afraid of them leaking out. But I made one copy. And I added some of the things I discovered about this place that I never got around to putting on the computer." I hoped I wasn't overplaying.

"No wonder you're so relieved."

"Sure am. But I feel a little stupid, too, for panicking. Could have saved myself a lot of trouble this afternoon. The funny thing is, without my losing those files, I probably would have forgotten to add the new Coastline notes that I'd put away with that single copy. And I wouldn't have found them until far too late for the story."

"Why's that?"

"I put them in Dave's desk. You know, Dave Zeeger, that investigative reporter I told you about. My ex-boyfriend, the one who's been in California all these months. I still had a key to his desk, and I figured that if anybody tried to get a peek at my notes, Dave's desk was the last place they'd look." I hoped this would make more sense to whoever was monitoring the cigar room's tapes than it did to me. In fact, I was counting on it.

23

Homer had left signs of a strenuous game of telephone tag. He'd tried to catch me at Coastline, but I was already gone. Then he'd left me a message at home. By the time Robert drove me back to my apartment after we'd really gone out to eat, it was too late to return Homer's call. I knew I could get him first thing in the morning.

Before I had a chance, even before I'd brewed my first espresso, Robert phoned me with the news. I forgot Homer for the moment. I had to get to work in a hurry.

Robert had already picked up some interesting conversations from our electronic moles. Most important to me was a phone call Gianni had made from his desk, undoubtedly after eating his first chocolate-covered raspberry.

The sequence of events played out like electronic baseball. My conversation with Robert about losing my computer files had apparently been quickly relayed from first base (microphones hidden somewhere at our table) to second base (the telephone at the host desk in the cigar room), where the news was passed to Ottavio (monitored by our chewing-gum microphone) so Ottavio could relay it to his boss. Gianni ran with it to his desk—third base—where he called some unknown person to warn that I'd stored a hard copy of my notes and some even more damaging material in Dave's desk.

Home base was Dave's desk, where I'd be watching for someone to search for that nonexistent copy. I hadn't expected our plan to come into play so quickly. Now I'd have to hurry to the office before the rest of the staff started arriving.

I slipped into my sandals, grabbed my purse, and ran down the stairs. That was the only exercise I was going to get, since I'd promised Robert I'd take taxis until I was out of danger. I jotted down two reminders to myself: (1) Call off my lunch date, assuming I didn't catch the computer thief before that, and (2) track down Homer once I did. Now I had more precise information to give Homer about Coastline's bugging operation, and in a few hours I'd probably have caught the *Examiner*'s spy as well. Samir's plan had been as smooth as dinner at Taillevent. I'd also call him to thank him.

I hadn't anticipated the *Examiner*'s saboteur acting so fast. By the time I got to the office, Dave's desk had already been rifled.

I was devastated. I ought to have allowed for the possibility. I should have come straight to the office after Coastline and stayed all night. We should have bugged Gianni's phone, even though Samir insisted that would take too much time and require an unacceptable level of risk.

We hadn't imagined Gianni would pick up my misinformation so quickly. I'd been too cocky once I realized that Andy Mutton, who always seemed to know what I was doing as soon as I did, must have been Gianni's contact at the *Examiner*. I'd made the mistake of assuming that after last night's misinformation was passed on, Andy would behave in his usually slow-moving sluga-bed manner to approach Dave's desk. Hoping for some miracle, I went over to Andy's desk, but he was gone. I hadn't really expected otherwise.

In addition to my crushing disappointment over not having caught Andy red-handed, I was scared. Now that he'd found Dave's desk empty, he and Gianni would know I was on to them, that I'd set him up.

It was time to come clean, to turn the controls over to higher authorities. First, I called Homer. I owed him a head start over the newshounds.

He wanted to know how I'd heard about the bugging devices at Coastline, but I had that handy journalists' excuse ready. I'd vowed not to reveal my sources, I said sanctimoniously. There was a lot more I didn't tell him, not even about the destruction of my computer files.

Homer didn't suffer from the deprivation. Apparently my information and the accumulated results of his two murder investigations would be enough for him to get a search warrant for Coastline. We didn't talk about the FBI, but given the excitement in his voice, I figured he was going to skirt that issue with quick action. He was so grateful for my information that it was easy to get him to promise to keep me informed every step of the way. I told him I was writing the story, which was wishful thinking on my part.

Next I went to Bull, but I stopped by to fill in Helen first. Falling right in with my plan, she accompanied me to Bull's office. I'd get further as part of a team than as a loner. Just as I'd hoped, Bull was so outraged by having his newsroom infiltrated that he left aside the question of Coastline's bugging for the moment. That gave me time to soften him up before he assigned that story, so that maybe I could at least share it—equally—with Dawn, if not keep the whole thing for myself.

Like any newspaper editor, Bull didn't want the police to have access to his domain. Thus he wanted to find the culprit himself.

He looked as if he were tearing after a matador as he lumbered at top speed across the newsroom. Jaws dropped. Reporters at the farther reaches stood up to see what was happening. Andy wasn't among them.

When he reached Dave's bent and scratched desk drawer, Bull bellowed a string of words we'd never print in the paper. He picked up the phone and dialed the switchboard operator, demanding she call the night guard at home and summon him to show up in his office in an hour. Then Bull pulled from his pocket a small box he'd brought from his bottom drawer. To my astonishment, it was a fingerprinting kit. He proceeded, in front of the entire newsroom, to brush the desk and its drawers with gray powder.

Nothing. Dave had been away for so long that the

office cleaners had eventually erased all traces of him, and last night's thief had been smart enough to wear gloves.

An hour later, the sleepy, ashen-faced night guard was standing in Bull's office wringing his hands. Other than the usual night cleaning crew, only one person had entered the building, as far as he knew. But that was the extent of his intelligence on the subject. He couldn't identify the person. He didn't even know whether it was a man or woman. He'd dropped his glasses when the person had entered, and without them he couldn't see more than to register the motion of someone walking to the desk and holding up something that he assumed was an *Examiner* ID.

My guess was that this misery-drenched guard had taken his glasses off for a snooze and was caught asleep by the invader. I'd seen him asleep myself when I'd stopped by the office at night, and he was slow to shake himself awake and reach for his glasses. Maybe the culprit even knocked them to the floor before the guard awoke. All he had to do before leaving was wait out of sight until the guard fell back asleep.

Bull was full of bluster and noisy outrage. He would be satisfied with a quick and easy show to inspire fear in his troops. Finding and punishing the culprit would require too great a commitment of resources. Scaring him would be enough for Bull. I grew quietly full of determination. I wasn't going to let this computer thief off the hook.

My priorities shifted. Thus, when Bull proposed that Dawn work the Coastline story and that I back her up, I didn't even protest. He reminded me that I'd need time to fill in the notes I'd lost from the computer. I nodded in agreement, but planned to set that task aside for the moment. I had my own investigation to pursue.

With my phone set to forward calls to the computer center, I returned to my friend Edie and her amazing keystrokes. This time her cooperation had a price, but I didn't mind. I'd have been glad to give her sister a list of restaurants I thought might need a pastry assistant even if Edie hadn't been setting aside a pile of work to help me, especially since she volunteered that she knew it would be unethical for her sister to use my name when she applied.

I'd been thinking through when I'd last seen my lost notes, and had determined that they had to have been purged within the past eight days. Edie showed me the printouts—stacks of them—that record the stories that had been killed, and left me to examine them on my own. I started scanning the lists for the slugs I'd given my notes, then backtracked. Andy wouldn't have been so dumb as to keep the same name on the files. So I looked for anything that related to food. I wanted to scream in frustration when I realized that most of the entries didn't have names at all, just numbers.

I tried scanning the "last action" column for Andy's name, but after running through a few of the closely printed pages, I realized my mind was switching off and my eyes were skipping entries. I started again and ran my finger down the columns as I went. That seemed more reliable.

By the time I finished my first run-through of eight days, tiny black splotches were congregating in front of my eyes. But I had some possibilities. I took my list of stories spiked by Andy and handed their numbers to Edie. She called them up from the storage tapes while I tapped my foot in an impatient rhythm.

What we found was interesting: In addition to notes for three food stories that had already run, Andy had trashed a long and exceedingly inept pornographic poem. It wasn't what I wanted to catch Andy with today, though.

Back to the beginning. I returned to the printouts, hoping they'd inspire a new approach. They didn't tell much, just the date and time purged, originating desk, number of lines in the story, and a name under "last action." I shuffled through pages, trying to free my mind to come up with a new method of attack.

The number of lines. That could help. Most stories were short, ten to twenty-five inches—under two hundred lines. Mine would have been almost twice as long. I started through the lists again, noting the numbers and names associated with all stories over two hundred lines.

My list was growing depressingly long. I didn't feel I could enlist Edie to search through so many stories. About halfway through the printouts, though, I came across my own name. What story had I killed that day? I couldn't remember. I jotted it down, just to satisfy my curiosity. The next day's list showed a bigger surprise. Four purges with my name. I knew I hadn't spiked four stories in one day.

I felt that heart-racing sureness that I'd hit pay dirt, even though I didn't understand why these stories would have my name as "last action" if someone else had killed them. I'd figure out the details later.

Edie was getting up from her chair with a notepad and pencil in hand, so I hurried to stop her. "I found it. I think I know now what I need you to look up." I put my hand on her arm, which made her jump.

"Got a meeting, Chas. I'll call these up for you when I get back. It shouldn't be more than an hour."

I looked around the computer center. Everyone else had gone to lunch or to the meeting except for one assistant left to monitor the phones. He wouldn't be able to help me. I couldn't stand waiting an hour. I'd explode.

"Just five minutes. This will be quick. I've got to have this before lunch," I exaggerated. Well, lied.

Edie looked over to her boss, who'd stopped at the conference room door to survey his realm. "I'll be about five minutes longer," she called to him. "You won't need me for the first part anyway."

He nodded. I wanted to hug Edie for the confident way she deals with her boss, not to mention her compassion for us always-frantic reporters.

"Five minutes," she warned me, and sat down at her computer. "What have you got?"

I handed her the list of the stories with my name on them. She ran through her mumbo jumbo of keystrokes and we waited while the computer loaded the tape from that day. I tapped my feet; Edie kept looking at her watch. The first story showed up on her screen. An old Table Matters column I'd cleaned out of the system. I shook my head. She keyed in the second number.

"Not found," the computer declared.

She checked the list and realized that in her haste she'd mistyped the number. She tried again. Another typo. We were both too nervous. I read the number to her aloud as she typed it the third time, and checked that it was right.

The computer froze.

"Damn. Let's try another computer. This one's been acting up lately."

We moved to another desk, and Edie signed off for its absent occupant, then signed on in her own name. Reacting to the tension, she slowed down to a super-calm state, as computer people learn to do, while I felt my pulse racing and my heart pounding. I was breathing like a swimmer after a race.

"Read me the first number."

I did. I tried to tame my breathing. I silently counted the seconds—extra slowly.

Bingo. A section of my notes came to life on the screen. I didn't understand why it was only a section and began to panic that maybe the thief had somehow erased the rest without it going through the purge process.

"Is this what you wanted?"

"Almost. Can you do a history on it?"

Edie hit some keys and called up all the actions on this story. It showed nothing, not even my editing. It must have been a copy, an abortive copy.

"Try the next one. Please."

Edie's boss was waving to her from the door of the conference room. She held up five fingers.

"You're going to cost me my job, Chas," she said, but it sounded like a perfunctory complaint, and she was already typing in the next number.

More of the same.

I was obviously barking up the wrong tree.

"Why do these have my name under last action,

when I wasn't the one who killed them?" I asked Edie as we waited for the next number to load. The process was slow because it was on a different tape.

"Last action doesn't refer to who spiked the story, but to the last person who edited it," Edie explained.

I'd gotten it all wrong. No wonder I hadn't found Andy's name with the stories I was seeking. My throat constricted. The next two numbers were going to be my last chance.

Edie was maddeningly calm. I silently urged her to speed up her pace while she stopped to adjust her chair, then rolled her shoulders and neck to loosen them. Mine were screaming with tension.

The computer churned endlessly. I was sure it had frozen. Even Edie started drumming the fingers of her left hand on the edge of the keyboard.

The number appeared. Edie typed in the code to bring up the story it represented. There it was.

My notes. One complete file of them. One of the two missing pieces. The smoking gun.

"Do a history." My voice was hoarse, nearly a whisper.

"That's it, huh?"

"That's it. The first half, anyway."

Edie tapped out the instructions for the computer to show every action that had been taken on this story and who had taken it.

```
ORIGINATED: Wheatley
EDITED: Wheatley
EDITED: Wheatley
FILMED:
```

Filmed—that meant it was printed out.

It wasn't "Mutton." Andy hadn't been the one to leak and trash my notes. It was Dawn.

"The bitch."

Edie looked alarmed. "Chas, what are you really up to here?" She searched my face and didn't like what she saw. "I think I'm getting in over my head. Perhaps you should talk to my boss before I go any further."

I wanted to handle this alone. Immediately. I didn't want it to get lost in a labyrinth of proper procedures, territorial rights, and union grandstanding.

"Look, Edie, you've already gone this far. I just need one more step. I need the next story. Then I'll have all my notes back. I won't bring your name into this, at least not unless I've filled you in on the whole story and you give me permission. Please, I can't bear to lose all these notes."

"Just one more." She restored this purged story to my directory and called up that last number. Predictably, it was my second set of notes, and once again the history pointed to Dawn as having printed it just a few minutes before it was spiked.

I was thanking Edie's back as she hurried off to her meeting. I danced my way upstairs to retrieve the untrashed files on my computer. Before I did anything else, I made two printouts of each, then transferred the files to my private—almost private, as I now thought of it—directory.

24

I postponed Robert. I set aside Homer. I didn't even consider Bull. The one person I wanted to talk to immediately was Dave. He had as much reason to mistrust Dawn as I did, since she'd once broken up our relationship with tales of having slept with him. On the surface, we'd made up—each combination of us—and I was no longer jealous of her. But I was still wary, and Dave had grown jealous of her for additional reasons.

She kept stealing his thunder. Whatever story he was pursuing, she'd come in with it faster and better. He'd been the *Examiner*'s king among investigative reporters, and she'd knocked him from his throne. Thus, while she hadn't parted Dave and me by seduction, she'd ultimately played a role in our breakup by outshining him professionally, leaving him depressed and distant. He took the assignment in California in hopes that a change of scene and a new challenge would restore his competence.

Dave, even more than I, was stunned that any reporter would steal a colleague's notes. He took particular offense that it was an investigative reporter, who above all knew how hard-won such details can be.

He, too, realized that Andy Mutton would have been a less infuriating culprit, since he's such a sloppy excuse for a journalist that he'd steal my notes as casually as he'd appropriate a box of chocolates addressed to me. But Dawn, for all her faults, was a nationally recognized reporter at the height of her profession. A Green Beret of a journalist. For her to be destroying a colleague's work like this was unthinkable, and for her to be trading secrets with Gianni was criminal.

Dave agreed that since Bull and Helen's offices were empty at the moment, I ought to try to quickly track down Dawn on my own. His guess was that she'd have disappeared by now, but in case she hadn't, every minute would count. He had some ideas about where to find her and volunteered to also try.

He added, "Tell Homer, too. But only Homer. If he's not there, don't tell anyone else in his office why you want to speak to him." I was way ahead of him on that.

Five minutes after I hung up, Dave called me back. "Chas." He paused.

"What's wrong?"

"That's how she trounced me. It wasn't that she was a better reporter than I am or that I've gotten too slow. She had an inside track. She was part of the action, and I was being cut out of it. She was given the benefit of this spy network, as long as she kept them out of the news. Oh, God, Chas. It was right under my own nose. We all should have known she was too good to be true."

I listened for a while and felt my heart wrench along with Dave's. He railed at Dawn, at Bull for believing in Dawn, at himself for not unmasking her. And himself again for making me pay for his misery.

"Chas, I want you back. I'll show you that I'm ready to have you back and treat you the way you deserve."

We'd see. Part of me felt like springtime and apple blossoms, but there were corners of my mind worrying that his apology was too facile; and even more, tomorrow he might resent that it was I, not he, who'd unmasked Dawn. Dave was professing a great leap forward; I'd feel more trusting of steady small steps.

As Dave had predicted, Dawn was nowhere to be found. She hadn't been in to the *Examiner* today, though she'd been expected to turn in a story. Nobody answered her home phone. Dave, too, came up blank.

He also crash-landed from his great leap back into my good graces.

"Guess you won't be working with Dawn on this story after all," Dave joked, but it sounded rehearsed, strained.

"Nope, just me and my computer, writing it all alone," I said, the thought of it making my chest thump in excitement.

"I doubt that."

"What do you mean?"

"You know Bull won't allow his restaurant critic to have the sole byline on the biggest political scandal to hit Washington since Watergate. This is Pulitzer material. He'll need a brand name, a recognized investigative reporter."

"Like you," I said through gritted teeth, belatedly seeing the point.

"Like me," he agreed. "With your help, of course."

I didn't waste a minute. I took the evidence of Dawn's destroying my files to Bull as soon as he returned to his office. Then I told him I was at work on the Coastline spying story, which was connected with Dawn in a way that I'd soon pin down for him. He muttered noncommittally and began to shoo me out so he could set his bloodhounds in search of Dawn.

I stopped at the door and said, "By the way, I've got to call Homer Jones and tell him about Dawn."

"You'll do no such thing, Wheatley. This is an internal problem, not a police problem, and should be handled within the newspaper."

I couldn't yet tell Bull everything I knew about Dawn's connection with Coastline's eavesdropping operation, but I argued that it was our civic duty to tell the police in case they could use the information in their own investigation. Bull didn't budge. I stormed out of his office.

I was about to dial Robert's number when my phone rang. It was Dave, who hadn't seemed to notice my chilly reaction to his last call.

"How'd it go with Bull?"

"I told him about Dawn. He reacted about as you'd expect."

"That's a pretty terse report. Is something wrong?"

"What more would you expect an assistant to report?"

He paused. "I get it. I wondered if I was being an asshole about this."

"Wonder no more."

"I apologize, Chas, I really do. I was so carried away with getting revenge on Dawn that I stepped way out of bounds. Forgive me. Please."

I'm a fool for a "please."

I set aside my hurt for the moment and told him about Bull's refusal to let me call Homer. "I feel terrible holding out on Homer this way. He'll find out, and he'll know I kept it from him."

"I know how to get to Bull," Dave promised. "I'll call you back soon."

I've always understood that half of the secret of being a successful investigative reporter is being able to manipulate your editors for your own journalistic ends. Figuring out how to do it is another matter. I still had a lot to learn from Dave.

Bull called me into his office a bare ten minutes later.

His bloodhounds had come up empty-handed. Dawn's car was still in its garage, her mail was still in its box, and none of her colleagues' leads panned out.

"Wheatley, I think you ought to take this thing with Dawn and quietly pass it on to your policeman friend. It might be even better coming from Sherele; but since she's not available, I'm asking you to do it. Do you mind? I don't want to sit on this too long.

"And before I forget, of course now that Dawn is

gone, you're going to have to take charge of the Coastline story. I already know you're busy with your column and all, so I don't want to hear it. You can squeeze it in. Skip lunch."

That would show Dave what Bull thought of restaurant critics.

"What did you do to get Bull to relent about Homer? You brainwash the guy?" I called Dave as soon as I got back to my desk. I knew that the best way to get Bull to act on your idea was to make him think it had been his idea, but I marveled that Dave could get him reversed so quickly.

"I used my magic words: *New York Observer.* I told him that if Dawn's antics were leaked to the *Observer*, as they were bound to be by somebody in our newsroom, that pink sheet would make us look like fools. But if the situation became known through official channels and appeared to be linked to a major story such as this Coastline investigation is going to be, the *Observer* would try to tell 'the story behind the story' and make the police look like the fools and us the heroes."

"Very clever. How did you convince Bull that somebody here would leak the story?"

"That was easy. You know how Bull's always desperate for the *Examiner* to be making news. If nobody else leaked it soon enough, Bull himself would. The crucial question was how the *Observer*—and everybody who copied it from there—would play it."

I resisted crowing to Dave about Bull assigning me the story. Dave had, after all, saved my relationship with Homer.

* * *

I reached Homer on his cell phone on the first try. He was at Coastline with the search warrant, so he was in no position to talk. I quickly outlined my discoveries about Dawn and said I had some reason to think her theft was linked to Gianni.

A few minutes later Homer called me back from a more private location and thanked me for my tip. He now could link Dawn to the spy network and had just launched a search for her, extending to the airports, bus terminals, and Union Station.

Things were happening fast, he said, so he needed to cut our conversation short. He'd have plenty of new details for me by the end of the day, he promised, though probably not enough for more than a sketchy story for tomorrow's newspaper.

I didn't tell him I already had more information than I needed for my story, thanks to Robert's and my counterspying escapade. That was still my secret, probably forever. Now that Homer was tipping me off before he called any other reporters and feeding me as many exclusives as he dared, I could pretend that all my information was coming from him.

I had my story pretty much written by the time Homer called me back at the end of the afternoon. I wasn't surprised to hear that most of the bugs were gone before the police arrived. As Samir had predicted, the cigar room had been swept clean of those that Gianni had planted. Thus Samir's plan turned out to have been vital.

What's more, it had worked brilliantly. The bugs Homer and his police force had uncovered were three: one embedded in chewing gum on the underside of the host's stand, another in the men's room, and the third in a malachite candy box on Gianni's desk. I'd counted on Homer's lust for sweets; he'd never be able to resist sampling those chocolate-covered raspberries. Then he'd have to justify his weakness by pretending to thoroughly examine the box. And as I'd expected, he was smart enough to pick up the faint clues that something was amiss with the box.

I was relieved that one of the policewomen had thought to examine the trash can in the ladies' room, where, under the plastic bag, was a tape recorder tuned in to those three microphones.

"We didn't get much off the tape, but enough to put our case in good shape. I also wanted you to know that one of the calls was to someone—obviously Dawn—who was told that you had a copy of your notes hidden in Dave Zeeger's desk. That ties in neatly with your discovery of Dawn's destroying your computer files, doesn't it? Amazing how handily this has all come together."

"Just amazing," I agreed.

"This is off the record, Chas, but do you know what I found on Marchelli's desk? Those classy chocolate-covered raspberries you wrote about last year. The guy sure knew how to live the good life." I didn't embarrass him by asking how he knew there were raspberries inside those chocolates.

"What would it take for you to link this spying operation to Denise's murder?" I graciously changed the subject. "I assume that's where you're hoping to go on this."

"You can't make wine in a day."

I'd put Homer on the defensive. A mistake. He

closed down and became a cop again. A cop under pressure. "I gotta go, Chas. I want to thank you again for all the help you've been. We'll talk again soon."

Before Homer hung up, I made him promise to call me with any new information. But his mind was clearly elsewhere, and all I got was an absentminded, "You know I will, sweetie."

I could have stayed around and moped, waiting for Homer to call with more news, but playing a passive role would drive me crazy. I had a better plan.

For tomorrow's paper, I wrote as much of the story as I officially had. When it was ready to file, I walked into Bull's office to tell him. He had his back to me and was pressing buttons on his speaker phone, cleaning up his voice mail messages. I leaned on the door jamb to listen; it was a rare chance for some insight into what Bull's job is like.

The third call caught me in the throat. It was Dave's voice.

"It's been a while since I've had the opportunity to call you a big shit, Bull, and it feels good. I agree with you, of course, that I could milk the best out of this Coastline story, but experience isn't everything. Chas uncovered the scandal and found the evidence against Dawn. Being inexperienced didn't stop her. In fact, it probably freed her to think creatively. She deserves the story. She's proved she's a capable investigator. You already know she's a great writer, and nobody at the paper, me included, has more credibility with our readers. Furthermore, if you don't give her this story, you might find her looking for a job at the *Post*, and I'd cheer her on."

"The *Post* already has a restaurant critic," Bull said, without turning around.

By the time I'd finished working over my story with the copy editors, I was ready for a celebration. I knew just where I wanted it, too.

Before I left the *Examiner*, I called Homer's office. Some growling voice told me he was too busy to come to the phone and would be occupied for some time. That was exactly what I'd hoped to hear. I didn't leave a message.

I was hungry, which meant Homer would be starving. I hurried down Seventh Street to the heart of Washington's Chinatown. It's a measly two blocks long, but if you know your way around, you can find some dishes worthy of San Francisco or New York. First, I stopped at Eat First—forget the pun. Small banners on the wall showed what I was seeking: rice-paper-wrapped chicken and shrimp-stuffed eggplant with black beans. The sablefish with ginger and scallions was tempting, but its sauce has a tendency to congeal if it's not eaten piping hot.

A couple doors away is the Golden Palace, which serves its dim sum all day and into the evening. I picked up baked pork buns and custard tarts for dessert. I detoured to Sixth Street because the kitchen at Burma tends to be slow. I put in an order for tea salad and fried tofu salad, then left to finish my shopping while they were being prepared. At Full Kee, I could watch the shrimp dumplings being boiled for my soup, since the huge woks are in the window. I made sure my package was double bagged to hold the heat.

I stood in the quiet darkness on H Street while I reviewed my menu and struggled over whether I should add a few flaky sesame rolls from Tony Cheng's Mongolian Barbecue or even a brisket sandwich and collard greens from Capital Q Texas Barbecue. No, that would be overkill. Or more to the point, my paper-bag feast might be too bulky for me to carry. I fetched the salads from Burma and headed for Homer's office.

My timing couldn't have been better. Homer was just returning from what the receptionist euphemistically called "an interview."

When he caught sight of me, he gave me a discreet hand signal to stay put, then turned away without a pause as he continued talking to his colleagues. They were thumping each other on the back, high-fiving, cuffing each other's jaws, all that tamed roughhousing that passes for affection among men. The others got in the elevator, but Homer stayed behind as if he'd forgotten something. "I'll catch up with you guys," he said, as the doors closed.

He walked over to the receptionist, who pointed to me with an apologetic shrug.

"Can I help you?" Homer asked me. I knew him well enough to realize that he didn't want anyone to guess he was talking to the press. Since my beat is restaurants, my face is unfamiliar to the homicide department. I played along, telling him I had a problem I hoped he could solve.

"Let's discuss this in my office," Homer said, loudly enough for the receptionist to hear. He ushered me down the hall.

When he closed the door, Homer was all smiles. "Do I smell shrimp?"

"Chinatown's best."

"Great idea. I'm starving. I could eat a bear."

"No bear today. Just Eat First's paper-wrapped chicken and stuffed eggplant. A couple of dim sum. Burmese salads."

"Enough. Enough. I'll tell you anything you want to know."

"Anything?" I asked, as I started unwrapping the soup.

"Anything I'm authorized to tell."

"In that case . . ." I said, lifting the plastic container of soup to show it off, then putting it back in the bag.

"Is that shrimp dumpling soup?"

I nodded.

"Anything at all."

I unwrapped the soup again as Homer made a quick call to a nearby bar to tell his colleagues he was going to be longer than he'd expected. He'd catch up with them in a while.

Then he pulled a tablecloth from his bottom drawer and draped it over his desk—papers, telephone, and all. I set out the bowls, spoons, and plates I'd cadged from my office cafeteria.

I let Homer dig into the soup and polish off a baked pork bun before I started grilling him. He wasn't hard to grill. In fact, he was bursting for a chance to boast.

"I've got it. The links, the details, the whole thing. I shouldn't be telling you all this, but we've got everything we need. Enough to convict Gianni of Denise's murder and more. We've even found another connection to the *Examiner*."

"Besides Dawn?" That stopped my spoon in midair.

"Yep. It's a minor part of the operation, as far as I can tell, but Gianni had a habit of passing on information to journalists he found useful, especially if it was something that might hurt his competitors. He had a small but steady relationship with that food guy. What's his name? Lamb?"

"Andy Mutton?"

"That's it." Homer was unwrapping spice-drenched rice-paper chicken from its foil envelope.

I should have known Andy couldn't have scooped me on the prosciutto scam without help.

I paused with a forkful of floppy lemony tea leaves, stunned that Homer had pinned down so much so quickly. "How did you get all that?"

"Ottavio sang. I hardly had to work at it. He was so angry with Gianni that he was begging us to take his statement."

I could barely hold back my laugh. I should have known.

Homer was wound up. He didn't wait for me to respond. "Ottavio somehow thought that Gianni had cheated him. It was that bug under the host's desk. Apparently he didn't know about that one and figured Gianni was using it to spy on him." He broke off for a mouthful of stuffed eggplant.

"You don't say." I couldn't wait to tell Robert and Samir.

"I guess they were both conning each other. Gianni apparently didn't know about the bug in his candy box and considers Ottavio a traitor. So he's willing to rat on his maître d'. But Ottavio has better cards in this case. He's afraid of being swept up in a murder charge, so he's making sure we have enough evidence to convict Gianni alone."

I heard something in Homer's voice that alerted me, so I took a flyer. "Homer, I don't want to join in the blackmailing, but please don't forget who put you onto Gianni. What are you holding back from me?"

"I don't know how much I dare to tell you, Chas. This is high-level stuff. You're right; there is more. A lot more. Just cover my tracks on it, please, or you're going to have to be my soup kitchen when I get fired, too." He tilted his bowl to spoon up the last drops of broth.

"You know I'm a master at covering tracks." Actually, he didn't know the half of it.

"Okay, here's the real story. If Ottavio can be believed–and he says he has access to more tapes to back him up–he's going to bring down a lot of other people along the way. The guy's claiming Gianni was responsible for leading Kenneth Starr to Monica Lewinsky, for the deep dirt in the Sinatra bio, and for enough insider-trading information to account for at least two stock-market corrections. He knew the Indians were going to test the bomb before the CIA did–which doesn't sound all that hard. And apparently he sold information that proved very useful in several elections. The Justice Department, the Federal Reserve, a good chunk of Congress–they've all spilled the beans at Coastline. He said Gianni's greatest frustration was that the

Israelis weren't cigar smokers. But he claims that Hillary was, and even Chelsea."

"Before they heard about Monica, you mean."

Homer laughed and popped a flaky little custard tart into his mouth.

His meal was over. Every carton was empty. He started to gather the debris from his desk, examining each container to make sure nothing was left. He looked deflated.

It wasn't the empty cartons that were a letdown. "It's unbelievable how far and wide this corruption extended. I finally understand," he said mournfully, "why the Redskins have had such lousy seasons."

I've never been so eager to get back to my desk. I couldn't wait to get started typing. From a pay phone on the street, I called Bull at home, and he met me at the office with two other editors in tow. They tore up the front page and hovered over me while I typed and deleted and retyped long into the night. It was the first time I'd ever had a chance to stop the presses.

Within a week Gianni was in jail and Benny was out. My stories on Coastline's spy ring had my phone ringing constantly. At the *Examiner*, colleagues who before had only asked me what new restaurants I'd recommend were stopping by my desk to exchange political gossip. It was hard to get any work done.

As soon as the Coastline news dwindled, I had to work nonstop on my restaurant-scam story. My nationwide column was due to be launched in a week. I stopped answering my phone and let my voice mail and e-mail boxes fill until electronic scoldings at every turn were warning me of overflows.

I didn't care. I had work to do. More than ever before in my life.

The day my column appeared, I abandoned the office and took a long walk to celebrate the coming of fall. I followed the bike path past Reagan National Airport, as it is now called, along the Potomac to Alexandria, stopping at a picnic table along the way and watching sailboats tack across the river past the Jefferson Memorial and Washington Monument. The city never looked more peaceful, cleaner, more wholesome. I imagined having swept a corner of it, day after day throughout the summer until my small section gleamed.

Helen and Sherele had decided to throw a party in honor of my new syndication and my Coastline series, but I didn't want anything official. They conceded to something small and informal, but were taken aback when I insisted on having it in a nursing home. I couldn't celebrate without Samir attending, and I couldn't be sure he'd be in shape to attend if it were elsewhere.

While Helen and Sherele cooked up the party, Benny did the cooking for it. The nursing home kitchen staff welcomed him reluctantly, but by the end of the evening begged him to return to give lessons on his white bean bruschetta, his snow pea salad, and his clam-and-spinach lasagna. When the cooks raved about the toasted-coconut cake, though, Benny asked me to bring Helen to the kitchen. She'd made the cake. She knew it was my favorite.

In the dining room, wheelchairs and walkers glided and swayed to the music. Nobody waited for partners once the dancing got going. Even Bull lumbered into the clearing that served as a dance floor and gallumped in a vaguely rhythmic way. Though Homer had arrived after the introductions and well into dinner, he managed to eat his share, then worked off quite a few chocolate-covered raspberries twirling and dipping Sherele. I missed Dave sorely.

The octogenarian deejay needed more breaks than most. In one of those quiet moments, I noticed Lily flirting with Robert. She'd had an argument with Brian and come to the party alone, but I hoped they'd make up soon. I'd hate to have to share ex-boyfriends with my daughter. I wandered over to Homer, who was alone at a corner of the buffet table, spooning up the last bits of the corn and country ham timbales.

"You did a great job as an investigative reporter."

"Thanks. I think I'll be glad get back to the more delicious side of life. Enough of serial killers."

"Well, Gianni doesn't exactly make it as a serial killer. Just two murders."

"And a suicide he caused."

I noticed Samir heading his wheelchair our way. I guessed he was positioning himself for a little eavesdropping, and I was glad to assist him.

"You don't often unravel three deaths so easily, do you?" I hoped my question didn't sound lame.

But Homer is a talker. And he loves to go on about his work, the few chances he gets. "Once Ottavio saw that cooperating could save him from a murder charge, it was just a matter of sitting back and prompting him with a question now and then."

"First, he told you about Denise's murder, as I recall."

"That's right, the one that Benny'd taken a fall for. I feel bad about the guy spending that time in jail when he was telling the truth from the beginning."

"You mean about not hitting Denise."

"Apparently Gianni made that up. Benny and Denise's argument was a lucky break for Gianni. Remember, Benny said that Denise was tense and irritable that night, and that's why they argued. She'd found one of Gianni's bugs when she was stealing some of his cigars and took the opportunity to try to extort some money out of Gianni."

"She was naive. She didn't guess how dangerous he could be, right?" As I said this, Samir edged his wheelchair forward to hear better and bumped Homer's leg. When Homer turned around, Samir set his face in a vacant stare and dropped his head to a limp angle. He let his mouth hang open.

"Excuse me," Homer said, and patted Samir on the shoulder. He turned back to me and continued as if Samir weren't there. "He'd already murdered once—that we know. That other Ottavio guy. It seems that Gianni's contacts had sent him a new cigar room manager named Ottavio Rossi, but he had a little accident on the way and showed up a few days late. In the meantime, in a coincidence that cost him his life, this other Ottavio Rossi applied for the job and was hired by mistake. When the real Rossi showed up, Gianni realized he'd made a terrible error and the wrong Rossi had seen too much."

"Nabbed him right off the street in broad daylight,

huh?" I forgot I wasn't supposed to know that. I hadn't told Homer about the other coincidence, that I'd met the murdered Ottavio right before he was snatched.

"Nobody knows," Homer said, not registering my error. "Probably done by a hit man."

"But Gianni didn't hire a hit man for Denise."

"No, that was apparently in the heat of the moment. Denise enraged him; he says he didn't even mean to hurt her. But once she was dead, he saw the opportunity to place the blame on Benny. He'd stabbed her with one of Benny's knives, and he made sure to leave a broken piece inside her."

"And then there was the suicide."

"We'll never know exactly what happened there, but we're sure Gianni was blackmailing that Jamaican."

Homer reached across the buffet table, having noticed a piece of coconut cake hidden behind a water pitcher. While his attention was diverted, I gave Samir a thumbs-up and a wink. He flashed me a bright, intelligent smile before he let his face go slack again.

"This is fabulous cake, isn't it?" Homer began talking between bites. I nodded. "There are still a few pieces I haven't quite fit together, but every case has those. The placement of the bugs was surprisingly amateurish for such a slick operation. With all that expensive acoustical tile lining the walls, I'd have thought there would be microphones at every table. And while I understand the reason for one in the men's room, I was amazed that Gianni bugged his own desk."

Samir was giving me a wink behind Homer's back.

"Did you ask Ottavio about any of this?"

"Didn't get much on this from him. He did

say that they'd put bugs in some fancy heavy ashtrays, but people tended to steal the ashtrays. Tried putting them in flowers, but people took the flowers."

"Hard to imagine," I murmured.

"Gianni had an interesting defense at first. He blubbered that he didn't know why we were so worked up about a few microphones. Everybody does it, he insisted. Even Daniel, that great restaurant in New York, is said to have video cameras trained on every spot in its dining room."

"Did you point out that Daniel does it to observe the service, not to record and spy on its patrons?"

"I wonder."

Lights were flashing and the deejay was playing "Goodnight, Irene." It was bedtime for the nursing home. I turned to Samir and swiveled his chair to make him obviously part of our conversation.

"Homer, I'd like you to meet a friend of mine, Samir Said."

Homer reached out to shake Samir's hand, then did a double-take. "Excuse me, what was that name again?"

"Samir Said," Samir said, as he gave Homer a firm handshake.

"I know your reputation. Very impressive. It's an honor to meet you."

Samir nodded his head with all the eloquence of a bow.

We said good night and walked toward the door, where Sherele, Lily, and Helen had gathered.

"I heard he was an amazing guy in the old days," Homer said. "Too bad his mind is gone."

25

Dave was standing right at the gate, leaning against a wall with his arms crossed, examining each passenger as if memorizing faces for a test. So I had a minute to take him in before his eyes rested on me. Tall—over six feet—and loose limbed, he looked as if he was barely resting his thin frame against anything. That lanky nut-brown hair shaded his eyes so that he could observe discreetly. Dave looked as soft and crumpled as linen in the tropics, but I knew he had the resilience of Gore-Tex. Seeing him made my fingers and toes tingle. Yet our kiss felt awkward

At the end of the nursing home party Helen had told me she didn't want to see me for a week. I needed a break, she'd decided. Not necessarily a vacation, but at least a change of scene. The *Examiner* was sending me anyplace I wanted to go to review a restaurant for my next column—which was two weeks off, since my scam story was running in two parts.

I was toying with London or Paris, or maybe even

Beijing, when Dave called. By the time we hung up, I was packing for San Francisco.

"I'll take care of staking out a restaurant for the first night. I've got just the thing in mind. I promise, it'll be somewhere you've never been and that will make a great column. And if you don't like it, you'll have time to find one on your own the next night."

He didn't have to try so hard. I really didn't want to go to Paris alone anyway. I'd much rather try to patch up our relationship, even if it meant dining on Dave's idea of memorable pizza (he'd probably found a Berkeley branch of Maryland's Ledo pizzerias).

Dave tasted different to my lips. His shoulder seemed bonier to my hands. I looked at his face and was surprised at the details I'd forgotten. He was looking at me a little warily, too. We'd have a lot of reacquainting to do.

"I hope you don't mind after all that flying, but I've planned a rather long drive for dinner."

"Whatever you say. I'm in your hands, at least for this meal."

The trip turned out to be a good idea after all. Being in the car meant that we weren't diverted by my looking over his apartment or unpacking. We had only each other, against a background of endless crowded and ugly highway.

It was an awfully long way to go for a pizza. Sacramento?

With each ten miles, though, we drew closer to our old camaraderie. The day began to grow dark, and I forgot about the road altogether, just reveled in laughing with Dave, railing at Bull and Dawn and all our common nemeses, filling him in on everyday gossip.

I had no idea where we were going and no longer cared. But when we stopped on a small residential street, I was surprised. Were we going to somebody's house for dinner?

Dave went to the trunk and handed me a box. Inside was a gorgeous pair of the flimsy spike-heeled footwear Sherele and I always referred to as "fuck-me shoes." I batted my eyes, licked my lips, and affected a whispery Marilyn Monroe "Thanks," as I slipped them on. Dave also pulled from the trunk a nubby linen jacket I'd never seen, a beige that exactly matched his hair.

Jacket and tie, and high heels for pizza? Pretty funky.

"Welcome to The French Laundry," said an equally beige-and-linen-clad maître d' as we stepped into the garden of a two-story stone house, roses and roasting meats perfuming the air.

"How did you ever get a last-minute reservation here?" I turned to Dave in amazement. This small Napa Valley restaurant is often called the best in the country, and even two months ahead it's as hard to book a table as it is to get into Stanford.

"Another trick of the investigative-reporting trade. I'll teach it to you sometime."

I was so excited that my mouth went dry and my palms began to sweat. This was the restaurant I'd most wanted to try in the entire country, but I hadn't even considered it possible for my impromptu trip. The garden was more beautiful than I'd supposed, lit only by fat, white candles in hurricane lamps. The small trees between the tables weren't trees at all, but rosebushes in a myriad of colors repeated in the flowered skirts that draped the tables.

Dave didn't look uncomfortable when the sommelier handed him the wine list with such reverence it might have been the family Bible. He didn't flinch when the waiter described a five-course menu, then a ten-course tasting menu.

"We want to try it all," he said to the waiter, while I sat openmouthed. Dave hated French food. He insisted he was allergic to it, that it made him sick. And his idea of dinner was one course, preferably on the coffee table in front of his television set.

The very first dish gave me an excited shiver. Tiny cones were presented, filled not with ice cream but with tuna tartare. Simply the best tuna tartare I'd ever tasted.

"Let's make a meal of these. Order a dozen more," suggested Dave. I'd have gone along with that.

But then came something equally delicious, a demitasse of soup that tasted like lobster froth. The next dish left all the others in the dust. "Oysters and Pearls" was a tiny portion of pearl tapioca, lemony rather than sweet, topped with lightly poached Malpeque oysters and more pearls: Sevruga caviar.

This time Dave did order more. "Could we have another round of these?" he asked the waiter.

"Certainly," he answered, as if he'd been hoping all his life someone would make such a request.

After such a breathtaking beginning, Dave was ready to try anything. He even appreciated the "Tongue in Cheek," whereas ordinarily he'd have looked a little queasy at the mention of beef cheek and veal tongue.

"That was fabulous," Dave groaned after the fifth dessert, which the waiter had pressed on us when he saw how much we'd enjoyed the four others he'd insisted we try.

"They're so small, they hardly qualify as a whole dessert," Dave had justified, following the caramelized apple *tartlette* with the whimsical snow cone of Meyer lemon sorbet. Every dish was so tiny and precise we'd been joking that the kitchen must be furnished with doll-size ovens and surgical knives.

We discovered a lot that night. We discovered that French food does not necessarily make Dave sick, and that ten courses and an extra four desserts can actually be consumed and enjoyed by one gastronomically resistant adult male without serious effects.

Revise that: without negative effects.

The dinner, the evening, the long-delayed reunion certainly had serious effects. The next day we woke deliciously exhausted and happily aching, amidst a tumble of pillows and lace in an utterly California-Victorian B&B. A couple again.

"Dave?" I piled half the pillows under my head and scooted to a near-upright position.

"Hmmm?" He piled the rest of the pillows over his head. I removed them and kissed my favorite curve of his neck.

"I still have one important problem to solve."

He opened one eye, then drew me down so that he could return the favor by kissing the equivalent spot on my neck. "I thought I solved all your problems."

"All but one."

"Where is it?" He began pawing my body in an antic search. Laughing, I built a wall of pillows between us. He tore it down and returned to exploring my body. More gently.

Later, I tried again.

"Dave?"

He heard it in my voice. A real conversation coming up. He stuffed two pillows beneath his head and sat up. "What's your problem, love?"

"It's about Homer. How do I let him know there's a mole in his department without having to tell him I planted those bugs that remained after Gianni had been warned to remove all of his?"

Dave paused to mull over my dilemma. "He heard the tapes, didn't he?"

"You know, I didn't think of that."

"So he knows somebody called to warn Gianni."

I felt a tendril of dread weaving through me as I considered the implications. "Do you think he really believes that Ottavio and Gianni planted those bugs to spy on each other? Should I be worried about his suspecting me?"

He looked at me as if I'd finally guessed the *Wheel of Fortune* answer with only one letter to go. "I'll just have to go back to Washington with you so that we can have dinner with Homer and Sherele and assess the situation together firsthand."

"That'll solve it, I'm sure."

Dave stretched, and ran his fingers through his tumbled hair. "What time is it?"

Instead of checking my watch, I pulled aside the curtain and looked outside. The sky was streaked with pink and the sun was setting.

"Time for pizza."

Helen's *Coconut Cake* (Serves 12)

1 cup whole milk
2 tablespoons butter
2 cups flour
2 teaspoons baking powder
¼ teaspoon salt
4 eggs
2 cups sugar
2 teaspoons vanilla extract

TOPPING:

6 tablespoons (¾ stick) butter
⅔ cup dark brown sugar
1 cup (4-ounce can) shredded coconut (preferable to flaked)*
1 tablespoon vanilla extract

Preheat oven to 350 degrees. Butter and flour a 13- × 9-inch baking pan.

In a small saucepan or microwave oven, heat milk and butter to scalding. Set aside. Thoroughly combine flour, baking powder, and salt and set aside.

Beat eggs in an electric mixer. Add sugar and continue beating until thick and foamy. With mixer turned on, gradually add hot milk, then vanilla. Beat in flour with mixer at slow speed. Pour batter into prepared pan.

*Shredded coconut (sometimes called Southern-style) gives the cake a crunchier texture, but flaked coconut can be used if necessary. Look for canned coconut, which is more moist than coconut packaged in a bag; it's fine if it comes sweetened.

Bake at 350 degrees for about 30 minutes, testing after 25 minutes with a toothpick. Cake is done when toothpick comes out clean. Cool cake slightly in the pan.

Prepare the topping: Melt butter in a medium saucepan or in a microwave oven. Stir in brown sugar, then add coconut and vanilla. Spread topping over the cake as evenly as possible, making sure to reach to the corners.

Turn oven to broil and place cake 4 to 6 inches below the heat. Broil until bubbling and dark brown, turning if necessary to assure even browning. The topping should be beyond golden, a definite brown, but be careful because it can burn in an instant.

Let cake cool to room temperature. Cut into squares at serving time.